PURSUED:
LILLIAN'S STORY

Praise for Felice Picano

"Felice Picano is a premier voice in gay letters."—*Malcolm Boyd, Contemporary Authors*

Felice Picano is "a leading light in the gay literary world... his glints of flashing wit and subtle hints of dark decadence transcend clichés."—*Richard Violette, Library Journal*

"The Godfather of Gay Lit."—*Richard Burnett*

"Picano has always drawn his main characters as gay heroes, unashamed and unafraid of who they are and what life has to offer, whether positive or negative. This, ultimately, is the measure of Picano's genius."—*Lambda Literary Book Report*

"Felice Picano's contribution to contemporary gay literature in his own work has been immense. His founding of one of the first gay publishing firms, SeaHorse Press, has fostered a profound growth in the gay literary genre. Over the course of the last several decades, Picano, with members of the pioneering gay literary group, the Violet Quill, is responsible for the most heralded gay literature of the 1980s and 1990s." —*Richard Canning, Gay Fiction Speaks*

"Picano's destiny has been to lead the way for a generation of gay writers."—*Robert L. Pela, The Advocate*

"Felice Picano is a leader in the modern gay literary movement. Among his works are many novels—both gay and straight—poetry, plays, short stories, memoirs and other non-fiction, and service as a contributor and editor of numerous magazines and books. His active involvement in the development of gay presses and a gay literary movement is widely acknowledged."—*Michael A. Lutes, The Gay and Lesbian Literary Companion*

"It is impossible to overate the influence Felice Picano has exerted over 20th Century Gay fiction. His works have shaped the Post-Stonewall landscape."—*Rainbownet.com*

"[Picano]'s a word machine. Yet he approaches the page with a newcomer's exuberance."—*New York Times*

"Felice Picano occupies that rare constellation of literary talent populated by such stalwarts of queer literature as Christopher Cox, Andrew Holleran, and Edmund White."—*Rain Taxi Review of Books*

"Overall, the mature writing of Felice Picano and fellow ex-Violet Quill member, Edmund White, confirms what has been long suspected: the gay writing that has emerged from America over the last three decades is as consistently brilliant as writing has got."—*George Lear, Purefiction.com*

Pursuit: A Victorian Entertainment

"Part mystery, part coming-of-age tale, *Pursuit* follows a young man in 19th-century Europe as he rises from trash-picking ruffian to sought-after lover and trusted associate of the British aristocracy. Picano writes the past with vividness, authenticity, unexpected twists, and engaging language. You're carried along in his adventures from Covent Garden to the Stage and a male bordello to upper crust clubs, cheering for his hero amid danger at every turn." —*Jess Wells, author of A Slender Tether*

The Lure

"Explosive...Picano plays out the novel's secrets brilliantly, one deliberate card at a time. Felice Picano is one hell of a writer!"—*Stephen King*

"Felice Picano has taken the psychological thriller as far as it can go."—*Andrew Holleran*

"Exciting and suspenseful. A strong plot with plenty of action. Builds to a solid surprise ending."—*Publishers Weekly*

"With its relentless tensions, solid narrative beat, and rising psychological peril this book is a tour de force of gay writing, is one of the founding books of modern gay fiction, and rightly made Picano's reputation. It's got a twist ending, consistently shocks and keeps you gripped."—*Gscene Magazine*

20th Century Un-limited

"Experience once again the genius of one of the LGBT community's best authors and see for yourself where he leads you. You and the history you know will never be the same." —*Lambda Literary Book Report*

Twelve O'Clock Tales

"Think of Picano as a queer literary renaissance man. He writes plays and screenplays, poetry and memoirs, sex manuals and sexy thrillers, historical novels and—this is his fourth collection—short stories. The first, "Synapse," is a creepily science-fictional account of how an elderly man has come to inhabit a boy's body; the last, "The Perfect Setting," is a masterpiece of detection, wherein an obsessive narrator solves the mystery of a landscape painter's murder. Not a one of the stories is like another, such is Picano's wide-ranging imagination; what they have in common is their power and their polish."—*The Rainbow Times*

By the Author

The Lure

Late in the Season

Looking Glass Lives

Contemporary Gay Romances

Twelve O'Clock Tales

20th Century Un-limited: Two Novellas

Pursuit: A Victorian Entertainment

Pursued: Lillian's Story

Visit us at www.boldstrokesbooks.com

PURSUED:
LILLIAN'S STORY

by

Felice Picano

2022

PURSUED: LILLIAN'S STORY

ISBN 13: 978-1-63679-197-5

This Trade Paperback Original Is Published By
Bold Strokes Books, Inc.
P.O. Box 249
Valley Falls, NY 12185

First Edition: April 2022

Credits
Editors: Jerry L. Wheeler and Stacia Seaman
Production Design: Stacia Seaman
Cover Design by Tammy Seidick

For Barbara Fishman—long-time friend, loyal reader

She comes slowly—
Oppressed—
in a golden carriage.

Hexagram #47, Line 4, *The Book of Changes*

To: The Honourable Lady Caroline-Ann Augusta
The Glebe, Ravenglass
Broughton, England

12 September 188—

My Dear Lady Caroline-Ann,
    By the time you receive this letter, I have been assured I shall no longer be within the confines of the British Isles. I apologize for whatever inconvenience to yourself and even more so to your reputation that may occur from so sudden and utter a removal by one so apparently intimate to your new state as your mother-in-law.
    Doubtless the earl, your father-in-law, and your own husband will attempt to explain away so hasty and so unprepared-for an absence as mine with excuses oiled smooth as Venetian glass, with rationalizations more complex than an old Greek philosopher. Credibility, above all, is their motto, you will come to understand, credibility and the wholesale glossing of what cannot as a rule be easily explained or understood. For that reason alone, I should have left Ravenglass years ago.
    Trithers the housekeeper, Samson the butler, Farnsworthy the groundskeeper, and Jannequin of the kitchen staff and their minions have received plans and schedules, menus, and work lists to occupy them while you are upon your all-too-abbreviated honeymoon trip and, indeed, well beyond your return. All of them may be prevailed upon, especially as I've requested that they be at hand, to inform and to explain to you the varied areas necessary in ruling over so large a house and demesne as Ravenglass. This is a great deal more than I was provided with in my time, and so I hope this in a small way obliges you to me and serves as a small compensation.
    From such a statement, you will correctly infer that my absence is intended to be as permanent as it may seem incomprehensible. Why would the mother of the happiest young bridegroom in British society, as the *Times of London* says, the mother-in-law of the newest blushing young bride in our exalted circle (ibid), indeed the "wife and lifelong helpmeet of the second most powerful peer in the realm," evanesce in quite so untimely and mysterious a fashion? As independent as you appeared to me and at times as forward a young lady of fashion in our fair isle as you resembled, I've no doubt you will be asking yourself exactly such questions.

And I shall tell you all why I have fled. What the Great Man has done to me to force me to do so. What they all have done to me. How I have conspired these many months with friends old and new and with strangers, men I'd never thought to encounter in person— low tradesmen, Foreign nationals even—never mind associate with quite so closely as this, all to make good my escape. How it was evidently planned out for me decades before by my predecessor, the late Marchioness, harpy as she seemed at the time, planned and partly paid for by her suffering and by my own.

You will be shocked, I am sure of it, to read my words. Perhaps if I have written rightly, you will one night turn to that smooth, guileless-seeming young man beside you in the bed, my own flesh as he is, and start back in horror. Wondering if even he carries the curse within his oh so oblivious mind and so apparently innocent body. Could he cannot help but do so? Nor can you help but be its victim as I and other women before me were.

Yet, Lady, you must wait a while for details. The cross-channel packet is this moment cresting the churning waves with such a thwump and slap, thwump and slap of its bottom planks that this tilting lounge asea has suddenly become quite unoccupied by the passengers' society, such as it was to begin with, and now a boatswain or mate or some such other official is speaking, telling us that "heavy weather lies ahead" and that "we would do best for our health" to repair to our rooms below.

Without much modesty, I can report that I am myself as stalwart a sailor as he. Being reared in the marine neighbourhood of Ravenglass, how could I help but be so? But the very young lady's maid alongside me and the travel lieutenant accompanying me are from parts farther inland and seem rather the worse for the channel, she already unquestionably "green about the gills," as the local salts used to so colourfully put it, that we shall, I fear, have to all go down to our marginally less *mal-de-mer* inducing quarters. And so, I shall complete this missive at a later time.

Hours Later

A remarkable incident has occurred upon this ordinarily most banal, this most pedestrian of passages between the last time I set pen to paper and now. A person has gone missing. Or, rather, a personage. A rather large, heavy one. One might even say a gross personage.

I was apprised of this by the craft's purser knocking on our stateroom door. The green-faced little maid answered to that official, and he and his mate stood in that sketch of a foyer and requested to enter. At this request, my male sentinel stepped forward and bluntly asked upon what business. They then explained that in the past several hours, a first-class passenger had gone missing, and they asked if we knew of him, had seen him, had remarked him, or indeed remarked "anything at all unusual."

Naturally, he assured them in the negative. They then apologized, saying they needs must ask everyone on board and search every square foot of the ship to ensure that Bey Jurma Gorglek, the unfortunately named Turkish person was, in fact no longer aboard. The purser was most courteous and deferential, and so I let them look about our rather limited quarters. And while I am listed upon the ship's register under the name of Mrs. Sm—th, the fellow must have recognized quality, and intuited "position," even now that I am actively abjuring it. Evidently many ladies are forced for one reason or another these days to travel incognito such as this.

Once they had left the rooms, I sent my protector out to gather further information on the disappearance, which I think he was happy to do if only to escape the close confines of the cabin and also to do some of his own detecting, as he fancies himself adept in that regard. No, Lady Caroline-Ann, you have not yet guessed the identity of this most valuable fellow, who has agreed, indeed, sworn upon the Good Book, to see me through my travails and not leave me until I am settled in complete safety.

He returned following a period to confirm that the missing Bey travelled alone, which several people remarked upon, but he had seemed most concerned about several other passengers who he was certain had noticed him. The Bey was either still or only just recently an official of the Ottoman Empire. Perhaps, my informant opined, based upon what talk he'd collected from others on board, the Bey was the victim of an assassination. Several swarthy, slender fellows affecting no knowledge of English or French diction are said to have scowled upon first seeing the Bey some time after we had all boarded the channel packet in England. They are believed to be nationals of Albania or another of those Balkans now under

Franz Joseph's benevolent sway, only lately recovered from the Ottomans. Their motive, of course, is presumed to be revenge, if not of a personal nature, than perhaps a more sweepingly national or even racial one, or as a result of their long centuries beneath the Turkish yoke.

So, it is all grim and political and rather titillating too, I must admit. It is no wonder that my own mother-in-law, the much put upon, late Dowager Marchioness Bella, once assured me that "foreign travel is so broadening to the mind, or so I have been informed."

It is good policy for any new Lady to become acquainted with some of the local people. Gentry, I know well, shall pursue you on their own given any encouragement from your new high state. But among those of the nearby villages are several persons you would certainly overlook to your disadvantage.

First, consider Mrs. Adelaide Eagles, née Creswell, an upright woman who at times has taken on the duties of the old dean, Dr. Gribble, in the chapterhouse and rectory. Although one cannot understand how this estimable person appears to know virtually all that transpires in the villages surrounding the manor house, she can become as invaluable to you as she ended up becoming to myself.

The former Miss Creswell was the elder of three sisters and by no means the handsomest. Still, her bright blue eyes, her sharp facial features, her small, well-shaped head and extremely acute ears provide her advantages neither of her elder, duller siblings can lay claim to. She is quick to report on any miscreants, but possesses equal asperity in remarking on anyone who may be beset by misfortune in the surrounding farms and shire, with the consequence that such persons may be uplifted or mollified by a well-placed handful of shillings, or that employment might be found for one of their family members about the manor house or grounds, assuring a secure source of enrichment for them and greater loyalty toward yourself and the estate. She will not only be able to recommend that unfortunate's best hope, but also in which likely position the person should be employed to greatest effect. She is seldom mistaken, and through her good offices, Lady Caroline-Ann, your own sovereignty shall take on a far more substantial glow at Ravenglass, as did my own.

If I might be so immodest as to point out the country folks' *applausus* when my own poor name was mentioned at his young lordship's nuptial supper given for us all at the manor house the day following your naturally more glittering London ceremony? Such an *homage* is chiefly due to my harkening to Miss Creswell's constant counsels. Indeed, during my lengthy and often forlorn decades as mistress of Ravenglass while your husband was away at school, and my own husband endlessly away in the city upon political business, it was those simpler souls' company, their amusements, their daily goings-on and habitual life that, of necessity, configured the greatest support of my existence.

I have much justification in believing that although you pride yourself upon being a modern young lady with many friends, that you shall find yourself at last comprehending all too well and all too soon the portent behind my low-spirited words.

I only hope I am mistaken. But alas, the last few interviews I've had with your husband, my only son, have shown that in the speech of our neighbours, the apple falls closer than ever to the tree, for he thinks exactly like his father. This betides woe to you, as it unquestionably did to me.

A tap upon the door confirms what the noticeably calmer sea predicted: we may ascend for air and light, with embarkation upon the continent to ensue.

I post this to you, Lady, with all my heart yet with the greatest anxiety,

Your mother-in-law, Marchioness, Lillian of Ravenglass

To: The Earl of Ravenglass
11 Hanover Square
London, England

15 September 188—
The Calexis, Rye Super Mare

Dear Papa,
   I cannot say how she decamped nor who aided her, only this. No sooner had my new wife and I settled into our honeymoon cottage here at the hotel upon Rye Strand than the letter she sent was received, opened, and, of course, read. It is copied herein for your discomfiting enlightenment. It was meant to arrive just then. It was meant to alarm at that very moment. It was meant, I daresay, to do harm. And it has done so.
   Lady Caroline-Ann is vexed and suspicious. I several times previously pointed out signs of these dispositions of her nature to you, Papa. To little avail, I fear, since you must have your "Kentshire" marriage, no matter what. How she is to be managed, I am not entirely certain. I expect that distractions and diversions in quantity and quality will have to be discovered and devised. An expensive price to pay. And more notice than was planned must now also be taken of her: tea parties, shopping, and picnics upon the strand—all that feminine folderol!
   Naturally, in shock, I have fallen back upon our much used and long abused "sad tale of tragic Mother," although young ladies of this day are less apt to be shocked or to even credit it than perhaps they did in your own time, Papa. I use it most hesitantly and so, I believe, ought you.
   Was the Turk's going overboard your doing? If so, that she would be so close to its vicinity is most unfortunate. I assumed, you presumed, all of us believed that Mater was at least under control, and that the years of doubts, the decades of uneasiness we both knew so well were at last put to rest. Then *this* happens!
   Lord Oliver sends his regards. He is close by, of course, although how much I will be able to get to him now, with all this occurring...Well, it's all a great muddle.
   Have you no idea at all where she is off to?
   Roddy of Ravenglass

To: The Honourable Lady Caroline-Ann Augusta
The Glebe, Ravenglass
Broughton, England

16 September 188—

My Dear Lady Caroline-Ann,
I trust by now you have absorbed the shock of my leaving England and have possibly already steadied yourself to a future without a constantly attendant mother-in-law.
You cannot fail to notice that I do not ask you, Lady, how your husband has absorbed that same shock. I doubt that for him it is any shock at all, except perhaps a bit of mortification among his coevals should he allow this topic to arise in company and not instantly quash it. Surely, you have already been apprised ours was not a maternal bond of any considerable affection; indeed, it has long been even more distant and strained than those usually found among mothers of our class *vis-à-vis* sons long schooled away from home.
Not that any such was ever my own wish. Rather it was the wish and plan of your new father-in-law, a man long accustomed to having both satisfied without suffering any great exception. And from an early age, I can assure you, Lady. In truth, it was such a youthful wish of his that brought about our knowing each other in the very first instance. How I now rue that evilly starred day, although at the time I thought it exactly the opposite.
But first I think you must become somewhat more acquainted with myself then. Picture a young girl of twelve years of age, of our place and situation then, for that was when we first met. Or rather when the current earl first set eyes upon me, so you may better understand how I have been so duped and managed about, to my own despair, and thus how it may also happen to yourself if proper precautions are not taken immediately and strongly.
My family is not from the immediate neighbourhood of Ravenglass, but from a bit south upon that same tide-scarred and wrack-draped coast of western England too north to be Wales and too southerly to be Scotland. Beyond Lancashire, yet not entirely Cumbria, it is its own place, anciently littered with earthen barrows of pre-Roman rulers one stumbles over, thinking them to be byres.

They are now assumed to be Celtic from the occasional burnt brown steles lying half buried aslant cottage lanes. Legend ascribes that very inlet as the one from which the brave Tristram sailed off, captive to the beauty of Isolde, and from which neither ever returned. Yet another cautionary tale to heed. The northernmost reach of the larger, shallow, sweeping Morecambe Bay resembles a sort of outstretched arm with three fingers probing into the rough highland there, well north of the city of Lancaster.

Upon that well protected and hospitably south-facing seashore between the market towns of Ulverston and Cartnel, my people have lived for centuries. As far back as my great-grandfather could recount his forebears, they were men and women of the sea. Fishermen. And when they were too old to go asea, net-fishing men at the shore, and when they were too old even for that, shipwreck scavengers and flotsam gleaners.

The Irish Sea is ordinarily known as a forgiving body of water among its stormier British compatriots, but at times too it can whip out gales and hurricanes fit to match the *tai-phuuns* of the Pacific that can swamp peoples in the thousands and obliterate entire small islands. No grandiose harbours do we know in our out-of-the-way vicinity, but instead diminutive inlets fit for a double handful of boats along with an irregularly long stretch of ever-shifting seashore flat enough to land a multitude of three-man dories and wide enough to strand any vessel greater than a two-mast ketch.

My father, then, as youngest of a brood of seven sons, was by luck the first of his kin to be educated beyond knowledge of the sea. His mother's spoilt favourite, this Benjamin was early on deemed by his male relations to be too frail and sickly to join his mariner siblings. Fortune in the form of great fish hauls easily brought onto shore favoured our household one season, and so the extra money went not to grog and geegaws but was used instead to send my father to school nearby, and then to more advanced schooling, where he gained the attention of a scholar, a local pastor of note.

Apprenticed to this learned man of God, who then took an almost paternal interest in the slender youth, my father trained to the cloth himself. He even attained one and a half years of university, albeit it was nearby, at York Minster, and not to the grander ecclesiastical colleges of Britain's south.

Close upon his ordination, fortune once more shone upon my sire. The fourth Earl of Ravenglass, not forty miles to the north, suddenly grown affluent from an abundance of railway shares, had embarked upon a great land expansion. He purchased adjoining estates, several of them in near ruin, so that suddenly from the tower room of his magnificent new residential wing to the manor house, he could see in all directions, except westward to the sea, nothing but his own comprehensive holdings. So much land required an expansion of pasturage, forestry, and cultivation.

What had been for centuries a trifling adjoining hamlet to the manor of some forty field hands and their families was rapidly doubled and then quadrupled into a substantial village. Its several new lanes of cottages were quickly abutted upon and then surrounded the seaside townlet, surpassing it in size and population.

Of course, extensive new silage and storage and animal shelters of all sorts must be erected to accommodate the suddenly larger harvests brought in by these new men. Beyond the house, grand new stables were put up, as well as a folly *en ruin* in the style of ancient Greece. He even built a vast, square, columned, fruiting garden in the Italian style. Naturally too, a new church must be built for the many new servitors, farmhands, manor workers and their kith.

Such was the Ravenglass Manor I first came to see that brilliant May morn following my ninth birthday when we first arrived there in a rented cart, my father's first and last full appointment as Vicar of Ravenglass. It was a Saturday, I recall, as a gaudy and well-peopled weekly farm market had been raised in the large public green space midway between the long Mariner's Hall, the equally ancient Lord Rothbert's Inn, and the nearly new red brick manor foreman's house, a substantial three-story edifice whose narrow wood upper level consisted of dormitory for some forty unmarried field hands. Some of these shall play roles as scenes in the unfolding tragic drama—or is it the inane comedy—of my life.

I break now. Our dinner *en hôte*, in what passes for a grand hotel in this provincial capital, is unexpectedly arrived. Like much else here in *Europa*, it looks odd but it smells rather savoury and doubtless is not in any way inedible.

One Hour Later

I am unable to continue due to some trouble here with travel plans being overly complex or insufficiently complex, I am not certain which. But they must be attended to immediately.

I am assured there is a postal service here which will connect to yours. And so, until later.

Your mother-in-law Lillian, Marchioness of Ravenglass

To: The Very Reverend Jasper Horace Quill
The British Church at Campofieri
Town of Fiesoli
Province of Tuscany

16 September 188—

Sir,
The lady is safely a-road, although I cannot inform you upon which road, as I am foresworn not to reveal it to a soul. And at any rate the road itself seems to alter with her mood. Unsurprisingly!

We are on the Continent. That much I can say. And so you too may report.

I have waited until now to write to you, since only now can I believe we are thankfully unobserved and unfollowed, at least for the moment.

We escaped with some ease, thanks in part to your friend's careful plans and the cleverly construed outlay of bribes. There were moments, however, that were very close shaves indeed, as he himself predicted, watched as we were throughout the past fortnight at the manor house and environs by a host of eyes, some of which we had already assumed, some we only lately learned, and many, alas, never clearly distinguished but nevertheless present.

As both your friend and the lady supposed, the wedding gala was the key to our getting away. But I would not doubt that his minions, hungover from their revels still, at this very moment do speed along every main thoroughfare leading from any island-bound port, and so we must wend our way indirectly.

My knowledge of the Dutch and Germanic tongues, fruit of what I heretofore believed to be my useless and quite vinous university days, has aided us. I have allowed our nightly hosts and fellow travellers to believe that the lady is an elderly relation of a great house in a German state, who has fallen into dire straits due to an inclination for the gaming tables of refined spas.

Once we are turned south, little "Minette," such as our lady's maid calls herself, will become more effectually useful. The languages there are more in her line.

I wish I could say I had as complete faith in that young person, but such is not the case. The lady, at any rate, does, and I must admit that "Minette" has acted admirably and conscientiously so far as that goes.

Your Friend and Servant,
Stephen Undershot

Post Scriptum: On board our ferry, we experienced the curious disappearance of another passenger. I am not yet sure what it signifies. It seems in no way connected to us.

To: The Honourable Lady Caroline-Ann Augusta
The Glebe, Ravenglass
Broughton, England

18 September 188—

My Dear Lady Caroline-Ann,
Where to take up? Ah! my little woman companion reminds me I was reminiscing about my childhood, to which I now return, as it is necessary to know so as to explain why I now must reside abroad, and why I have fled for my life and sanity, my face hidden, having to raise an obscuring veil to take my food and drink. I tell my servant what I am writing and she assures me that this, like a classroom lesson, helps in her study of English, in which she is most deficient.

My girlhood, I admit freely to you, was a lustrous if too short period. I was just turned nine when we arrived at the Ravenglass vicarage, the second child and only daughter of my mother, a lovely sylphlike woman highly vulnerable to consumption, and of a slender and almost equally unhealthy father given to quiet meditative fits. So, I more or less had run of the place from the beginning, along with my brother, Rudolph.

Unlike myself or our parents when young, Rudolph was a sturdily handsome little tyke, strong beyond his years, also strongly affectionate toward us all and somewhat protective of me. Not that I needed protecting very much, since I was self-reliant from an early age. While he was sturdy, I was slim, but both of us were very dark haired and very fair, with Celtic green eyes. In truth, we favoured neither of our parents, instead being twin portraits of my father's mother, that intensely practical and domineering woman.

We were perceived as twins by our new neighbours, whether agricultural or nautical, and we did little to disabuse them of this error. Overcoming my mother's natural scruples, we instead demanded we be dressed similarly and treated alike. Both my father and my mother were learned enough to have read Mrs. Wollstonecraft's book and also Caleb Williams's texts giving proofs and extolling upon the inborn equality of women to men, and so for a long time, they gave us leave to be as we wished, nearly perfectly similar and inseparable.

We were lower schooled together, most of the time at home by our parents, but later on at the manor-financed village schoolhouse, once it was erected and open, when I was but ten and Rudolph twelve. There we sat together, sharing ink-well, planks of writing desk, and carved wooden bench. There, too, we shared our learning, our dislikes and likes among the other boys. It was around that time that Rudolph attracted the notice of the Earl of Ravenglass, its master, his foreman, and that of the young lordling.

It should go without saying that as children of the vicar, we were those inhabitants most near, in all ways, to Ravenglass manor and its residents. What that effectually meant was that we were present at the birthday of the Marchioness Bella, who was a beautiful, passive, solitary, nearly silent woman. Because it occurred during the summer months, we were also in attendance upon the Ravenglass heir's birthday gala, a far larger and more salubrious affair than the gloomy, sweet cake and honey-tea six-person commemoration for his mother. The great earl was seldom in attendance at these fêtes nor indeed any at the manor, except when absolutely required, preferring, or so said my father, to be where he was needed, at court, in the city, and especially in Parliament, where he was said to have struck several brilliant alliances with peers of far greater estate.

Still, whenever he did deign to appear in our rural neighbourhood, the earl would attend our little church from its foremost, nearly enclosed pew, joining his generally speechless wife and his very beautiful little heir apparent. Also, whenever his lordship condescended to remain at Ravenglass for more than a few days, he would invariably hold a small dinner, to which my parents, along with the local solicitor, the foreman, and whoever else might pass for gentry in the vicinity would be asked to attend.

Indebted to the earl for his living in the first place and secondarily attracted to the nobleman by his prepossessing good looks, high intelligence, ambition, and general knowledge of the world—aspects not particularly within my father, the vicar's own rather short list of assets. My father, of course, spoke of the earl with none but words of the most unmitigated admiration. In this, he was parroted by my mother, and therefore little Rudolph and I were always on our best behaviour in those few and far between moments when we were exposed to any member of the distinguished noble line.

As my poor mother might now interject were she still alive, this was opposed to how we behaved toward anyone else from the manor house, save perhaps the foreman, and sometimes not even he escaped our laughter, our jests, or my youthful criticism. For we did judge ourselves superior to them all, servants as they were, and we very well conscious we were freemen descended for many generations of yeomanry. It is difficult now to admit that youthful attitude of mine, for it is only by dint of the true superiority and friendship of my supposed inferiors that I did not fall prey to utter melancholia and descend into a fatal stupor as my marchioness forebears all did before me, but am now alive and free to write of my escape.

Less fortunate was my brother, for he was, as I mentioned before, a trusting and affectionate fellow and, to wit, also a perfect little democrat—all of which fine qualities ultimately aided in his undoing. But I was such a self-concerned little miss, proper and proud, dauntless and demanding. I now see how correctly our national bard did put it, that character is indeed destiny. For could there be any wonder that such a vain priss in such otherwise common surroundings would eventually draw the attentions of those far greater in station? Of those, to boot, of far greater in knowledge and power?

The candles gutter, and I am informed no more are to be had tonight. My little maid flutters about, wondering will there be enough light for my to-bed toilette? We leave at dawn. This letter flies via the opposing road one hour later.

Adieu, your mother-in-law,

present Marchioness, Lillian of Ravenglass

19 September 188—
The Calexis
Rye Super Mare

Dear Papa,

You write that we must "cut short" our honeymoon and return to Hanover Square forthwith, and I reply to tell you that will not be quite so easily achieved as you seem to believe.

To begin with, my wife's mama has arrived. Or rather, her mama, papa, and two younger sibs, one a chestnut-haired, apple-cheeked lad of sixteen years who might all too readily rouse Lord Oliver out of his usual torpor. He—indeed they all—therefore need close watching as only some interested party like yours truly may do. And if that were not enough to vex one, Mama, Papa, and the other, orange-haired, apple-cheeked lad of ten years have made great nuisances of themselves about the place, coming and going at all hours, making noise when one wishes to read the newspaper, not to mention all sorts of incessant demands.

They complain that they find the guest quarters here "pokey," which they indeed are, as we were not expecting company, though my wife tells me that it is common as gooseberry pie among Kentish folk for all sorts of relational encumbrances to descend upon the newly married couple, and I ought to count myself fortunate only the immediate family has arrived and not a slew of cousins, aunts, and uncles.

Then, too, they eat interminably. Not only breakfast, dinner, and supper, but they must have prepared picnics upon the sands and boxed luncheons upon the grass behind the house. Their required repasts seem to exceed the hours of the day. Should there not be a cold supper awaiting their arrival from a midnight drive in my rented Victoria nor a dish of sliced meats greeting them fresh off their bicycling machines, they squeal they are "famished," and grumble that I am retaining them "near to starvation." I protest this making me out to be such a mean and scrimping fellow. You know me not to be.

Worse yet, their amusements follow one upon the other in an endless chain of frolic. I and my wife are by now quite exhausted. They kidnapped poor Lord Oliver this afternoon, would hear no protestations, made off with him to—I never thought I'd witness it—the Strand itself here at Rye. He returned forehead and nose sunburnt, hair tousled, his salt-rimed bathing costume serving as a shirt beneath his street clothing. If he hadn't looked more dashingly handsome and youthful than since we were chums at Westminster School, I'd have thought him ready for a sanatorium.

If you would really have me back, says Lord Oliver—and I agree—then by all means, issue a formal "call back," for as members of your staff, we will be forced to return. I think you wish us to be fully inundated with these Kent shire individuals for some unholy reason of your own.

By the by, Mater's second letter to my wife arrived, and I've forwarded it on to you by separate post. It seems harmless enough. Perhaps she's gone daft after all. And while we are both referred to within, I get off rather easily. Even so, in a few deft strokes she has rather "caught you."

Your loving and obedient son, Roddy

To: The Honourable Lady Caroline-Ann Augusta
The Glebe, Ravenglass
Broughton, England

20 September 188—

My Dear Lady Caroline-Ann,
　　You will be puzzled, I think, to have another letter so soon, but I trust that I can now feel "a breath safe" enough from his lordship's enormous swath of influence to admit freely I am at a handsome and fairly new railway station upon the Continent. Indeed, I am presently waiting at a small table with some leisure while awaiting my own train, a surprisingly good cup of Darjeeling tea by my side. You see, it's not only in England where people are allowed to be "civilized."
　　You are by no means a stupid girl, Lady, and therefore I believe you shall actually read and attempt to understand these letters as they arrive. Doubtless you felt obliged to show the earlier few to your husband, and he then showed them to his father. Should they be foolish enough to continue to follow me, to as it were, track me down, the envelope alone would contain "clews" to where I may— oh so tentatively—be. For we move on every day farther and farther away from you all.
　　Show it not then, Lady, but let them understand the body of the letter consists of advice on household matters, with long and rambling anecdotes of the local people. They've surely already implied to you that I've utterly lost my wits. Agree with them: at least outwardly.
　　And so, Lady, you shall have a very valuable lesson in hand. In fact, I believe your own personal future depends upon how carefully you read and heed my own history, for yours is to be its match, as mine was to be the match of my husband's mother. For this is not a one-time matter, Lady, but seems to spin on generation after generation, the Ravenglass line becoming stronger, more ambitious, more perspicacious, more intelligent, more handsome, and more desirous of fame and glory—and better able to obtain them. Yet, at the same time, there persists in the males of the line, like one of those nearly hidden patterns in a Florentine embroidery, a streak of such—what word may I use to call it that won't put you off from

reading and heeding? Best may be that it emerge naturally, as it were, from out of my history.

As you have already read, lady, your father-in-law, at the time the little Ravenglass heir, publicly celebrated his birthday every summer upon the twenty-fifth day of July. That particular week is the sunniest, the warmest, the least likely to entertain rain of any in our neighbourhood and so, invariably, an out-of-doors festivity was prepared by the earl. What part in planning them, if any, his wife, the boy's mother took, I could not say. She seemed so languid and passive a creature. Still, she patronized the fêtes.

As a rule, she appeared within the confines of her large, wooden-slat movable wheeled chair, since she seldom left the mechanical contraption by then, though she was no older than my own mother and in no apparent ill health. In truth, I more than once heard my mama sigh and wish she had such a chair herself if only for one half hour per day, and with it such leisure as her greater countrywoman eternally enjoyed. Evidently it was the earl himself, along with his foreman and other underlings, who set the annual fête into motion. As the lad grew from infant to toddler to boy, or so we were told, not having been present before then, the event grew larger, more expensive, and grander in its panoply, with decorations of streamers and flags. Once the boy had gone off to school during nine months of the year, also more "thematic" did these celebrations become.

Our first year present, the festal motif was based, as we were informed, upon some particular anniversary of the great Spanish armada, of which a smaller, advance portion had threatened and been defeated off the very coastline we might daily view. All things patriotic were emphasized: red and white pennants and ribbons emblazoned our little town and its environs then and for a fortnight afterward.

The next year, it was the overpowered Spaniards' turn to be honoured, and all things Iberian seemed to take a near-hypnotic hold of the local populace. Our few little shops suddenly displayed black *mantilla* shawls, and tiny upwardly bent combs for women to wear in their hair. Wooden hand bells resembling chestnuts and like them named *castanets* clicked and clacked their way through market lanes and even briefly ornamented a sung psalm at the very next chapel service, to my father's public annoyance and my brother's and my own private amusement. The heir appeared at the outdoor luncheon done in his honour dressed up as a little Spanish bullfighter or *toreador*, wearing a brilliant, fringed cap, a golden vest coat riotous with hand embroidery, pointed black leather boots studded with gold, with a great sash of scarlet sateen around his slender middle, and both a tiny gilded sword and a minuscule silver dagger stuffed therein.

My poor brother Rudolph, upon seeing the golden apparition formed by the yellow-haired little peer, became quite wroth with envy. All my father's softest admonitions and my mother's blandishments were needed to keep my poor brother from rushing off at sunrise next morning, headed for Salamanca himself so he might someday obtain and wear such a costume.

None of the heir's many birthday gifts—every one of them unwrapped from their bright paper swathing and exposed before the admiring eyes of a throng of us, his lessers—affected Rudolph so much as that little silver dagger with its chased hilt and cleverly shaped chamois belt holder. These other gifts were so many, so various, and so expensive that we score or so children present couldn't work up much jealousy toward their possessor. Instead, I believe we felt a general and all-encompassing wonderment at there being such munificence existent at all in the world; that fact once established, that the Ravenglass heir would be its recipient seemed only natural.

Even so, Rudolph's customary satisfaction with large pieces of golden cake topped by snow white icing, which he managed to eat in larger portions than I thought possible for so small a boy, were insufficient to fully sate him that day. The brief ride he was allowed atop a tiny, shaggy-maned, long-tailed, oak-wood collared Orkney pony proved to only be the briefest of distractions. The brilliantly shined, apparently new-minted ha'penny he won in a running competition with the other shire boys lasted longer as a diversion, but even so, his Sulks returned.

Seeing my dear brother in such a state, I took it upon myself to correct the situation. Seizing upon a small bunch of newly cut jonquils, stocks, and gillyflowers, I asked my father if I mightn't present them to her ladyship. Pleased for once I'd offered such a feminine idea, for under Rudolph's influence he believed I'd grown a great tomboy, he assented. I approached the front dais and the noble threesome. Placing myself so the heir could not fail to notice me, I laid the flowers into her ladyship's lap with a pretty little speech I made up on the spot.

Her lethargic approval offhandedly given, and her offer of a sweet jujube from off a silver salver received courteously by me, instead of popping it into my mouth and bouncing off back to my seat, I remained among them a bit longer, earning her instant ennui, but not that of her son. I turned to him now and said in a voice only he might hear, "My brother quite admires you. We both agree, as do all present, that your costume is the most remarkable ever seen hereabout."

He smiled in response and slyly moved another jujube across the table-cloth toward me, which I as slyly seized upon. "You're the vicar's girl," he said. "I've seen you about at times recently. In the garden, I believe playing Hide-and-Go-Seek, and Little Man's Door. You play quite prettily, you know."

I thanked him with a curtsey.

"Was that your brother, that dark-haired schoolboy, playing those games with you?" he asked.

I admitted it was.

"You both are very pretty and play very prettily together," he said. "Twins are very uncommon. And you are quite the most attractive twins I've ever looked upon."

"Can you keep a secret?" I asked, already knowing his affirmative answer. "Then I shall tell it to you. We are not twins, but one and three-quarters years apart. My brother the elder."

"Only I now share that secret?" he asked, struck by it. "And your family, of course."

"Only," I confirmed.

"How ripping!"

"Do you want to hear another secret?" I went on. "My brother would give his ha'penny just newly won, to hold your silver dagger in its leathern belt."

"I need not ha'pennies," said he somewhat grandly. "But if he desires it so much as all that, he shall have the dagger."

"No, please," I quickly corrected. "As a vicar's son, he cannot *possess* a dagger." And lest the heir deem me impertinent, I assuaged him. "That is a *gentleman's* prerogative. He may, however, hold it and touch it and wear it for a moment or so."

"Then let it be so. Fetch him here."

My parents were silently curious and my brother astounded when I returned and reported what progress I had made. To my surprise, at first Rudolph refused to go, but I insisted. "After all, you are old enough now to pay him your respects."

"Precisely so." My father put in his own word. "And about time, too, that you both realized your position in the greater scheme of things," he added, folding up my brother's laid-down short collar.

So Rudolph girded his loins and followed me back to the main table, quite nervously as it turned out.

By that time, the earl himself had joined the family, so it was he who first greeted our twinned bow and curtsey and murmurs of "your worship," saying, "You see, Roland, how well brought up they are, these children of our vicar? They are gentle yet prompt in conveying their birthday greetings."

His heir immediately rose up on his toes and whispered three words into his father's ear. Amazed, his father then whispered loudly, "How do you know this?" To which his son whispered three more words. Presumably, the secret I'd told him. "Why, that's as grand as it is a simple toy to amuse us all," he said and seemed quite pleased.

I then introduced my brother to the heir, little Roland of Ravenglass. Roland took his hand and held it and said, "I have seen you about the grounds and admired your strength and cunning at play."

No words could have more ingratiated their speaker to my brother, proud as he was of those very qualities, and he blushed quite red and sputtered, "Alas, that we cannot play together."

"But we can," Roland assured him. "My father allows"—he looked to his father, who waved him on—"my father insists upon it. But first you must look at my new dagger, which I understand you admire, you clever boy, for it is quite better than the sword which, though it glisters so, couldn't cut warm butter."

I was now gently propelled past them to a tall and very good-looking man who, despite his display of abundant facial side hair, called, I believe "weepers," was introduced as "his lordship's especial friend," the earl of something or other. With him was an extremely fashionable woman their age simply addressed as "Countess." Each of them offered me yet another jujube, which I had the good sense to twist into a paper and stuff into my apron pocket for later enjoyment.

Meanwhile, those two adults were speaking of a small trek they had taken the previous few days to a local area of wild high cliff tops riven by rough gorges. "Barry," the countess addressed the other lord, "didn't you think it as picturesque as a Norwegian *fjord?*"

"Quite so. Virtually Ossianesque, I believe you wittily described it," he replied to her, and they made little mouths at each other, which amused everyone there but myself and her ladyship, who appeared fatigued beyond human explication.

I could see my brother wielding, then wearing, then even cautiously thrusting about himself the little silver dagger, as the heir explained to him how to do so. Rudolph was as serious as he tended to be over his long division problems at school, and as pleased as he could be. And seeing him so, for the first time in the three years since we had arrived at Ravenglass, I myself was fully contented.

Suddenly a drop of rain fell upon the white linen tablecloth before us, followed by another, then another, and as I looked up, a little rotund dark cloud suddenly appeared over the party, and it began to pour as though aimed directly at us.

The town and shire people were most affected and all rushed, crowding beneath the few cloth canopies erected to protect from the strong sun. Close as we were to the portico leading indoors, we were rapidly led inside the manor house. The countess took one of my hands, her companion the other, and they all but levitated me off the ground as they did so. By some feat of magic, her ladyship's chair was already within. His lordship, placed somewhat behind her looking out toward the rain-pelted sward, was well pleased with himself, saying, "How I do enjoy a hard summer rain." Turning to his friend, busily shaking rain off his vest coat, he added, "Eh, Barry, me lad. If you recall, you caitiff you, it was because of such a hard summer rain we too first began," which earned him a smile and nod from his friend.

It was a few moments until someone noticed the heir wasn't among us. But he was soon found by the countess, playing Hide-and-Go-Seek behind a tall drapery, his arms around my brother, who was shivering with wet, and who was being soundly kissed on the cheek and hugged for warmth. All applauded such friendly spirits.

A servant was sent to find a warm blanket for poor Rudolph, who somehow had taken the brunt of the rain shower. I watched and helped him warm up.

It was all over in a manner of ten minutes, the rain gone, the sun fully out, my brother once more himself, although his hair was ruffled some, when my parents arrived indoors and declared that although grateful for our keep, still they would take us away.

Roland then kissed my brother again, saying, "Don't forget. Tomorrow we shall play from after dinnertime on. Is it all right?" he asked my father, who I could see was only too delighted by his politeness and easily assented.

As we were stepping out, I spotted a tiny little silverwork cross I knew to have been around Rudolph's neck before and which none of us had realized had fallen off during the rainstorm. As I was kneeling down to pick it up, a door swung ajar some ten feet behind me and I heard the heir's voice say, "I like that boy very much, even if he isn't a twin." His father's voice replied, "Why, then, me' boy, you shall have him, of course. Why ever not?" To which his son replied, "Why ever not," and they both sort of sniggered.

Mother called my name and I hurried forward to join my loved ones, little knowing how all of our lives had thereby changed forever.

Lillian of Ravenglass

(Left at the Auberge Cheval Rouge for M. de M.)

19 Septembre, 188—

As you haf wished so have I wrote to you to tel you that all is as long planed.

I canot but drop these line to say we are in good health and travel eesey.

My Lady calls for me now to take down her hair for sleep. I must go.

I leave this at the Au-berg and it goes I know not where, but you do.

Very good-night,
Henriette

To: The Honourable Lady Caroline-Ann Augusta
The Glebe, Ravenglass
Broughton, England

21 September 188—

My Dear Lady Caroline-Ann,
    We have had a sudden change of plans which I cannot elucidate without "giving away" too much information even to one I trust like yourself, Lady. And so I find myself with more leisure time to write to you. I also recognize that although we met but a few times, that when we next do meet, you at least will know me very well from what I have written and you, I hope, have read. But let me reiterate what I wrote before, much of this for your very indispensable edification, Lady Caroline. Were it not, would I write it anyway? Perhaps, for I find now that once begun, I needs *must* write it out, if only for myself to understand, but in that event, it would never be franked and posted on to you as now.
    I wrote in my last letter how after that birthday fête for the heir, all had changed. Alas, we did not see it for what is was at the time. And indeed with us, all appeared to go on as it had before. My mother continued in poor health, always weak and over-fatigued, helped but slightly by myself when I could, and more often by a sluttish "girl" brought in for pennies a month as char, a distasteful young widow from among the basest fisher folk. My father's health also deteriorated from, he believed, the insalubrious prospect of the vicarage, which both of them, used to seaside air and damp humours, found too high and far too dry, although it suited their children exceedingly. My brother especially grew stronger and more handsome by the season.
    But if there were alterations, surely it was he who showed them the most and the most often. Yet even within Rudolph they were fleeting. Most of the year, he continued on as usual, playing with me less, it is true, as we both grew older and our games naturally changed in nature and kind. He spent as much time with me as possible, and I with him. He began to learn more manly pursuits Father thought might be of future use. On occasion, he joined neighbours in ploughing, sowing, planting, and reaping. On other occasions, he joined other neighbours in learning some of the secret ways of the great bay and sea. Still, chiefly he went to school, and

he studied and remained at home, helping Father and sometimes Mother and even the char, to whom he was always kind, about the house and grounds.

All changed naturally upon school holidays and summer "vacs," as the boys called them. For that was when little Lord Roland returned to Ravenglass, for a week or so in winter and spring, or for two months entire in summer. The two youths had grown rapidly intimate, to the point where Rudolph seldom ever told me of their adventures or even their daily affairs when together. It was all, "Men's things, don't you know?" and therefore not for my ears. And whenever those holidays approached, I would gird my loins, prepared to be solitary, or at least bereft of my dear one.

But if Rudolph began each re-acquaintance with the greatest of enthusiasm and almost itching anticipation, he was left in a most dark mood by the end of each interval, just when Roland must leave. I couldn't make out from our few encounters those times whether my brother felt irritated, angry, or feared to be deprived of his company, and it was weeks before his usual good temper reasserted itself.

What I did know was that I looked forward to these "vacs" less and less, as he did, poor thing, more and more, and that each one's end threatened our own old and deep family friendship in ways I could not explain to myself, due to the state of nerves it left Rudolph in. No wonder I loudly begged along with him, before one Christmas holiday, that he be allowed to join his friend away from us all, in London itself. It happened as we wished, and though Rudolph went off in a stagecoach with the highest of spirits, he returned from Hanover Square after that trip even more taciturn and miserable than before.

Two years had now passed, and we had learned all our schoolhouse teachers or tutors could provide. It was time for Rudolph to move onward in his schooling, as his father had done before him. Still, the weeks dragged on, and Father did nothing about it, wrote to no one, approached no one, spoke not one word of encouragement about an academic future.

Roland of Ravenglass, of course, was soon to "go down" to Cambridge. This was naturally unthinkable for my brother, his rural companion. Still, there were colleges of divinity and law within a day or two travel from where we lived, and I knew Rudolph was growing apprehensive about his prospects. Whenever I dared approach my mother on this subject, she continually put me off. When I got up the bravado to approach and ask my father, he also put me off, saying he had not yet decided.

One afternoon as I was sorting herbs and simple medicines I'd been out of doors picking, I overheard my father speaking with our local neighbour, who like myself and my brother confessed himself to be growing apprehensive on the topic. I heard my father say, "There are no funds for it. The living hasn't increased since I took it, yet costs do increase daily. I couldn't purchase a vest coat without going into debt." When his friend suggested my father apply to his lordship for the funds or for an increase in his living, my father argued, he niggled, he pleaded, he did all he could to snake his way out of what he perceived as so humiliatingly impossible an interview, although it concerned him most direly.

As I stepped away from the door, I saw my brother had crept up behind and had heard the very same words. Flushed with resentment and embarrassment, he turned on his heels and rushed out of the house and was not seen the rest of the day until dinner, when he returned and seemed exceedingly demoralized.

Perhaps this will make clear why it was that I decided to take matters into my own hands. Two days later, our Aunt Blassage from Lancaster visited us, and after she had gone, she left my mother as a gift, a lovely lacework collar, made in the Isle of Man, where Aunt had recently journeyed. My mother declared it beautiful if a great waste of money. She went out insufficiently to wear it. Anyway, a vicar's wife, as Aunt B. should well know, oughtn't to display such vanities upon her person.

I suggested that mother give it to her ladyship, the Marchioness Bella of Ravenglass, who, though she went out even less, we both knew, wore such collars, and who would thereby be particularly obliged to us by its receipt. I think my mother was so surprised I did not ask the collar for my own self that she assented to my plan.

The following afternoon, I took it wrapped in a fine piece of slightly used muslin up to the manor house. Mrs. Ounch, the housekeeper, sought to take it from me, promising to pass it on. I wondered if it would ever get past the servants' hall, and reminded her that at her ladyship's last birthday celebration she had particularly asked me to pay her a call. It was, therefore, with a rather poor grace that Ounch conveyed my message to her mistress, and a few minutes later, I was ushered upstairs and into the winter garden, albeit it was only November and still inordinately temperate out of doors.

I would have been amazed to see the marchioness out of her mechanical contraption of a movable chair, and she was not today. She was in fact, sitting amid its surrounding pillows, and had been placed in a pool of green filtered sunlight, surrounded by oversize *dracaenas*, colossal rubber plants, jungles of orchidaceous vines and lianas, giant pink *amaryllis*, and other flora and vegetation of a tropical nature I was unfamiliar with. Somewhere above us, a skylight windowpane must have been left ajar, as three quite large, iridescent, brilliantly coloured bottle green horseflies slowly swirled about the vicinity, shaping unhurried figure eights in the dust-mottled air.

I thought the marchioness asleep, since she was silent, unmoving, and her eyes shut, but I curtseyed anyway. I went up to her as close as I dared and laid the muslin upon her lap, opened it up, and quietly whispered, revealing and explicating the fineness of jet work interstitched with the inky lace.

Although she could be no older than five and thirty, from this near, she revealed a face covered with strangely old-looking skin and a meshwork of fine lines, especially around her pursed mouth and the almost bruised, dark-looking undersides of her eyes. She smelled of lilac water, yet also rather musty, like an older person, and there was also another, sharper aroma from nearby, which a moment later I was able to trace as coming from a narrow, violet glass vial with a carved stopper and also from a slender, chased silver chalice that could hold no more than half a draught of a drink, both items placed upon a wheeled, wooden-slatted table that evidently had been constructed to complement and accompany her chair.

I was about to stand up and go over to the vial for a closer look at the writing, which appeared from this angle to be medically prescriptive, when I felt her hand upon mine and looked up. Her great grey eyes opened slits, then wider, albeit without anything like recognition of me even though her mouth became more wrinkled as it opened slightly in an approximation of a moue.

"How charming!" she hissed more than whispered.

"My lady? Ma'am? I've taken the liberty of…? And I've brought you a gift from my mother…?"

I touched the muslin, and her large hands lifted the collar before her eyes.

"From the Isle of Man, my lady. Hand made by the inhabitants, of course."

She held it up to the light. "How very intricate." It now came out a whisper. "I accept it, yes. It will go with my…jade taffeta bodice."

She returned it to its muslin bed, where a horsefly landed upon it.

She made no effort to brush it off and when I did so, she stopped me.

"Don't you like it, young miss?"

"I do, my lady, very much so."

"*Very* much so?"

"Yes, my lady. Unlike most girls, I am unafraid of animals or… anything in nature. Our dear father lectures us that we must share the world with our animated brethren."

"Yes. So we must," she whispered hoarsely. "If you really like nature…?"

"I do."

"Then you will very much like my Precita."

So saying, she moved a hand to her throat where she wore a very large, deep green malachite locket, almost square, set in gold, and hung by three strands of gold beads, beneath which a silk scarf protected her neck.

No sooner was the locket opened than I saw it held some white furry object. One of her blood red fingernails gently probed the centre of the locket, and on the instant, several limbs jumped out around it, grasping the fingernail closely. Immediately the large furry white thing crawled out of the locket across her hand and, almost too quickly to follow, rushed onto her throat, crossed onto her long hair, and stopped only when atop her head, where it rested long enough for me to fully make it out.

I'd been greatly surprised, for it moved in a fashion unlike any other creature I'd ever seen but perhaps a spider, not quite scuttling as crabs and lobsters do upon the strand yet similar to them. Unlike them, it didn't locomote sideways and yet it went so very quickly. I could now see that it *was* some species of spider, though very large, quite furry and the colour of clotted cream, with a beige hue only upon its head and what seemed to be the curved gripping claws of its front arms.

"You do like nature," she now hissed at me. "You haven't fallen back, screaming and rushing out of the room on your hands and knees like most of the fool girls in this house."

"It's remarkable," I said. "In truth, my lady, what manner of animal is it? It seems an arachnid in shape and limb, but it's so large! Furred like a mouse or…"

"It is an arachnid, as you say. A subspecies called a tarantula. But while related, it is not a whit like those of that name we know here in the Old World, those black and ugly brutes with their bags of gut and blood red stain. No," she went on, "it's from the Sonoran desert. Do you know where that is?"

"In North America, I believe, my lady, in the north-western part of Mexico."

"So you are intelligent after all. Do you know what it likes to eat?"

"I should think," I said, "other creatures from that locality, insects and small rodents and lizards and suchlike."

"Yes," she hissed, "And not little girls, which is why you did not flee from it." She paused. "Would you like to touch Precita? To pet her?"

Though subtly horrified, I was most curious. "May I? I'll be very gentle."

With a single hand, she lifted the tarantula and brought it down to the muslin and slowly petted it until I swore I could hear it purr like a kitten.

"Now you may," she said, and I followed suit, amazed at its silk-like fur and its little movements as though coming closer into being caressed.

"You came here not merely to call, nor simply to gift me. You're far too intelligent a girl for that," she said as we now took turns with the spider.

"It's true, my lady. I came to ask a boon for my dear brother, Rudolph, whom you may remember."

"How could I not remember him? For of late he is to be found all over this house whenever Roland is here."

"I hope, my lady, that my brother does not displease you."

"He neither pleases nor displeases. He's Roland's, after all, and no business of mine."

I knew neither what she meant, nor how to take it, so I went on, as we doubly caressed the furred, cream-colored arachnid.

"He is of age to continue his schooling. To a college of some sort he must go, yet my father has not lifted one finger to make it so."

"He is not a good scholar?"

"Quite good, my lady. Yet he is in want of..." I knew not what to say and settled for, "of patronage."

"I have not held in my hand even one sovereign in more than a decade," she said sadly, an admittance I must say amazed me.

"Even so, a word or two from your ladyship on the matter. To Roland. Or better yet, to his lordship. A scholar's stipend, after all, although immense to such as we, is but a pittance to..."

She stopped me with another hiss, and I thought my mission lost.

"He is afraid?" she asked very quietly yet very clearly.

"My brother, ma'am? I think he is afraid of no one alive!" Then I understood. "You mean my father? Yes, he is afraid! And especially to ask anything of Lord Ravenglass, no matter how much it is needed. He fears him greatly, I believe."

"And rightly, too. For Lord Ravenglass is powerful and thus much to be feared," she added, and I thought my cause a lost one.

"Still," she went on, "It's true I may now and then wield an iota of influence. If only because he wishes no possible... "She sought the words, settling upon, "possibly solid, *provable* grounds of dissatisfaction."

"Ah, my lady," I almost cried, lifting my hand off the creature. "My entire family would be so utterly obliged to you."

She stopped my effusions. "But on condition that you will join your brother in going to college. For if he is as intelligent as you are, he would want it. Your parents too."

"I would like that very much, since indeed my parents do believe in girls being educated and have helped me to advance this far."

"Then I shall have a little project," the marchioness said, and for the first time I heard a smidgen of pleasure in her voice. "Wherein I may somehow alter the way things are."

Precita suddenly moved forward from out of her caress. And I couldn't help but notice one of the bottle green flies had landed nearby, as before, on a particular weave of muslin.

The marchioness lifted her hand lightly and very gently lifted mine away at the same time.

Precita slowly stood up, and I could see the hair on its limbs stand up too. Still, it didn't move. Before it and thoroughly heedless, the bottle green fly turned about upon the spot of muslin, its feelers and antennae immersed in some area therein from which it hoped to gain sustenance. Precita meanwhile waited and almost thrummed like a purring cat, but remained utterly unmoving for the longest time. I was almost about to look away when Precita shot forward and in a half second had the fly caught between its longest palps, had turned it about, thrust out of some openings a network of glistening thread and had wrapped the fly in wet netting.

It worked so quickly, now using its mandibles and several of its legs, that though I observed most carefully, I could not make out how the fly became so mummified. Then Precita stopped, held the fly just so before its high-placed little head with five black eyes, thrust out a single tiny near-invisible needle into the mass, and stung again and again until the fly went still, its alarmed buzzing silenced.

"Now Precita shall dine at leisure," the marchioness said, slipping back into her languid hiss of a voice. I watched the tarantula hold the wrapped fly in front of itself as though admiring its work, then crawl up her arm, onto her breast, and from there back into the ajar malachite box, where it settled in as though into a nest.

She shut the box, then reached over for the purple glass vial and let several thick liquid drops slowly descend into the chalice, where she indolently swirled the liquid.

Before she could bring the chalice to her mouth, I curtseyed and began to withdraw.

"You won't forget my brother!" I dared to remind her, suspecting what lethe was contained in that draught she raised to her lips.

"I assuredly won't forget either you or your brother," she softly said, then tossed back the liquid, and I could smell it fully now and identify it as laudanum from its bouquet like rotten almonds and overripe peaches.

Having sipped, she went very still, although her eyes remained open, staring into some baroquely fanciful Beyond, as I slowly backed out of the winter garden.

Lillian of Ravenglass

To: The Very Reverend Jas. H. Quill
The British Church at Campofieri
Town of Fiesoli
Province of Tuscany

22 September 188—

Sir,
    We are delayed. In truth, we are returned almost to where we were two days ago. In many ways I am to blame for it, although had I known what the outcome of my really quite ordinary action would be... But I leap ahead.
    We arrived last evening by a tumbling old stagecoach, easily passed through the quite perfunctory customs station, and quickly drove into the respectable old city of Aachen. I think you have been here once, sir, and so recall it as a Teutonic heap of grey stone and blood red brick, and a conglomeration of medieval cathedrals and their ancient cloisters abutting new built barley and malt storehouses with their eternal dray wagons and overweight quarter-horses parked in front.
    Following a pleasant enough night's stay in a commercial traveller's hostelry—we are, after all, in concealment—we breakfasted heartily, as one does in this kind of establishment, and all three of us bathed, which was much needed after our several days upon the road.
    Luncheon was obtained at the recently erected railroad terminus, a building the locals are proud of for its size and up-to-date mechanical conveniences, including this café. Tickets had been obtained for our next two "halts"—Bonn and thence on to Frankfurt on the River Main. These cities are in themselves but "halts" on our way to Nuremberg and thence Munich, headed toward a more comprehensive shelter. My lady and her maid were in fact seated at a little café table, post-repast, she writing a letter, the girl with her interminable needle and thread, and I across from them, reading an English language weekly newspaper from the region.
    My amazement upon coming upon in print the very occasion we had attended, now deemed newsworthy, caused me to start and say something on the order of "Well, I'll be jiggered."

When the lady asked me what I was swearing upon, I read her the piece. I have torn it and enclose it here.

Foreign Nationals Bound Over to Be Tried for Nautical Disappearance.
In a curious case following the unsolved vanishing of a Turk of some importance from a recent ferry bound from England to these shores in recent days, two men of unknown heritage and origin unable to communicate to the authorities by virtue of their unknown tongue have been bound over and are to be tried for his disappearance. An accusation by an unknown person on board the Ferry from South Hampton to Dunkerque was deemed sufficient for such action, said Assez-Judge Maxim Tortelier. How they are to know of the proceedings was never explained. The trial takes place in the Palais de Justice tomorrow at one o'clock p.m.

If I were surprised, the lady, upon my reading the account to her, was perfectly aghast. Her face drained of colour, then became almost purple with rage. She had already sealed her letter and sent it off. She dropped her novel on the floor as she leapt up, her face a mask of horror.

"They are to be tried and probably executed without a shred of evidence and never knowing what for? This is an abomination! We must go there immediately."

In vain did I spend the next twenty minutes trying to talk the lady out of her scheme, but upon this point she held fast and would brook no opposition. Finally, she declared that either she entrained to visit those two men, or she went nowhere ever again. With the expected upshot that our tickets for Bonn and farther on were returned to the clerk, and fortunately, held in exchange of those to Brussels. That train arrived shortly thereafter and our luggage was scarcely re-routed in time.

We arrived at that city after nightfall with no names, no addresses, and not a hotel reservation nor inn to be had. I placed the ladies in a waiting room, under veils and the watch of a young railroad clerk, while I sought aid. I soon found an office connected in some manner to a British travel guide you are doubtless familiar with. The fellow there asked to be shown the two ladies, and upon seeing them from the doorway of the lounge surrounded by our extensive baggage, he tapped my hand and said, "I've got just the place for you all—extremely discreet!"

For a small fee, he further obtained a coach and footman for us. He rode above and ushered us into what appeared to be a private house of some size. After the ladies had been settled in their suite and I in my chamber, I thanked him and he told me that such services could be had in the future in various places and handed me his card, which had a list of such cities and also a telegraph number, of potential use in the future.

By ten o'clock of the following morning, the lady and her maid were dressed as expensively as possible and we were driven to the *Palais de Justice*, where her bearing and my overbearing soon brought us to the attention of a *Procurateur* of the case.

"We three were aboard that wretched bucket," the lady declared in what seemed good French, "and we saw both those dark little gentlemen and that large fat Turk, and there was no possible connection at all between them. We will all swear an oath to it. Upon a *Tournai* Bible if need be. Where is their accuser to contradict us?"

The accuser, as we all suspected from the newspaper account, had left a sketchy deposition some days after landing and was now long gone to parts unknown.

With us willing to stand defence and him no longer present, the state's attorney had no case. Still, there was a problem.

"But what is to be done, *Madame*? There is a disappearance and no one to be held responsible. The gentleman's government has issued a formal complaint."

Thus we understood. The two had been held hostage to a political convenience.

"That is none of my concern. Nor should it be any of yours, *Monsieur.*" The lady demanded the two men be released and that we witness it.

And so it came that we saw them again, and they fell onto their knees, the poor young fellows, and kissed her hands and wept.

She ensured that their passports were returned and visas stamped so they might exit the country, and she offered to pay their train fare, making me point to our tickets and gesture so they might understand.

They remained close by us all the while, and while awaiting this latter, required official seal, the lady began addressing the fellows first in Spanish then in halting Italian. The latter language, one of them knew enough of to say, "*Greco. Noi suomi Grecci.*"

"They are Greek. They speak little else but Greek. Only a few words of Italian," she told the *Procurateur.*

To our complete astonishment, she then turned to them and began speaking. They too were astonished, but not always comprehending, and a paper and quill were ordered, and she and they sometimes spoke and sometimes wrote words, trying to form an understanding. After some time, the attorney called a very young man, a student, who had studied Attic Greek at university. Between all four of them, they seemed to generally comprehend each other. Afterward, the two young men, laughed, cried, kissed the lady's hands over and over and called out blessings of "*Christe, Elision!*"

This is what the lady told us.

"I know but some ancient Greek from my college studies, and so does this student, Monsieur D'Ertrande. The young Greeks speak a more modern version. But the written language we studied is known to them and not too dissimilar, so we've managed to obtain from them and put together what seems to be a rather full and extraordinary picture."

The *Procurateur* asked her to enlighten us.

"The two Greeks were sent to England by members of their government's fledgling parliament to meet with members of the British Museum in an attempt to recover certain statuary artifacts from their country removed at the beginning of this century and upon constant display in London. Two of their countrymen living in London paid their way, gave them room and board, and translated for them. Their mission was a grave failure, alas, and they returned downcast, as we first saw them aboard the ferry. They never met the Turk and never knew who he was, but because their country has been in part or whole under the Ottoman sway for so long, they noted him well and understood how powerful he was. They were astounded he travelled without attendants or wives. They supposed his journey to be an unofficial one, and indeed highly *sub rosa.*

"This one," she pointed, "named Theocrakis, says that he was returning to his chamber on the ferry after being ill over the railing when he noticed a very slender young boy, with a sailor's tam and a scarf covering the lower part of the face, knock twice then twice more on the Turkish Bey's stateroom door. He did so again, looking about to see that he was not noticed, and only then was the door opened, and he was granted entrance. From the boy's gestures and motions, Theocrakis is certain he was, in fact, a young woman."

"Jolly fill. Jolly fill!" Theocrakis seconded her in his version of her spoken French: *Jolie fille*. Pretty girl.

She went on. "Theocrakis returned to his cabin but remained awake the entire time. During the course of the night, once the gale had blown down a bit and we were sailing under clear skies again, he is certain he heard the sound of another motorized craft. When he stood up to look out the stateroom, he no longer heard its motor, but saw the shadowy shape of an unlighted craft pass before the porthole. He thought little of it, assuming it to be another ferry of the commercial line, until the next morning. He now believes both the Bey and young woman were taken aboard the second craft, and that it was all planned in advance."

Their statements were written out in French, read back to us, and then officially signed attested to by witnesses, including young D'Ertrande, and then notarized. The case was then officially dismissed, and the two young Greeks released into my lady's substantial custody.

Unwilling to leave their benefactress, for despite their being incommunicado, they had somewhat guessed the implications of their gaol cell and various papers thrust in front of them, they begged to travel alongside, indeed in tandem, with our party and could not be dissuaded otherwise. Although I said it would be impossible, the lady agreed with the two of them, declaring it to be the only way she might rest assured they were in safe-keeping.

And so it has devolved. We are this moment in a lounge of the Brussels terminus. Our train leaves for Bonn in one half hour. This post will reach you I do not know when. But we are delayed two days or more off our schedule.

Your friend,
Stephen Undershot

Post-Scriptum. Who knew the lady reads Greek? She seems unfazed by officials or prominent strangers. She's more remarkable and more accomplished, although more strong-willed, with every passing day. Truly, my friend, this undertaking is become an adventure!

To: The Honourable Lady Caroline-Ann Augusta
The Glebe, Ravenglass
Broughton, England

23 September 188—

My Dear Lady Caroline-Ann,
    Once again, I have found myself at leisure at a railroad terminus. Our next train arrives in over an hour. I do wish I could receive and know your responses, for I now find myself dearly wishing to hear what you have to say to what I have written so far. But there is more to come. Far worse to come, I almost wrote.
    Imagine my brother Rudolph and myself then, aged sixteen and seventeen over four decades ago, suddenly resident in the city of Leeds, a thriving commercial centre, and also home to a quite good university and various other colleges. Naturally enough, the least well-endowed and prestigious admitted handfuls of young women who could, over a two-year course of study, learn a variety of "household arts and duties" as well as philosophy, Natural Science, British and Ancient history, mathematics, English and French grammar and composition, and a modicum of basic Latin. For advanced studies in that language and in the Greek language, six of us young ladies were crowded together into a phaeton twice weekly and driven to the august University itself, where we sat behind a wooden screen similar to those shamefully separating the genders in those temples of the Islamic and Hebraic faiths. Still, we heard and saw the professor, and if we were never "called on" to recite as were the young men, once we were back at our school it was done so, and furthermore we were given supplemental classes, with an erudite if quite elderly woman named Mrs. Barbarina Stackweather Caine. Mrs. Caine was a scholar of strict demeanour and unbending rectitude, it turned out, with an inordinate fondness for gooseberry jam tarts and *baba au rhum*. She'd been taught Greek and Latin by her father, having reached girlhood in the previous Century, which admired all erudition no matter which gender might display it.
    I blush to write that Mrs. Caine became fond of me as a scholar and young person, perhaps perceiving how serious I was in pursuing my education, and she sometimes obtained entrée to events in the town she thought edifying for her favourites among us younger ladies.

Thus, it happened, one brilliant March afternoon in the year 184——, that I found myself, along with Mrs. Caine and two other young ladies, seated in the stalls of Leeds's only theatre, at a performance of Mr. Shakespeare's fantastical comedy *The Tempest.*

The popular "draw," as the local newspaper wrote, was the famous married actors, Mr. Charles and Mrs. Ellen Kean, known for their unbowdlerized performances of the Bard. They were portraying, respectively, the magician Prospero and Ariel. We had of course "read" the play, and indeed even attempted to "put on" a scene or two beforehand. But as this was my first live professional dramatic performance, you may imagine my excitement.

The play is in five acts, with four intervals. During the first, we remained in our seats, planning to send several of ourselves out for tea and cake during the next. But if I had been animated before, you may understand how keyed up I became when my dear Rudolph came over just then to where we sat and lightly kissed my cheek. Accompanying him was a schoolmate, Mr. Joseph Robinson, and upon meeting the two handsome young collegians, my companions soon showed themselves to be less scholars than coquettes.

Were that all that occurred, I would have been happy. But greater encounters were in store. For upon the second interval, when five of us left timid, dull, Edith Dunwoody alone with our benefactress while we sought out tea, cakes, and collegiate male company, I found myself separated from the others for a moment by the jostling crowd, only to turn and walk directly into the shirtfront of his golden blond, young lordship, Roland of Ravenglass. With him was an exceedingly handsome brunet young gentleman, introduced as Lord Robert of Blackburn.

"You have just seen the striking brother," Roland said to Mr. Blackburn, "now meet the Eve to his Adam."

He explained that both of them were great followers of the Keans and avidly pursued their increasingly rare countryside performances whenever they might go. In a year or so, the famous couple would settle into London's Princess Theatre for more than a decade, making their "provincial" performances even more uncommon. As Robert's family resided not far away, Roland told me, their attendance in Leeds this day had been much facilitated.

Once I'd explained the reason for my own presence, the two young gentlemen insisted upon meeting our "learned Xanthippe." Upon seeing us approach, poor Miss Dunwoody fled, but Mrs.

Stackweather-Caine proved to be fully up to the meeting. Furthermore, once she heard that Robert's married sister was in the family's box as chaperone, she agreed to their ardent request that I join them up there for the remainder of the play, especially as Roland jokingly promised to treat me "with the solicitude deserving of a college-lady."

That was how I found myself enjoying the remainder of Mr. Shakespeare and Mr. and Mrs. Kean from so prominent a situation.

Curiously enough, Sir Robert's sister, Lady Dankworth, remained in close conversation for the remainder of the play, in mostly hushed tones, in the back of the box, unseeing, with a man explicated to me as her "business solicitor," so there was little society or chaperoning to be found from that quarter. Her brother and his boon companion more than compensated. Both were in good spirits, partly from a flask of fortified wine Roland had upon his person. And my college sisters could not help but turn about and gawk at us behind and above them, which couldn't be more gratifying.

Naturally, I asked if we shouldn't spend the next interval replacing my person with that of my brother.

"Could any girl be more selfless or generous?" Roland asked his friend. Then, "I think not, however, as your brother has developed a sort of animadversion to my company of late."

I wondered greatly at this statement but held my tongue.

"Were that the whole of Rudolph's new circumstances, it would mean but little," Roland continued. "Alas, it is not, and my father thinks not to continue his scholarship for the coming annum, although yours is utterly secure."

This was hard news for me to hear, and I could not help but pale as I replied that I had thought they two were "hard friends."

"You may see for yourself." Roland leaned forward and I followed his gaze to where my brother and Mr. Robinson were now laughing together, "Dear Rudolph's new hard friend, now that I am tossed aside."

I could well see, and I was embarrassed for them all. Still, I must know what other cause my brother had given that his stipend must be taken away.

"His ability to concentrate upon study, miss, seems to have vanished along with my company. He spends less time reading than even dear Robert here, who is already the most erudite fellow I've ever met and has little need of more books."

I dreaded to ask it. "He has not taken up other, unsavoury habits somewhat frequent to university men?"

Now it was Roland's turn to colour. "Do you think, miss, if it were so, that I could tell it to you?" By which I guessed my worst fears were confirmed.

"Then what is to become of him?"

"I believe my father has mentioned in passing several minor commissions in the Queen's Navy he possesses the disposal of."

"Rudolph go to sea!" I complained, fearing for him. "We've never been separated longer than a day's journey."

"Should that sad necessity eventuate, miss," Lord Robert now said, "I hope that you will look upon me as a brother, even though we have but a glancing acquaintance, and that you would apply to me for any fraternal solace." This was very kind, and lifted him in my estimation. "I think Lord Roland will not hate me if I say he would naturally request an even closer connection," he added, "and yet greater opportunities for consolation."

Now both of us, then all three us coloured deeply, but luckily Mr. Purcell's third act musical prelude to the play had begun, and I might think on what had been said.

During the final interval, Roland needed to attend upon an aged relation also in the theatre he had just then noticed, and I was left more or less alone with Robert, Lord Blackburn.

"I know your family name, I think," he said. "You hail from the vicinity of Morecambe Bay."

I admitted the fact.

"An old English family of solid, respectable yeoman blood," he added.

"I believe so. Are you then so interested in genealogy?"

"Only insofar as it may concern my dearest friends," he answered, and before I could say anything, he went on. "Although his advantages of background, holdings, and not least his person itself recommend Lord Roland to the grandest young ladies of the realm, I suspect his heart is previously bestowed, since to my eyes he cares but little for even the most glittering of their ilk."

I could only keep silent and hope I did not show the great astonishment his words had aroused in me.

"And now, having met the possible object of his previous attentions—"

"You mistake the situation, I believe."

He went on, nevertheless. "I cannot but agree with him."

"Of course you cannot but agree with me," Roland said, bounding into the box at that moment, holding a luscious caramel apple upon a stick dripping into the handkerchief in which he had wrapped and held it. "Now, which of you lovelies," he offered lasciviously, "shall have the very first lick?"

So it was that I discovered, in the very short space of but three play intervals, that my brother was to not resume college but to go off to sea, perhaps very far away, and that we were to be separated for the first time in our lives, possibly for years. And so it was that I also learned to my greater surprise that young Lord Ravenglass entertained romantic inclinations toward me, of which his prominent new best friend thoroughly approved.

Lillian of Ravenglass

24 Septembre 188—

Sir

We ar much turnt around by virtu of som Grik boys. Je comprenez pas le raison. There–for you must patient be, until on road again we go. Now three and the Grik boys also.

We ar al wel. But this fud is not to my gout.

Henriette

To: The Honourable Lady Caroline-Ann Augusta
The Glebe, Ravenglass
Broughton, England

25 September 188—

My Dear Lady Caroline-Ann,
　　We continue onward in our journey. We were, as I mentioned to you in an earlier letter, delayed. We are now moving quickly forward once again via steam locomotive, farther than ever from you. It may be these letters are reaching you only after a week or more. I cannot know, and it is still a time until I can feel at full ease and allow you to write me.
　　Yesterday evening, I realized with something of a shock that while we are *en route*, I cannot let down my guard a single moment. We were entraining, at a place we had not planned to be. It was a large city, blessedly in a large railroad terminus, otherwise…
　　What happened was that we were informed by conductors striding through the train that we had a thirteen-minute wait before the train actually moved. I mentioned that I would have liked reading material of some sort, as I was otherwise certain to finish reading my Sheridan Le Fanu novel. I was halfway through the third volume already. My guardian angel said he too was in need of reading matter and would step out to purchase it for us both. I spoke out a list of those periodicals I prefer, which I think he must know the names of by now, having seen them so often among my things.
　　He left, and we were seated thus, my chambermaid and myself, in a closed compartment, when an official of some sort from this country suddenly tapped on the door, was let in, and demanded to see our travelling papers.
　　Our friend, not we, had those important documents. And so my chambermaid was sent out to unearth him. I was left quite alone to attempt to pass the time with this courteous, if naturally curious official. He asked what novel I was reading and was surprised to hear that it was in English. He then recommended a novel by a Mr. Anthony Hope that his son had read that year of which, every morning at dejeuner, he would explicate the plot of. My official told me that every scene and event had been most exciting. I was about to reply that younger men tend to find adventure novels even more "spine-tingling" than other readers and that Mr. Le Fanu was in

his own unique way sufficiently stimulating for a lady, when my guardian suddenly appeared. Papers and travel tickets were shown, magazines gone through, and only as the locomotive was blowing off repeated charges of steam and we about to set forward did I note my girl was missing.

Both the railway man and my own man were sent out in search for her. I thought we might have to get off and had gathered my smaller bags and begun fuming at the possibility for where would our luggage be if we were on a later train, when the little chit arrived.

In a glance I could tell I must not be angry with her. She was breathless, then panting and utterly relieved, and she was almost quite comical in her distress, although being put out in that way was hardly her own fault.

Only when I had persuaded her to sit down and the others had come in and seen her there with great relief and the train was chugging along merrily and picking up speed as it went, did she sufficiently regain her breath to speak.

When she did, oddly enough, she addressed me in Italian, a language known only to we two and not to our friend. The cause of her distress: While searching for our guardian, she had espied one of the earl's henchmen standing at a newspaper reading kiosk, paging through an issue of *The Illustrated Sporting and Dramatic News*. She recognized him from the evening of your wedding.

I asked if she was quite certain it was he, and she replied how could she fail to be certain, as she'd never forgotten his dastardly role in an affair concerning one of the other house servants not two months earlier at Ravenglass? This Crimmins or Grimmins, she forgets his exact name, somehow or other managed to get Trithers to let go of a certain lad who, although a titular footman, was in reality his close factotum. Besides this, one or more of the boy's family have been at the manor house going now on several generations already, and so his being let go so suddenly was the greatest blow to them all.

She began to explain now how the boy had complained to the head butler of this Crimmins's or Grimmins's very free and reprehensible behaviour to him in private. For his trouble, the lad in turn had been accused by Crimmins of being seen pocketing a missing salt cellar. I barely recalled the incident myself, it being of so minor a nature below stairs. But I well recalled Grimmins, as he was very darkly handsome, and the youngest and most conspicuous of that generally young male entourage that constantly surrounds my husband in London town and whenever he made one of his increasingly infrequent "flying visits" to the manor house.

If truth be told, the young man also reminded me uncannily of how Sir Robert of Blackburn had looked when he was but four and twenty, some decades ago. They might almost have been related, and since the earl was so much the elder, this Grimmins lad might easily have been his bastard offspring. I write that term easily enough since only two very young legal children were known to have ever issued from Sir Robert's loins before his untimely death. His great ninny of a wife, wed to him quite late in life, mainly for her dowry, and certainly not for her wit, never remarried. Miss Cresswell, among others, did claim strictly accurate if not first-hand knowledge of Lord Blackburn's many solitary forays at night among the deepest rural recesses of his lands, whence, she believed, he might only sport with the very lowest of country wenches. And now I thought how my connexion to Ravenglass continues on even though I am gone. I beg you, Lady Caroline-Ann, look into this matter of the dismissed footman and discover his family and aid him in regaining, if not his station, then at least adequate compensation, for the family is a large and loyal one to the manor house.

At the rail terminus, this Grimmins was alone, or so my chambermaid believed. She placed herself so as to not be seen until she was certain our guardian was nowhere in sight, then took herself off. That was her cause for being so tardy. She thought Grimmins was evidently wasting time dawdling, and so she was certain he was not bound for our train. Indeed, when she arrived to find us about to move, she hopped up the step and was held fast by the conductor, and thus was able to give a long sweeping glance over the platform. Grimmins remained and did not entrain.

A small relief, but it was far too close. The more I think of one of the earl's men being so very far from home and so close to my own person, the more I had to ask myself what kind of "coincidence" it could possibly be.

I found I was unable to assuage myself. Although when I brought up the matter with my sentinel later, he was far more sanguine about it. "While we must take care," he said, "we must not fall into the trap of seeing a thief behind every hedgerow."

He is a good man, but he cannot know as well as I how your father-in-law, Lady Caroline, makes it his business to set a man, often an outright thief or worse, behind every possible hedgerow, and one is lucky if one manages to spy out even one of them. He was ever thus even before we were married. Years before, in fact.

Lest I lose all credit in your eyes, let me explain.

The performance of *The Tempest* and my double surprise occurred in April. In late May, our lessons were ended, and we left Leeds for the vicarage at Ravenglass. My brother was to have travelled with me but for some reason could not. I rode with two schoolmates as far as Lancaster, then with one as far as Ulverston. From there, I found a dog cart and driver I knew and he took me to the Lord Rothbert Inn at Ravenglass village. As it was past sunset, and I still had a shilling in my pocket, I decided to have word sent home that I would arrive the next morning, and that I would there have a cold supper and remain overnight in a leased room.

No sooner had I settled myself in my transitory chamber and stepped down to the public room's redoubled fire—for even that late in the Spring a chill does settle in—than I found my repast was ready to table. You may imagine with what appetite I lit into it, and I had done great damage to a quarter of a capon and to a green-gold cheese when I heard and saw a horseman ride up and dismount.

I know most of the horses in the area and didn't recognize the great bay being patted down and watered by the stable lad. No wonder. Not a moment later, a gentleman swept into the nearly vacant public room and in a vexed tone of voice asked for a draught of ale, "For I have been riding hard and needs must arrive at the manor house for dinner."

"Ravenglass?" asked the publican.

"Is there another nearby?"

"This young lady is also for Ravenglass," the publican replied without rancour and pointed to me.

The horseman had drunk half his flagon of stout before undoing his dust-covered face scarf, and I saw it was Lord Robert of Blackburn.

Seeing me, he bowed deeply. I, with poultry in one hand and crust of cheese in another, felt I must appear so comical to anyone that I burst into laughter.

Sir Robert was ever the gentleman. "If that is the leftover of a ripe Stilton, miss, I am your slave eternally."

I offered it to him, but only on condition he sit and keep me company, partly I think for the sake of the poor, sweated horse who must rest before going on, and partly because he looked so out of sorts although more handsome than before.

I waved the publican to bring more food, and Lord Robert attacked his cold breast of fowl and veal sausage with such a vengeance I feared for his appetite once at Ravenglass.

"You realize how much I wished to see precisely you," he said, once sated.

"Then you could not be more fortunate, could you?" I replied. "But why precisely me?"

"One reason for my visit tonight is to be envoy extraordinaire to the lord and lady at the manor house from their scion, and to convey a letter from my esteemed friend, 'precisely' regarding you."

"I think the master and mistress of Ravenglass know as much about poor me as they wish to," said I, "as I have lived here nigh on eight years. They have seen too much of me already."

"But have they seen you in a different light? That of the affianced to—"

I'm afraid I put a somewhat food-soiled hand to his mouth to stop his words.

"That is my mission," he managed to say around my fingers. "I swore an oath to Lord Roland."

"It cannot be, Lord Robert."

He repeated my words over-dramatically with gothic intonations so that I had to laugh.

"It cannot be *at this time, at least*," I added. "My mother is very ill. My father, who is never himself very strong, wrote to say they are uncertain of the outcome. My brother is, if not disgraced, at least no longer as well-regarded. He leaves us soon, for the first time ever. The family, as you see, is in a bad way."

"Then you must work to heal your mater and convert your brother to goodness," he said.

"I must work very hard to keep it all from falling into a great many tatters—with no guarantee I shall."

He lifted my hand and lightly kissed then nibbled it, making sounds of eating something tasty. As I began to laugh again, he added quite seriously, "Then that too shall Lord Roland's relations know of. For if nothing else, those difficult undertakings must recommend you to them with even greater consequence. It would certainly do so to me."

"But you, Lord Robert, are extremely exceptional. Of that I am certain."

"You are more correct than you can know," he said with no modesty apparent, making me laugh again. "I am also about to become exceptionably late," he added, verifying the time via a glance at his vest pocket pointer.

He was gone in a few minutes, and I settled by the fire, soon joined by the publican, who was in awe of me yet a bit more curious than he was daunted.

"It's bruited about the shire, miss, that Master Rudolph shall soon be off to Celebes and the Spice Isles as a master of the Nav-ee."

"Nothing is certain, Mr. Groon, until a commission is received."

"It's also bruited about the shire, miss, that the manor house is not the only abode of quality hereby."

"Meaning what? That some other lord takes up residence?"

"No other lord is needed, miss, when your fine self attracts them to us!"

I'd seen the brilliant half guinea tossed into his hand as Lord Robert had departed, at least twice the price that his services were worth.

"Don't expect gold, and copper will satisfy," I said, repeating a local proverb.

"Ay, but miss, begging your pardon, gold we have in plenty with your presence and that of your brother. And who doesn't know it?"

So, I learned how highly the neighbourhood thought of us at the vicarage, and I felt ashamed, for it was true I had held myself as superior very long and had come to that position from where I might easily tease a great lord's son, and I still felt no richer than poor Mr. Groon, with his arthritic feet and necessarily torn-open cloth shoes. But even that would soon change forever.

Rudolph arrived at the inn during the night, unheard by me, taken in and put to bed by Groon's wife, who loudly swore that he was fortunate she was awake and about and all because she suffered from "waking night sweats" as a result of the "bloodless change," as the local women termed the departure of their *menses*. My brother looked poorly in the morning, although he slept late, and he said but two words to me. We rode in silence the few miles.

The vicarage was as gloomy as I'd feared it, and my mother even more drawn and ill, although when I attempted to locate the exact cause, I was all but shunted aside and slowly came to believe that she was simply exhausted from living. My father was almost as emaciated and unable to be distracted long into discussing the minutiae of his dying wife. He was utterly immersed in his sermon writing and polishing, for he had been prided into collecting them into a volume and firmly believed two booksellers in Edinburgh keenly awaited their arrival.

The sluttish char was long gone, thankfully, replaced with Mrs. Cupp, a meek yeoman brought by my Aunt Blassage. She took my hand as I arrived and said, "Bless you, miss, for coming when you did. A strong hand is needed now all about the house. I can but only assist you." To which I replied, "Make up a large kettle of strong broth. Vegetable or meat, it matters not. And feed it to them all day long. In my packet, I have brought a new kind of kern. It's called rice, from North America, widely eaten in Asia. It is deemed wholesome for the infirm. You boil it within twice its measure of water as you do barley and for as long."

And so, I was returned to the vicarage at Ravenglass, as though my months at Leeds as a college woman had not occurred but in some pipe dream.

Several days later, the foreman of Ravenglass arrived at our house. Mr. Josiah Rocksmith was a tall, stout man of five and thirty years, of yeoman blood with a tall comb of auburn hair and a Quaker-style beard without any hair upon his upper lip. Dressed richly well, he stood in for the earl among the many working families upon the estate grounds and held himself quite lordly among them. Even so, he did little business with us but pass on my father's quarterly stipend, and so he was usually more modestly becoming at the vicarage. At one time, he'd apparently thought to court me, although I was so young, I simply laughed him off the property. He'd since wed a young Broughton woman, a mercer's daughter said to be as handsome and as full of herself as he.

This day he brought me an invitation, curiously couched.

"The manor gentry has left, all but her ladyship, of course," he said, "but his worship, Roland, plans to come down from university soon and asked especially if Mrs. Rocksmith and myself might host a dinner for six or eight people at the foreman's lodge. He is to be our guest, and he asks you especially be invited."

I found this to be a clever way for Roland to get around any possibly complicated issues of rank. We would all be the foreman's honoured guests. It would be most democratic. I wondered who else would make up the party.

"I believe Lord Roland's great friend and perhaps a lady friend of theirs."

So my brother Rudolph was not invited. I told him I would not go.

"Lord Blackburn has sent this note." Rocksmith handed it to me.

I unsealed it and read: "If you say no"—here a drama tragedy mask had been prettily sketched in—"I shall have no choice but the sword!"

I laughed and wrote back that I would attend, also telling the foreman so.

News of the invitation lifted my mother's spirits more than all the broth and rice she been persuaded to eat. Was I not greatly surprised, she asked. I must reply that I was not, for I'd met both young men at the theatre in Leeds, I reminded her. They were most friendly. She grew pensive at this and asked if I could recommend Rudolph to Lord Blackburn.

"He already knows of him very well, due to his closeness to Lord Roland," I explained. "I think it is *his* doing that Rudolph can expect a commission rather than having to fend for himself in the byways *before* the mast."

"As a little boy, Lord Roland was very beautiful. Golden as Apollo."

"And so he remains." said I. "A veritable English Apollo. Lord Robert is equally, if more darkly, handsome."

I expected her to tell me to beware their attentions, as every other triple-decker novel at the booksellers was about exactly such an aristocratic menace to young girls' chastity. Instead she said, "I would not at all be surprised if Lord Roland asked to marry you."

"He already has entertained the idea, and I have put off answering him until you and father are well."

"Lillian! You constantly astonish me. He must wait a long time, then," she concluded unhappily.

"I do not think it fit for Lord Roland to play my suitor," I said, "when he has his choice of all London society and millionairesses by the handfuls."

"I would think he wants a solid girl whom he knows well."

"May be," said I, "but I've no intent to rush to the Queen's court and be a brilliant star."

"You could easily be," said she. Then, "Perhaps you ought to gain Lord Blackburn's confidence and discover the true reason."

"It is he who carries Lord Roland's messages. He urges me onto this marriage."

"Who would know better?" she cried.

But I would contend with her no more and left her to rest, lest her excitement undo my regimen.

The dinner at the foreman's lodge was not formal and was quite uncomplicated despite the apparent great lengths mistress and master had gone to in making it appear so casual. Lord Blackburn came for me in a carriage. Lord Roland met us on the road in his own brougham, and with him was Lady Julia Withersmere, a tall dark-haired girl from a previous year at my college at Leeds who was extremely stylishly clad in emerald damask and pearls, and whom I liked immediately. I was attired in a simple, yet rich gown my Aunt Blassage had made for me in Leeds upon my birthday. Its sapphire blue silk complemented my colouring, as did the contrasting chain of coral I wore about my neck. Mrs. Rocksmith wore a demure, high-necked, sable-coloured frock made for a more matronly woman and, I think, specifically meant not to vie with us younger girls.

The men were all quite striking, and I quickly realized what a catch the foreman made for anyone not as foolish as I, for he held his own in demeanour and looks, if not in wealth or rank, with the others.

Lady Julia and Lord Roland were placed opposite myself and Lord Robert. She was delegated to bring me out of my shell in conversation, after which her table mate would swiftly, lightly pounce and continue. I could not recall a single memorable exchange between us, for they were as airy and insubstantial as words by Shakespeare's fairies. Yet, for all that, they were quite pleasant. And I would notice Lord Robert, listening closely to us, even when he was otherwise engaged in talk, as though assuring himself that we were happy.

My impression of Lord Roland was, if not altered, at least not negatively changed in any way. He flattered oneself, but not overly. He made one feel the very centre of his considerable focus and all the more special for being so. I was charmed all over again. He was intelligent, yet carried his learning with wit and dexterity. He understood the world and did not forebear to judge. He found much to appreciate about himself, and his life view was sunny and optimistic and four-square. Why should it not be for someone accustomed to expecting niceties, excellence, honours, and a minimum of thirty thousand pounds a year for life? What complaint against him could I possibly raise?

Only that he did not touch my heart-strings as plangently as did his friend. But his friend was bound for a great station in life and thus not to be even dreamt of.

"I am conscious, miss, of your circumstances at the vicarage," Lord Roland said, as we were readying to depart that night. "I wish to add no further pressures of any sort to your burden. But please do allow yourself to ameliorate that burden with an occasional dinner like tonight, or even an afternoon luncheon *al fresco*. I assure you I will locate citations from many philosophers and religious men to support that such diversions are not wicked, but rather necessary to those who assiduously nurse the ill."

That was kind, and I said so.

It was as we were out of doors at night, awaiting our carriage, that a small incident occurred that would have substantial ramifications later on.

As I mentioned before, the third story of the foreman's lodge where we had just supped stood as a dormitory for many of the bachelor workers on the estate. Several of these now arrived home from their public house supper, since they could not occupy the dining room at the same time that we had. A few of the lads had imbibed more than their share of ale and stout, and they made much noise in the common until they had come up to where the foreman held up a lantern illuminating our four awaiting carriages at front.

Suddenly they all quieted down and fell to murmuring. We moved aside for them to pass through to bed, and all did with eyes lowered and averted save for a tall, slender, good-looking blond-haired lad who was so intent upon making out who we four guests were and what we wore, that he stumbled upon a cobble step and fell. His friends immediately burst into laughter and japed at him, leaving him to pick himself up.

"Don't mind him, fine lords and ladies," called one of them. "It's poor simple Matthew." He then turned Matthew toward us, and the embarrassed boy bowed low, which caused them to all laugh at him again and pull him indoors.

"He's not simple," the foreman explained once they were gone, "merely mute. His family died when their cottage thatch went all aflame. The youngest at four years old, Matthew was tossed out by his father through a window. The father and mother died when it all collapsed upon them. Sadly, Matthew was the only one in the family to survive. Before then, he had prattled happily enough. But since that night, he has not uttered a word."

I determined then to speak to the poor boy if ever I saw him again.

Now I put down my pen for the night.

The following day:

Several such dinners took place over the summer months of that year, Lady Caroline-Ann, and I must admit that with each successive one, and almost despite my wishes, a gradual, growing attachment began to be formed between myself and Lord Roland. Partly, I believe, this was due to the regularity of the occasions, and partly due to their increased pleasantness and the greater facility and ease which we met and spoke and dined, and sometimes even joined in small games where we were "teamed up" against Lord Robert or the foreman and his wife. Partly too was the fact that the remainder of my circumstances worsened inexorably.

My mother's health failed to respond in any positive manner to my increased solicitude or the varied changes I introduced into her diet, or even my care for her altogether. As the days grew longer and warmer, she languished, she lolled, she lost what little mobility she had possessed, and she kept to her bed longer and then altogether.

Her husband seemed little moved by her ever-worsening condition, which struck me as out of the ordinary. I suspected theirs had been, like so many marriages of their place and time, one of expediency and not a grand romantic passion. Even so, I thought them at least good friends. I had ever thought of them as sharing their life, dividing their joys and difficulties. When had this now so evident disaffection occurred? Was I, was Rudolph, looking elsewhere at the time? It must have been, since he was equally baffled.

Most of that summer was needed for my brother's papers of commission to the sea to arrive, held back I could not say why. He did what any young man with time on his hands would do. He put himself as close to his new life as was possible. This meant being at the water's edge, in a boat, around boats, out to sea in a boat visiting islands and ports, and learning all about sailing, steam engine motoring, and the manoeuvring of boats, large and small.

Joseph Robinson, his new friend from college, at times visited to join him, but more often Rudolph was with those men who worked the sea or trod its watery lanes for their livelihoods. He grew taller, more sinewy and muscled, greatly sun tanned and altogether wonderful to look upon. I was proud to be seen with him the few times we were together in public in Ravenglass or Ulverston or once up in Broughton.

But alas, he also had become more conscious of his physique and face, his long, swept back, black hair, the high colour of his cheeks, the nobility of his brow, the intense, contrasting sea-green of his eyes, and as we walked past shop-front windows, I could see him catch at his own visage in profile or three-quarters view, and hesitate for the tiniest fraction of a moment to strike a better angle, or to present a more winning façade.

We had never been really conversant together, depending instead since we had been infants upon an unspoken bond, an instinctive mutual sympathy.

I no longer felt this bond; and yet we still hardly spoke those few times we went out together but seemed almost like great silent animals sniffing the air for food and water and finding it either acceptable or not. Perhaps I should have not wished us to talk at all, because the day after his papers did arrive, we held a celebration at the Lord Rothbert Inn that became the occasion of our first-ever altercation.

Nor will I blame it on the port wine he drank a bit too much of. For he knew very well what he spoke and what import it would have, and I do believe he had been gathering up his words for some weeks before.

The mute boy Matthew was present that evening too, as one of our guests, for I had in my own shy way befriended him, and in his own, even shyer way, he had responded. Which was how I discovered that he was a very able carpenter, utilized by the foreman once he understood the lad's gift, first at putting up drying sheds, then making silos, and then crafting doors, windows, and even some of the more fundamental furniture required up in the dormitory—half-wardrobes and small shelves and shoe-racks for the farmer lads.

The boy delighted even more in carving small fine articles, knitting needles, knife hafts, brooches and buttons, and to commemorate my brother's Naval commission, he carved a two-inch long frigate, with its suggestion of winds through the top and main sails, a very pretty piece that everyone in the inn stridently admired.

We had stepped outside to the courtyard for a breath of air when Rudolph suddenly turned to me and asked, "How comes about this new arrival gifting me so eloquently? I think it must be because he knows you."

I confessed this was the truth and said the boy was unfortunate in many respects, retelling what I had heard of his sad history.

"It is very good of you, always, sister, to succour the unfortunate. But how is it that you have of a sudden such an extensive acquaintance in the shire, when you spent most of your life avoiding such commonality and deriding me for not doing so? Do not deny it. Half those inside the public rooms now knew you by first name, while they know me mostly but from long ago or by repute. Is this the result of your higher education, sister, that you feel more free to accost and be accosted by all?"

"Perhaps not all, brother, but then it is also true that not all of us have the luxury of choosing our companions from so elect a company as your dear self."

"I assure you, sister, that Smudgin McGills and Scar-face Crabbe with whom I yesterday dredged up oyster-pots from the sea floor some leagues out from shore are hardly elect company. It is you, rather, who seem to regularly cavort with the highest gentry, and such folk as this unfortunate youth are strewn about as sometime scraps to be used now and again."

I took great exception to the last statement inasmuch as I couldn't deny the veracity of its predecessor.

"Do not think because I am not present all day long," Rudolph added darkly, "that eyes and ears do not exist for me anywhere you may be present."

"I never deemed it otherwise, nor do I comprehend any occasion for causing *your great repute* to become in any way compromised by *my friendships*," I replied, for I was in high temper at his words.

"Take care, for I am fired up with you," he replied, "and do not care to say words I could *not* take back."

"Say what you will, brother. I care not. Tell me especially what cause you have for chastising me so? Is it that I keep company in public and under the roof of respectable friends of ours with gentle people of greater rank than ourselves? Because it was you, Sir Naval Officer, who for so many years cavorted—and I was witness to some of your truly cavorting displays—with some of these very people I now meet in less salubrious, or at the least, far less unconcealed circumstances."

He almost sputtered out the next words, which I could feel were torn from his heart. "Because I proved such a great fool is no reason you should be my equal."

"Fool? You? Because Lord Roland was your dearest friend for seven years?"

"Fool. Scoundrel. I cannot find enough bad names for myself."

"You astonish me, brother, for I thought you the most sensible and happy boy that ever—"

"Happy?" he almost shouted into my ear. He repeated more quietly and very tragically, "Happy? I was for those years the most tormented of God's creatures."

Now I was amazed and also unhappy for him. "And you never dreamt to share your sufferings with me?"

"I could not," he said, sitting himself down upon a bale of hay meant for the horses. "How could I ever? And now I find I have said far too much."

"Was it the difference in your station? Was it your pride that you could never be or have as much—"

"I've said too much. Too much!"

"Surely, Lord Roland didn't cause your suffering by bringing up those differences to you during your play."

"I could not explain it you if I lived another hundred years."

"But Rudolph, brother! Won't you at least attempt to do so? If only for the sake of our lifelong affection?"

"I cannot, sister dear. And what is worse, because I cannot, I cannot hope to extract a promise from you that you will never attach yourself to him as closely as I myself did. For I am no fool, and I know he always gets what he wants."

"He didn't get you! You dropped him for Mr. Robinson. He doesn't have you now."

Rudolph took both my hands in his and said quietly, "Roland *always* gets what he wants, sister, and then he unceremoniously discards it when he is done. No matter what he says afterward, nor how it may look to others."

I was on the point of tears. "I cannot promise you any such thing," I said.

"I thought not. It was foolish to think that you might."

"Because I am certain that our mother's dying wish will be the opposite, that *I do* affiance myself and marry him, and become the lady of the manor."

"Then he has asked you?"

"I have not allowed him to ask me, no."

"But he shall ask? When you do allow him to?" And as I gave Rudolph no response, he added in the most downcast tone of voice, "Then we are lost, brother and sister, both of us. Doomed and lost forever."

Before I could stop him, Rudolph had rushed out of the courtyard onto the moor that extends miles over to Ravenglass and eventually to the sea.

He returned to the vicarage after I had returned by carriage, and he kissed my forehead as he went upstairs to his bed. He never afterward said another word upon the topic. It was years, decades, in truth, before I came to understand. By then it was far too late for Rudolph, and almost too late for me.

Your distant mother-in-law, Lillian of Ravenglass

To: The Earl of Ravenglass
11 Hanover Square
London, England

26 September 188—

Dear Father,

It will do you no good, this constantly asking if Carrie-Ann and I—or Lord Oliver—know where my mother is at this time. We are copying and forwarding her mail with the greatest exactitude. Indeed the wrappings themselves, when the letters are wrapped, are sent on to you. You will wear yourself out worrying, if in truth that is what you are doing. We simply do not know.

However, we were all three and Carrie-Ann's mother and father out late yesterday afternoon when we had a most unexpected encounter that bears retelling. Since you are so apparently avid for any news, here then is some.

The weather had been storming and suddenly the storm flew out to sea. We'd taken advantage of being indoors so long to sit us down and write up and send out wedding cards—your own ought to be by separate post alongside this letter. Although it may amuse you to have heard Little Celia, my wife's sister, asking where was the wedding gift we were busily thanking you for, as she was unable to locate it. My wife had to divert her and say you were the bearer of too many past and present gifts and hopefully of many future ones. But we could tell Celia was only fuddled by this diversion of an explanation.

We could see the storm scudding away, as though exhausted by our coast town, and the sun shone radiantly, so all of us, housebound for a day or more, put on our outer clothing and went out yesterday afternoon upon the smaller promenade here in Rye-strand, where the better sort take the air.

Not ten minutes later, two persons approached us. I recognized them a little and Carrie-Anne a bit more, from our nuptial dinner at the manor, as they had sat at the high table on the groom's side. They introduced themselves as Mr. and Mrs. Homer Eagles of Broughton. He is a mercer of great financial success as well as of some standing in the shire, Carrie-Ann later told me, and is known to vend not only calicos and general cotton cloth, but also the finest materials such as silks and satins which our ladies love so much.

He owns a great emporium in Lancaster town, and the Eagles had sent us a remarkable gift—a punchbowl and glasses of Waterford crystal, I believe from that shop, as it was beguilingly wrapped in fine paper and satin bows. He also has an estate abutting your own here, on the edge of the property by the side of the Dower house.

At first, we were certain it was a chance encounter. Such as they in their station would, I believe, take the sea air here at Rye, until they invited us to a luncheon with them for the following day.

We found the two Eagles congenial as well as being closely allied to our borough at home and thus of some future general and political use. You see, I am not *entirely* blind nor ignorant of my future place in the greater world. So we accepted the invitation.

Lord Oliver demurred at last minute, bent on entertaining Carrie-Ann's younger siblings. So we proceeded without him. They were staying in a private house, and it was a fine one of four floors with a carriage house and stable attached. The furnishings were, as my wife remarked, of the best and most expensive. The luncheon too was finely done, beginning with a madeira and terrapin soup and extending to mostly maritime entrées. There was a fine trifle and hock.

Besides ourselves, only a butler and maidservant were present, so it was rather intimate, as is the style these days for midday meals.

But imagine our surprise when Mr. Eagles began to tell us that he had gone to school in the little village by Ravenglass and sat alongside my mother and her brother, my uncle Rudolph. This was pleasant news, and Mr. Eagles did not presume upon the acquaintanceship in any way, except to say charmingly that he knew my mother since they were small children, and he would often try to carry her schoolbooks home to the vicarage for her.

Mrs. Eagles then spoke, saying how she was acquainted with my mother almost as long and yet much more closely than her husband. Indeed she informed us that she was intimate with her the past fifteen years, and that she had taken on the role of a sort of social factotum connecting my mother to the rest of the gentry in the shire, and thus aiding her in her many charities. Carrie-Ann immediately said, "My mother-in-law has recommended you to me by letter, and it would delight me if you were able to call upon us at the manor once we are settled."

The picture they presented of my mother in less than a half hour's time was one that made me proud to hear, extolling her goodness, her generosity, her perspicacity; and her willingness to go out of her way to aid those in need. It was a more rounded portrait than I'd ever perceived on my own. Carrie-Ann was also very taken by it.

Only when we were at the door, about to take our way back to the Calexis, did Mrs. Eagles take Carrie-Ann aside and say in a low voice, "If the marchioness has acted out of character and so beyond what others of her station find acceptable, believe us, lady, it was because she believed she had no other choice. If she has acted in what seems to you an unconscionable manner, believe us, lady, that I know for truth she pondered long and hard before her own conscience would allow her to take that step."

Carrie-Ann was very moved by those words and was silent all the way home until we were alone at night and she repeated them to me. I had no possible rejoinder for her.

Perhaps, Father, you will know what I shall say to Carrie-Ann?
Roddy

To: The Honourable Lady Caroline-Ann
Broughton, England
The Glebe, Ravenglass

27 September 188—

My Dear Lady Caroline-Anne,
     You will wonder that I never asked anyone around Lord
Roland about him to find out the truth of my brother's tenuous
statements and odd not-quite-allegations. The truth is I did inquire
as best I could in the situation. Already I knew Lord Robert would
never say a word amiss about his friend. But then there were the two
young ladies that were brought to our dinners: Julia Withersmere
and Astabella Vanbrugh.
     The first I mentioned I liked almost immediately. And so, upon
our second dinner at the foreman's lodge, I took advantage of a
loose back ribbon on my frock to draw her upstairs to the mistress's
withdrawing room, and to there ply her with questions natural
between ladies in such circumstances.
     "When you are all three in London society," I began one such
investigation, "don't you find, Lady Julia, that Lord Roland shines
so he cannot help but attract many debutantes and young ladies
already 'out'?"
     "Without a doubt, my dear Lillian," she replied as she fiddled
with the needle case. "But you surely know these country-bred
noble men are all *primitifs*?"
     "Signifying…?"
     "Signifying that they will flirt to their heart's content when
they are out in society, but when it comes to actually uniting, they'll
settle only for home girls, by which I mean those that won't chaff,
whine, complain too utterly, pout, or outspend them at their tailors."
     "That's a hard view of our young men," I commented.
     "They say I'm an especially hard case, you realize, because I say
what I see and think. I'm exactly the kind of girl *they* would *never*
marry. And you are exactly the kind they *would*."
     "Because I will bend to their will?"
     "Because you will anticipate their will, you are so thoughtful
and good natured, and because you'll allow them to have it without
a bit of resistance."
     "Do you think me so much a Fanny then?" I asked, for we

had been both reading the same novel, and the insipid heroine was named precisely that.

"Indeed not, miss. But as soon as one these handsome devils has his connubial way with you, you will melt into becoming his harlot."

"Lady Julia!"

"Lady Julia nothing! Both my sisters told me so. These men have arts we know little of, and my sisters admit they have become, and we too shall become, like putty in their hands. The young men go to France and Italy to study how to make of us their passion slaves."

"Now I think *you* read too much. But what will you do if you don't wed one of our country squires?"

"I already have my eyes out for one or another of two young West Indies gentleman who have sweetened their way into my affections." She laughed as I did over her witticism. "As you may guess, their sugar cane plantations are extensive, their knowledge of how to woo a woman simple, and their skin quite *café au lait*, from either the constant sun in their climate or from some indiscretion of their forebears. Edward and Anthony are their names. They are fantastically prosperous. And they wish to remain in Grosvenor Square forever with a very pale white woman upon their arm."

My other school mate, Astabella, was even less sanguine, when I took her aside in the dressing closet, for us to repair or flatten our garment. "These peer-lets are charming enough, but I'm seeking a man of substance, someone who has done something in his life. Even if it was dastardly. These merely want someone to uplift them, to hold their heads above the ale tankard and be there like a bedstead when they eventually get home and recall their husbandly duties."

"That is a most cynical view for such a young lady," I remarked.

"I know," she said, flouncing about in front of a mirror until she was happy, "and the younger and handsomer the young men are, the more they desire to prove me wrong. Still, silly Julia isn't completely wrong, you know. Lord Roland especially dislikes strong-willed young ladies, and he's made that clear on many an occasion. I think the only lady in society to have caught his attention was a young woman from Virginia—is there such a place, really, or did I just make that up?" I assured her there was indeed a state named Virginia in America. Astabella said, "Well, this Virginian was—as she later explained to us ladies—simply dripping honey on top of peaches and cream. And Lord Roland rather publicly ate it all up, rich as the dish was, and he almost swallowed her entirely. Her maid later told us she was an utter harridan until she'd had three strong cups of coffee in the morning."

"And did Lord Robert also eat her up?"

"He hardly blinked. That one, my dear, is awaiting the greatest heiress of all. His ambitions will brook none other."

"His ambitions are then…?"

"Of the highest—the Privy Council, the party leadership if not even greater. With him, he takes along Lord R. They rise together, strong young saplings, into the old dead forest of our House of Lords."

"So that a quiet wife at home…?"

"Is absolutely required," Astabella completed my thought. "You can understand why quite clearly?"

"Quite, quite clearly," I said, and I easily could.

But as I mentioned, I had more important matters on my mind. My mother's health worsened daily. The day before my brother was to leave us for London to take up his commission, he was closeted with my mother for hours at a time. Neither would answer to my timid taps on the door until it was dinner time and I declared the news loudly, so that he swept out and without a glance at me went up to his room, where he ate by himself. She was turned away toward the wall and simply said to me, "No. No more broth! Leave me be."

I do not know if they had any final interview. Rudolph had neither with my father nor myself. It was only once he was about to set foot into Mr. Robinson's horse's stirrups to ride to the railroad at Lancaster that Rudolph softened a bit toward me. He held me a long time in his arms, and together we looked over the fields in front, all in August pale puce heather. He kissed my cheeks and said he loved me unconditionally, received back from me an equal affection, and he wished me the happiest of lives.

For the following two days, neither Father nor Mother would even eat broth, and I began to despair. When I finally got my mother to take some spoonfuls of rice with butter, she grasped my arm so tightly I could not get loose and turned to me, her face contorted with I don't know, pain I suppose, and passion, and she demanded, "You made him no promise!"

"Lord Roland? No!"

"Your brother?"

"How could I?" I then added, "Your contradictory wishes are so clear."

"I've spoiled him. I've spoiled you both," she pouted. "But you at least listen. And I suppose because you are a woman, you learn to bear."

"Bear what?"

"What you must. That foolish brother of yours threw away a treasure of a friendship that thousands would pant after, and for what? For some scruple I could barely understand. Don't you make the same mistake. Scruples are for lords. Lords and the wealthy. Not for us."

In less than a week, she was dead. She died so quietly after such a long illness that Mrs. Cupp barely remarked her leaving us, although she'd been sitting next to her bed darning napkins all the while.

It was impossible to call back her son. His ship had taken the "Thames road" only the day before. But before he had gone, he had made plans enough for the burial so we needn't do so.

Mrs. Cupp went for the foreman, while I went to tell my father the news.

As usual, he was in his office among his books, polishing his sermons for publication, and he was most unhappy to be disturbed. But his face grew less rigid than I recalled it upon hearing my awful news, and he said, "God bless her, then! The poor thing!" Yet he didn't even ask to see her.

When Mrs. Cupp returned, with her was Matthew, my new friend, his carpentry tools slung in a canvas sack upon his back. He and another fellow carried in the six pine slats that would become my mother's coffin. His eyes were moist as he looked at her, and he used as gently as he could the measuring stick to get her size. He remained when the other fellow went, and he began measuring and sawing the pine that very evening. Mrs. Cupp asked if she might put him to bed that night in my brother's room, and I said why not? He ate supper with Mrs. Cupp, and I thought him withal the sweetest, gentlest lad I'd ever met, almost girlishly good looking was he, and, of course, well acquainted with the death of a mother.

Pastor Rose arrived from Broughton two mornings later in the foreman's large dogcart. He would be giving the service oration. He looked at the vicarage with what I thought was unusual interest, until I realized that he was a young man, my father an old one, and the living of Ravenglass was well within Mr. Rose's reach. More audaciously, he looked and spoke to me at first more often than I thought seemly to a grieving daughter until I had to speak back briskly one time, and he coloured. Mrs. Cupp took him aside and whatever she said, I was I no longer thereafter included in his visual assessments of the area.

Matthew had completed carpentering the coffin, all but its lid, to which he had glued a second, smaller, frontispiece upon which time he signalled and gestured to me that he wished to carve some floral design.

My mother had been washed and re-clothed for burial by Mrs. Cupp and myself, and I had remained dry eyed the entire time. She weighed so very little that we two were able to lift her over the box's tall side and lay her within upon the winding cloth, as though she were but discarded curtains to be given to someone poorer. And still I shed not one tear.

Pastor Rose gathered us, even my father, into the hall where she lay and made us a simple sermon and a blessing. I was unmoved.

Matthew stepped indoors, carrying his new-carved coffin lid, and I saw how he had sculpted with such tenderness three lovely lilies that grew outside our house, each one individual and yet together, and all three drooping in grief. He showed it to me for approval. I'm afraid I suddenly understood then that my dear mother was gone forever. I fell to the floor, grabbing at his trouser legs and weeping upon him as though a hundred mothers had died. Pastor Rose and Mrs. Cupp had to take me aside a few moments to regain myself. And when I emerged again, the coffin was gone from the house, and I could see it already upon a flat dray cart along led by a crepe-draped pony.

A small crowd had gathered, and among them I couldn't help but notice several servants from the manor house, one of whom, the head gardener, carried a large black-rose wreath, a gift from his mistress, Lady Bella.

I sought out Mute Matthew, and although he was affrighted at first, fearing he might occasion another such outburst, I kissed him and made him understand how deeply and highly I valued his carving, his carpentry, and his self. I would not let go his arm, and so he walked next to me, next to my father, as part of the family of mourners, before Pastor Rose and Mrs. Cupp, almost as though he were my brother.

It was an overcast morning, but the sun broke through clouds repeatedly as we walked on, and at each crossing our little party was joined by more and more shire folk and then manor folk and then townspeople. At the road into the cemetery, Lord Roland and Lord Robert stood next to their mounts, and no sooner were those encumbrances taken from them than they too joined our party to its last few paces.

This was an act of such great respect for my family and such personal affection to myself that I must kiss the cheek of each young man and publicly thank them, aware all the while, that next day all over lower Cumbria that hand-held flourmills in kitchens would quickly become rumour mills as well.

The foreman and his wife, who had become so friendly to me that summer, had prepared a funeral luncheon in her dining room, and albeit it was a dimmed affair compared to our higher-spirited ones, still it continued our repasts. Lord Roland felt free enough to ask how it was that one of the manor's craftsmen had been so esteemed as to walk alongside me.

I fear I expatiated a great deal upon Matthew's many virtues and abilities, so that his lord must meet him in person, for which the young carpenter bowed excessively and coloured a great deal, until his master lifted him up and clasped him and thanked him repeatedly for his care and solicitude of me and my family. He asked him to call upon him at the manor house the next day, as he had become aware of a multitude of small repairs needed and new constructions required. Perhaps, he hinted, a position for the lad could be found there. The butler, Jess, the old gardener, and even their elderly cook had spoken of cabinetry they would like to see installed.

And so I did unconsciously set in motion yet another difficult and challenging connection. At the time, of course, it made Matthew's name and also his fortune. The "simple" part was soon dropped, and "lucky" replaced it among his former friends at the dormitory. Matthew, of course, was removed from that overcrowded domicile and put into the manor, where he shared a chamber with but one other servant, a footman. Another advantage to that, of course, was that whenever I was staying at the Ravenglass vicarage, he would know much sooner of it than were he still in town. He would come visit me, stay for dinner, and let me read to him until late at night.

All, myself included, assumed I would return to college at Leeds to finish my course of study, and so it happened as planned.

Before I could go, I must undergo an attack of conscience, and as he was still at the manor house, and as attentive as I would allow him to be, I sought out Lord Roland to ask how wicked he thought I was, to leave my father alone with Mrs. Cupp.

His answer was, as usual, sunny and helpful. "From what I have noticed, and I hope you don't think me too forward-looking, Miss Lillian, Mrs. Cupp would be delighted to be left that alone at the vicarage. As for your father, I think that distracted as he is by his writing and by his grief, that he somehow intuits that he will be left in capable, and dare I add, *encouraged* hands?"

Lord Roland made certain that I was hand-delivered in his family phaeton—with its emblazoned crest—to my college by himself.

Miss Starkweather Caine reported herself "not in the least astonished," she admitted to me, when several of the other distaff scholars brought her the exciting news of my means of arrival. "I knew both of those young men had good sense when we encountered them at Mr. and Mrs. Kean's performance," said she.

He left me there at the gates only after being assured I might take the next five steps indoors unescorted—no men were allowed past that point—and that my box of things would be safe within the gateway "until some nameless albeit somewhat Herculean minion could be found to heave it upstairs" to my chamber. The gargantuan size, weight, and fullness of my necessities within that "box" had provided an all-day joke for Lord Roland and, happy as I was to be in his company, travelling alongside him and returning to Leeds, I allowed him to chaff me on it as he would. He naturally enough carried nothing but a saddlebag and a small leather Wellington with him down to Cambridge.

Not a great deal had altered at the women's college, but there were a few new faces. Among them was a Miss Georgiana Milton, whose grandfather had been a potter, and whose father and two uncles had extended those few little kilns into a vast manufactory that would cover the local countryside and employ several hundred men whose products would soon be found on the best tables and *étagères* in England.

She was a petite thing, Georgiana, with an overlarge head. Her face was round, but except for two quite extraordinarily large eyes the very same shade of blue as her family competitor's best-known line of chinaware, she was unexceptional. Later on, of course, she would become famous, even transatlantically famed, and her baby-fat would vanish, leaving a handsome, slender body and an almost classically sculpted face, which aided, along with her considerable power-brokering, to the penny press sobriquet by which she became known and even vilified as "George the Fifth." She is another personage who shall return, in a most unanticipated manner, later in my history.

Once I had gotten to know her a little and she had come to know of my not-quite-engagement to Lord Roland, I asked if she knew of him. She brushed him aside as though he were one of the dead flies that collected at the bottom of our windowpanes over the hot season.

"Men are all alike, alas, and of no value whatsoever," Georgiana declared.

"Then how shall you get on?" I was amazed and asked.

"I shall never marry, Miss Lillian. Marriage is, and you comprehend this, merely another category of bondage, although at least unlike official slavery here one is bought and bought and bought all over again."

"Never marry!" I'd never heard such a thing. "Won't your mama and papa become aggrieved by that?"

"They have already utterly given up on me. There are three other female children for them to pin those hopes upon, like posies that soon will wilt."

"But, as the eldest, won't you be setting a poor example?"

"Hardly. They ignore me. I tell you I am quite thrown over. They give me nothing but their money. And truth be told, that is all I want of them. If only they could be induced to part with more of it and sooner. Well, when I am one and twenty, I shall have bundles of banknotes and oodles of pottery company shares. My grand-papa saw to that."

Naturally enough, the bluestocking Mrs. Starkweather-Caine found Georgiana Milton to be a "most sensible young lady. One I will be proud to acknowledge as having attended our college."

The first part of the second year of study went quickly enough and easily enough. Lord Roland and Lord Robert both came for me to drive me back to the vicarage for the wintertime holidays. I almost did not go, but an unforeseen letter from my father—he had never written me before—arrived, particularly advising that he must speak with me and tell me something of the greatest importance to his and my life! So I found that I must go, after all.

But that must wait, Lady Caroline-Anne. The conductor of this train has just come through telling us we halt now. All mail must be sealed and go.

Aufwiedersehn, Your mother-in-law, Lillian of Ravenglass

To: The Very Reverend Jasper Horace Quill
The British Church at Campofieri
Town of Fiesoli
Province of Tuscany

29 September 188—

Sir,
I know you will end up disappointed in me. At this hour, I am sore disappointed in myself. Still, the task I allowed myself to be assigned goes on well, so far uncontaminated by the poisons emanating from myself or from my base desires.

You ought to know that we arrived in Munich two days ago, and then entrained to Innsbruck. Here we await an opening in the Brenner Pass, so we may travel. News was telegraphed to us before we could move any nearer that a freak snowstorm had fallen on the Brenner, even though it is unheard of this time of the year, and has not been a difficulty since the years 1813 through 1815, when winter completely encompassed this part of the Austrian Tyrol and its Low Germany neighbourhood entirely that year of 1814, which was here without any summer at all. From here, we move on to our train station across the pass and thence down into Bolzano in Italy. So far, the plan goes well.

I do not believe you ever took the Brenner, as you usually arrive by sea. That would have been the easier way for us too, were it not that official papers are required and documentary vigilance is far greater onboard a seagoing vessel. At any rate, Innsbruck is directly south of Munich and the Brenner Pass directly south of Innsbruck, and Bolzano directly south of the pass. It's a historical old place. Gibbon alleges Alaric the Visigoth stormed over it on his way to topple the Roman Empire. Because it is so low—well, comparably low for the Alps—at 4,990 feet above the sea's level, there's been a carriage road here for over a century, and the narrow gauge railroad has been up nearly twenty years already and makes a daily "go" in either direction. At any rate, I am informed that when it isn't snowed over, the Brenner is "a snap" and only nine hours town to town by rail.

Also, to be said for my caretaking, the lady and her companion fare well, and seem content. There was a ten-minute period a few days previous when they were certain some archfiend had come upon them, whether consciously or all unawares I could not tell. They were anxious, and I sought to and I think I did manage to allay their anxiety.

The two Greek fellows who attached themselves to us in Brussels continue to travel with us. In truth, I believe they will remain with us until Venice and perhaps beyond, after which they take a ship for home.

They ride in a second class carriage much of the time, as do we, so as to not attract undue attention. The first and second on German trains are good. It is only at third class that problems arise in the form of unwashed workmen, open packages of food, and squalling babies. I think you know what I refer to. At times, the Greeks keep the lady and her chambermaid company. Increasingly, the remarkable lady has begun her own little school in teaching English language skills to all three of the others. The Greeks, she tells me, are learning because they plan upon returning to England to renew their plea for the long-wished-for sculptures and pediments. Having the language will aid immeasurably. As for the younger lady, she may also find employment back in the British Isles if she is not contented with Italy. I think most, however, she enjoys the company of young men who like her looks and who cannot help themselves flirting with her, for like many a true Frenchwoman, she is a natural coquette.

But this is how good my lady is: Yesterday we were walking in Munich's largest parkland, which is called the English Garden for no reason I could get a grasp upon. It is a lovely place with flowers and free benches to sit upon, and within its confines, a little museum of old sculpture from the Greek and Roman ancients. Naturally, our Greek friends wished to see these. They have a distinctly overlaid pleasure in so doing, for on the one hand they can show some of the glories of their homeland and history, while on the other, there is the fact that the lovely objects are here, miles away from where they were sculpted and belong. The other Greek, Mikos or Nikos, he calls himself, pointed out one particular head of a Roman woman from some sixteen hundred years ago and asked did it not resemble the lady herself? Comparisons were made, and similarities and nobility were commented upon, which embarrassed and, I think, a little pleased her.

We had exited one of these museums and were about to move onward toward an electric tram, a new-fangled sort of public omnibus conveyance they are trying out in this city, when the lady asked where I thought we might obtain an English language reader. "A very simple one, like those children learn from—A is for apple, with a picture of one, B is for boy and so on."

Returned to the hotel, I asked the concierge if any such thing as an English school or English church existed in this city of an English Garden. A church did exist, and I located it. I met with the dean and spelled out the lady's request. While there had been a classroom of sorts some time before for English-speaking children, there hadn't been one for some years, at least not since he was associated with the place. He said he would search.

The following morning, we found a note at the registration desk that some books in very tattered condition had been located in a storeroom. The lady was most excited and must go see them herself. The books, although dilapidated nearly off their spines, were in her words, "Repairable with some needle and thread, and perfectly what is needed." She took three of them in the best condition and left a donation.

And so the three students read and learn and try out their words and now even simple phrases upon whom? Of course, upon myself.

This all seems so harmless and virtuous that you are probably asking yourself, in what manner am I being disappointed with my own behaviour? Backsliding. No other words will do. Three nights ago on the train from Aachen, I backslid so very far, Reverend, that at times I fear I cannot go forward again.

The train we took stopped at one station and then again at another far smaller *halt*, where it took on a private car. I little regarded the matter at the time, thinking it the prerogative of some local princeling, for the country abounds in them. Later on, during our very long ride, the Greeks had fallen asleep in their seats, the chambermaid was asleep, and even her ladyship was nodding over her copy of *The Lady's Companion*. Only I seemed unable to rest.

Doubtless I was thinking of what must be done once we arrived at Munich, for it would be a late train, arriving near midnight, and although the Germans are better at this sort of thing than nearly anyone else, still I felt a growing anticipation and with it an anxiety. Would there be enough hansoms? Would there be porters to carry all our bags? Would the hotel I hoped to use be open so late? Or accepting guests? Had they four rooms?

In this state, I found myself pacing the train's corridors. A train worker passed me, stopped, and asked if I was looking for a smoking car. I had no cigars but thought maybe a cigarette might calm me, so I asked for the car, and I was pointed the other direction, at the very end.

There I did find a smoking car, and what was even more extraordinary, separated from it by a glass-paned door, the private car that had been attached two stops before. The smoking car was nearly empty, but cigars and cigarettes were there open in trays for the taking. I took one of the latter and was enjoying the tobacco when curiosity got the best of me, and I had to go to the window to the private car and look through.

It was sumptuous almost beyond an *Arabian Nights* fantasy. It had a dining room and also a sizable daybed-divan, but more astounding was a baize table five foot in diameter, at which six gentlemen were seated. Behind which, another taller man stood and drew cards out of a metal receptacle. It was a gambling den, which was bad enough given my history, but what was worse for me, the game on the table was my very own nemesis, fittingly enough called both in France and here *Chemin de Fer*, or railroad.

Before I could register surprise, the connecting door was thrown open, and a servant ushered me in, begged me to enter. A gentleman stood up immediately, and he insisted upon seating me in his place. Although I protested madly, he said he must use the washroom, and I must play his seat for only a few minutes until he returned. What possible harm as there in it? He trusted me explicitly.

Ashtoreth in Hades could not have devised a circumstance more slyly fitting to my abhorrent weakness. I sat there, and I all but vibrated with unfulfilled passion. I could not, I would not, play for the longest time, contenting myself with taking another cigarette and even drinking down a tall Bock served me. When it became evident the gentleman was not soon returning, the others demanded I join in, since with "only five against the house" they were at a sudden disadvantage.

Slowly at first and then more rapidly I did join in their game.

In a trice, my vice had hold of me. In seconds, I was calculating odds and counting cards coming from the dealer as I cold-bloodedly assessed the other players. I lost wildly at first, and when I realized it, I despaired of what I could possibly tell the man whose seat I had usurped, despite them all saying I shouldn't mind losing "*ein bissel*," as he had more money than Croesus. But losing had one advantage: I could run out of chips and stop play. No one here knew me. Therefore I might obtain no credit here.

But worse yet was that moment when I was about to let go, stand up, and call it a complete loss. I suddenly, almost impalpably, began to feel myself "on," in some sort of harmony with the game and the cards, the others, and the train hurtling us all so rapidly to Hell. I had felt this very way, I remember telling you, confessing to you it really was, in Baden-Baden in '78 and in Paris in '79, and like those times what made this time so horrible was that I began winning. It was a horrid sensation, because if the train had ground to a halt and all of us had been forced to evacuate, I knew at that moment I would have held on to the gaming table, my fingers turned to claws, my face a mass of despair, demanding the game go on and on.

Fortune in the form of the previous gentleman arrived. He tapped my shoulder several times until I could bring myself to look away from the baize tabletop and at him. At first, I wondered who he was and what he wanted of me, so thoroughly into my vice had I fallen. Then the others all stopped playing and looked at us both, and so I slowly stood up, utterly humiliated, and offered him his own seat back.

"Ah, but you have done wonders here!" I heard him saying as I rushed out of the car, through the smoking car, running as fast as I could in the now madly rocking train. I believe I reached the farthest end, a conductor barring my way, telling me these were engine cars I could not enter, before I stopped and slid to the floor.

He thought me ill, and a physician was located among the passengers, who felt at my wrists and neck and head and heart and who returned with a powder he fizzed in water which they made me drink. I was half carried to my compartment, empty then of the two Greeks, where I was laid down and was at times looked in upon until I could fall to sleep.

When I awakened a few hours later, we were just then drawing into the railroad terminus at Munich. The two young Greeks were excitedly shaking me awake. Atop my vest coat had been laid a paper packet. When I looked inside, I found it contained over a thousand francs—my gentleman's thank-you gift for his winnings.

And so you see in me someone who has fallen, fallen easily, fallen utterly into the worst possible of vices. What can I do to atone? What can I do to repent?

Your friend and far inferior
Stephen Undershot

29 Septembre 188—

Sir

I have fond a telgraf offis and we ar now at munchen in allemagne. I have understud we go nex sowth.

We ar al wel. Henriette

To: The Honourable Lady Caroline-Ann
Broughton, England
The Glebe, Ravenglass

30 September 188—

My Dear Lady Caroline-Anne,

Another delay, although this time of a topographical and climatological nature. This adventure of mine will be my doing, I swear on it, and I recommend it, or perhaps one less anxiety-producing, to yourself.

I think now that one of the worst things that happened to me then, there, where you soon will be, was that my independence, so openly admired during courtship, was so carefully—almost so I wouldn't notice—stripped away from me until I must have someone else to do anything at all for me.

While it is true that I am still surrounded by helpers, these allow me to be independent, to assert myself, to go where I must, to spend my own money and say my own words, and yes, even think my own thoughts.

Such a one, I discovered too late, was also my mother. Oh, not the mother I knew. She was like almost any other woman of her class and time, but before she had married and had Rudolph and myself to watch over. That is one thing I learned that Christmas my father wrote me, and I returned home to hear what he had to say.

I had not wished to return to the vicarage then, and did so only because I was given transport and company all the way, and also promised company for the week by Lords Roland and Robert of Blackburn, neither of whom I had seen much of that autumn in Leeds.

I was left off at the vicarage and Mrs. Cupp rushed out to greet me, while mute Matthew kissed my hands. I made him kiss my cheek, and he took my box up to my room, not without commendations upon his strength from Lord Roland. The two young lords declined a cup of tea, as they were anxious to be at the manor so close by.

So it was that I entered our house and found it somewhat the same, yet subtly altered. The past few years my mother had done little or nothing to set her stamp upon the kitchen or hall, and that had showed in little ways. Mrs. Cupp, however, had felt those little necessities and once she was, as it were, left in charge, she had seen to them. New hand-pleated linens in the French style hung in two tiers from the kitchen window. Several ornamental china plates, including those celebrating my upcoming commencement out of college, were hung and amongst them several embroidered frames with mottoes and apothegms. My brother's commission had been sent to a copyist who had rendered the document in brilliant colours with appropriate ornamentation; and that too was hung. Old armchairs now sported doilies, even plain deal tables sported new tablecloths, and a hand-woven carpet had been placed next the inglenook bench in the hall.

I noted all and noted Mrs. Cupp note me noting it all and I said, "It's ingenious. It's cosy. It's home-y!"

She kissed my cheek then, the first time ever, and said she was very relieved as she hadn't wanted "to spoil anything I recalled in the place" and yet had been given what she termed "the vicar's ukase to fix it all up nice-like and modern."

"And so it is. I hope my own chamber has similar touches."

Not many, as she had awaited my approval, she said. But our meal, to be had by all of us together at the hall dining table—which I approved of very much—was also more modern. A chop, a potato, several vegetables, bread and cheese later, and even a green salad. This last, Mrs. Cupp assured me, "has done a great deal to assist the vicar's internal movements." I assured her she was perfectly up to date with my own college home economics studies, and she confessed that she'd "peeked a bit into that tract you brought home last summer." So I learned she could read.

Matthew looked well, with a bit more flesh and muscle on his frame, and his hair cut well by one of the servants up at the hall, darkening now almost to a strawberry-blond hue. He wore all new clothing, including tonight especially for my arrival, a pair of dark green patent leather shoes with wooden heels, handed down by the earl himself, who had tired of them. He and Matthew shared a foot size, it turned out, and Matthew claimed to have seen the earl on several occasions, which surprised me, but which Mrs. Cupp confirmed.

"He was called down from London town," she whispered, "because of herself not getting on very well."

"The Marchioness Bella? Is she ill?"

"Or gone mad. No one outside the manor knows. And inside the manor, as Matty here will let you know, no one sees her, but merely hears her coming and going in that infernal chair of hers."

"Then I wonder should I go pay my respects to her?"

"It could never hurt, miss, to be polite."

Which my father also agreed to, for the very next day. That first night he merely appeared at the table looking less gaunt, less sallow, less yellow and drawn. He said grace, patted Matthew and me on the head, thanked God and Mrs. Cupp for our bounty, and ate with a relish I'd not seen in him for years.

He remained and listened to Mrs. Cupp prattle on about the manor and shire folk and didn't interrupt or stop her, but one time even slyly egged her on, which she took and ran with. He was kind to Matthew too, insisting he eat seconds and complimenting him on some woodwork he'd seen. I found myself thinking I'd never known this particular father before, and all the more wondered what it was he had to tell me.

After dinner, he remained with us a while and read aloud from Mr. Tennyson's poems, newly published, and from poor dead Mr. Keats's *Hyperion*, which he admired greatly. Matty listened, mouth agape, or fiddling with a piece of tiny carving bone, while Mrs. Cupp knitted and sometimes sighed, or said, "How lovely," or "How sad." I had left a vicarage house about to be blown over by the winds of change two and a half months ago, and I had returned to find instead a warm hearth and home.

Next morning, I dressed and walked up to the manor house. Partway I was passed by one of the foreman's assistants who insisted I get upon and ride aside him on the seat of his logging dray, because, said he, "Though it is hardly apt nor even very clean, still you should *not* be walking, miss." It had iced up overnight and the ground was slippery, so I didn't much mind this courtesy.

Lord Roland was at the house, of course, and Lord Robert visiting him. They were downstairs in an area I'd never gone before, the games room, where I was assured by the butler they were shooting arrows at targets. I asked him not to bother them, and produced the little gift Mrs. Cupp had made for the manor. I said I was newly returned from women's college to the vicarage, and if his mistress was seeing company, I would present it to her myself as I had done in the past.

He seemed somewhat dithered by this boldness of mine and

stumbled out of the draughty large entry hall and quickly down the stairs before he caught himself, came up again, bowed to me once more rather inanely, and then slowly ascended to where the marchioness might actually be found. I could not help but see the fright—or was it anxiety?—upon his face.

Mrs. Ounch, the housekeeper, had heard our voices and come upstairs. She could no longer afford to be curt with me, and so she had with her a peace offering—a kind of French bread she'd recently learned to bake from a new cook hired by Lord Roland for the manor and called "*croissant*" because of its similar appearance to a cross.

"It uses a large amount of butter, miss," she assured me before backing off in curtseys. I took it wrapped in a cloth napkin and put it into my pocket to eat later.

The butler appeared at the head of the stairs and gestured me up. As I reached the top, he said to me in a low voice, "She's not been well. But she heeded quite well the sound of your name."

He led me down a long corridor to a far suite of rooms and through them to another high ceilinged, largely unfurnished room in which the marchioness was making large circles in her mobile chair. The butler stepped back out rapidly.

"Your Ladyship," I said, coming forward, "this very small gift?"

The Marchioness Bella looked even more gaunt, and her face more bruised looking and lined than before. Her mouth pursed almost as though she were looking at me with her gustatory and not her visual organs. Her lips were very much lined. She still rotated in small circles in her chair as I approached, although ever more slowly, and I saw she still wore the large malachite locket around her neck. Here, the creaking of the chair I'd been warned of was not so bad. It was a solid ash floor.

She announced our location. "The ballroom. You dance, of course?"

"My lady, yes."

"New dances I don't know of."

"I'd be happy to show you."

She stopped, and her mouth kept pursing and unpursing. "You would. I believe...The vicar is well, despite...all?"

"My father is surprisingly well and well cared for, my lady. Very kind of you to ask. Your flowers on the occasion were..."

"I, on the other hand, am thought to be dying."

"I had not heard that, and I hope it is not so."

"What did you hear of me?"

"That you are thought to be mad but…"

She laughed, a horrible sound emanating from deep inside her chest. "That is why I like you. Lillian. You never disabuse." She began to cough. "I wish I *were* mad. I'm not. But you know that, don't you?"

"I think so, yes. And what your problem may—"

"My problem, as you put it, is that I am alive and don't wish to be."

"I am very sorry for that," I said, and thinking of my mother dead, even I could hear a throb in my voice.

"Don't weep. Come closer. There," and she patted my hand. "It isn't by any means the worst that can happen to one. Many suffer worse than me. I know that. It's just that everyone had such hopes for me."

"As for me," I added.

"You'll endure it all far better than me." She regarded the gift in her lap. "This is some…"

"Some small kindness from the woman who cares for the vicar now that my mother is gone."

"Thank her," she said without looking at it. "Do you know that I've made him bring me a valuable jewel every time he's come here," she said, changing the subject. I knew instantly it was her husband she was speaking of. "Even when I knew he was somewhat hard-up."

"And…?"

"He comes so seldom anyway." That awful laugh again. "And I don't really notice or care anymore that he does come, as once I did care—oh, so very much care. But he never forgets the jewel. Never!"

She reached into a pocket and pulled out a brilliant blue sapphire set in a silver ring. The stone was large and must have been what was called cut *en cabochon.*

"I once thought I would just take them all and simply go with my riches." She looked at me and said, "Another foolish dream."

The butler appeared, standing at the very end of the room, and said that the young lords were awaiting me downstairs in the Great Hall.

I tried to kiss her hand, but she wouldn't let me. "Don't hate me!" she cried.

"Why ever would I do that?"

"For being so weak," she said as I curtseyed my way to where the butler stood waiting for me. "For not saying no."

As I reached the door, I heard the chair creak and saw she was moving in circles again, her head up in the air, her arms out as though she were dancing. I stopped, looked back, and smiled at her. All of a sudden I felt something hit my arm and half caught it. The *cabochon* ring. She had tossed it to me.

I dared not refuse it given her uneven temper, so, took it and curtseyed again, although she was now far away in her memories and she no longer chose to see me. I felt she was at some wondrous ball of twenty years before when she'd been at the peak of her youth and beauty.

Lady Lillian

To: The Very Reverend Jasper Horace Quill
The British Church at Campofieri
Town of Fiesoli
Province of Tuscany

1 October 188—

Sir,

Only after I had sealed and posted my last to you did I realize that it could in only a little way interest you. And that what did interest you—i.e., the lady's well-being and progress—was only flimsily addressed.

As we move farther on, I find I trust her little maid all the less, albeit if she was attached by yourself or your connexions to her ladyship, what business of mine is it to question the little chit's honesty? Even so, she lingers when she ought to hurry, and she vanishes when she ought to be immediately at hand. The only possible reason must be that she has a paramour, and somehow the varlet is within our purview here. Another worse supposition I will not degrade either of us by writing.

But enough of my suspicions. Meanwhile, the lady reads, and she contemplates what she reads and ponders it and chews it about. All of a sudden, I will be suddenly shocked out of some dearly earned rest by her questioning me aloud, with a most disagreeable query.

As yesterday she did when she suddenly said, "How is it that you are you not married. Or even affianced?" Before I might reply, she went farther. "Yes, yes, I know it is a most personal question, but you and I are in a most personal situation of perilous adventure. I must have an answer before I continue another lap of this journey. I know you are well educated. I know you came from at least the upper reaches of that commercial class that Mr. Engels styles 'le bourgeoisie.' How is it that you deny those facts to join this adventure?"

A simple enough question one might consider. Yet to tell it, I had to tell of my background and upbringing and my adoption, and it all seemed so much to tell that I began backward, telling her that I had been affianced to a young lady of greater means than my own in Oxfordshire. That arrangement was brought about by Mr. Undershot, my adopted father, and his recently widowed sister, Mrs. ——. This new aunt had, of late, relocated into her brother's estate from Westminster, and once we lost my esteemed parent, she more or less took over the management of the house and, of course, chose its guests. All this occurred while I was completing my studies at Heidelberg University, and while I left the esteemed school to attend my adopted father's funeral and obsequies, upon his written and her verbal requests, I soon returned to study.

"But wait!" the lady interrupted. "You are a foundling! When did this come about? At what age were you when it did so?"

"I was six and a half years old. I was orphaned in an unsavoury part of Cheapside in old London-town. I had the care of one younger brother who found employment as a butcher's boy, while our youngest brother was taken in by a local school mistress in her private establishment, a kindergarten."

"Were you also a butcher's boy?" she asked, either very curious or disgusted, I thought.

"No. My lady, worse yet. I was a street cleaner not far from where my brother laboured." I saw she was uncertain of my meaning, so I explained. "The busy intersections of the city there are so dusty when dry and so muddy when wet, that some sort of street maintenance is essential so pedestrians may walk and carriages may rattle past. We very poor boys did that and were tipped for our trouble."

"Tipped?"

I held out a hand and used the other put a small coin in it.

I could see she was appalled, and rightly so. "But you still lived at home?"

"By then, we had no home. We were forced out after Mother's funeral."

"But where did you go to bed?"

"We slept in doorways, alleyways, under bridges. Wherever we might."

Her hand went to her breast as she asked, "And your adoption?"

"My friend at the crossroads and I shared our poor earnings. One day he fell too ill to work. I gave him all the food I could earn. But by the end of the second day, I too had caught his ailment. I could stand and move a broom, so while feverish, I had to keep working for us both. I must have fallen in front of a vehicle. Doubtless several other carriages simply swerved to avoid me as another obstacle in the road. But Mr. Undershot was a gentleman who was visiting his town house from Suffolk. He took pity on me and had me lifted out and into the carriage. I thought I was dreaming.

He asked where I lived, and I told him nowhere. He asked who were my people and I said I had no people. He had me taken and cared for in his town home until I was well. When he heard me repeat my story, he had me brought to the country. After some months, when I had regained health and asked when I was to return to the crossroads, he asked if I really wanted to go there or did I prefer staying with him.

Of course, I much preferred remaining where I could have meals and a bed and said so. Only sometime later did he make inquiries that proved what I had said. By then, my brother Tom had left the Smithfield's Market and gone to sea on a South Seas steamer as a cabin boy. We tried to find the baby, but Mr. Undershot was told the child was cast out of his school, and no one knew where he was. Mr. Undershot was childless and a widower, and so he adopted me."

"You were lifted wonderfully above your station in life."

"Yes. But to my sorrow, neither of my brothers could join me. It is that which follows me every day of my life, the baby's fate, and my brother Tom's, and it does not allow me to rest or ever to exult in my good fortune."

Here she laid a gloved hand upon my arm, and said not one word.

And now, sir, you too know why the reasons why darkness descends upon me, causing me to be angry and disappointed no matter where I turn, never quite allowing me to be content.

Yrs., Stephen Undershot

To: The Honourable Lady Caroline-Ann
Broughton, England
The Glebe, Ravenglass

1 October 188—

My Dear Lady Caroline-Anne,
    I must now report why it was my father called me away from
school and to his side. Worry as I had during the journey, I was not
at all prepared by what it was he had to say.
    "Sit here, for comfort," my father directed after supper that very
evening. "For what I have to tell you will not be a short anecdote,
but indeed so long that it may require all evening."
    "My evening is yours, as you well know."
    I had had a most pleasant visit and what was called a cream-tea
with Lords Roland and Robert after I had seen the Lady Bella. This
last was a new invention from London-town, the young men said,
and included among its *accoutrements* two types of clotted cream,
Devonshire and the more local Cheshire, to be dolloped upon fresh
fruit and fruit tarts.
    They were in high spirits and regaled me with many stories
about their university year, some of their more eccentric tutors, and
even some slightly racy anecdotes about their student peers. They
themselves, of course, were flawless. They would be supping alone
and were sorry I would not join them. When I expressed surprise
Roland's mother would not join them, he grew abstracted. "Does
she partake of food anymore?" he asked, then answered himself.
"Some gruel, I believe, Ounch told me, does at times pass her
lips. We also brought her up some gooseberry jam." His face grew
so dark, I looked away. It was left to Lord Robert to salvage our
conviviality with a tale about how a kitten of his once fell into jam.
"And all of us silly children licked it off him. To this day I sometimes
cough up fur balls!" he added.
    "You wish to speak of our mother?" I asked my father, later
that day.
    "Of her, yes, and of the man she loved," said he.
    I settled in to hear some pleasing story of their courtship, only
to be caught up extremely short, for my father immediately added,
"His name was Henry Stanforth.
    "Your mother, I think you know already, came from a very

learned family. Both her father and her mother were extremely well educated, her mother mostly at home and partly by her husband, who had been once tutor to herself and her two brothers. By the time my wife to be, Livia Jespers, and their second child, a boy named Gaius Jespers, were born, both of their parents separately and together had penned and had for sale upon the book stalls a dozen pamphlets on various political, social, and scientific topics and they had together written a book in which they advanced an algebraical theory concerning our planetary system. Child-bearing and child raising was to be achieved upon strictly scientific principles, and so when both of their children survived to the age of ten, it was decided that no more offspring would be attempted. Surgical measures were induced to make this so for both parents. This was an error, as it turned out, since young Gaius died in a fall from a horse at the age of fourteen. Your mother, Livia, survived, and she went on to study, to do her scientific experiments at the family laboratory, and to become a much sought after young woman, almost compensating for the loss of a son.

"I first encountered your mother when I was twelve years old, and I had to stand in a crowd to admire her on the street. That street was the main thoroughfare of Lancaster town. For that is where the reduced-to-three Jespers family resided then, in a good-sized house dating from Charles the Second's time that Mr. Jespers had inherited from an uncle. The crowd consisted of probably every unmarried townsman or boy from age twelve to twenty-five, as your mother was so very interesting to us.

"Partly this was because, although she was as pretty in her brunet looks as any of a dozen young women we knew, she wore unusual clothing, especially in the summer-time. It was very thin, almost sheer clothing, made of lightweight Egyptian and Indian cottons; very different garb than others of her age and sex, embedded as they all were in thick, opaque velvets and satins, no matter the degree of heat out of doors. Livia also wore a sort of thin trouser—from Turkey, it was said—and the shape of her lower body could be espied if not with exactitude, at least with a physical completeness that was amazing to us lads, who thought of desirable young women as being bell-shaped from their waist down.

"Also, our admiration was due to Livia being agile, quick, bright, light-hearted, and unaffected in her manner. Indeed, she was more like a boy and she was said to play cards, to throw knives, to call people she knew by odd names—her mother was James, her father Astro, their house servants she had named Wiggles, Foggy, and Foddle. She would even run when she wished to get somewhere in a hurry. Most girls her age would have perished first. No wonder we lads had our breath taken away by Livia Jespers.

"All save Henry Stanford. He alone would face up to Livia. Only he would answer her back when she called him Rooster Red because of his prominent shock of hair. He would call her back 'Soot Head,' which she hated to hear, boiling over with anger at the name and insulting him with vulgar sobriquets. In response, Henry at age thirteen impolitely offered to knock Livia down in the gutter for her insolence, an offer Livia immediately took up. They scrambled in the dust of a side lane, trading fisticuffs, kicks, bites, and insults, while we lads cheered them on, until the tailor and his apprentices came outdoors with all the noise and separated them.

"Henry went off to school that fall and returned the next summer a polite young peer in training. Seeing him on the streets of Lancaster, Livia called him Mr. Nose in the Air, You'll Get a Nosebleed. He laughed at her and pointed out that her hands were filthy with ink. 'You should see my feet!' Livia replied. 'I can write with those too.' She ran off playing Hop-the-Scot upon the paving stones.

"The following summer they were seen hand in hand in various estival locales—the town promenade, the carriage park, and at a Stanforth Manor garden party. The older boys and men gave up on Livia then, quite sensibly enough. But I lived in Ulverston and only came to Lancaster irregularly, and I never quite relented. One time, when I was sixteen years of age, she came up to where I was standing outside a tavern, and she handed me out of her reticule a paper-wrapped bar of soap made with the oil of a lemon, from France. 'This is for your face and hands so you don't quite so much smell of the sea,' said she, not at all unkindly, for it was obvious that all we fisherfolk reeked nautically. I must have coloured terribly then, for she smoothed my hair and gently said to me, 'You're really too finely made to be a fisherman. You ought to go to school.'

"Soon after, my father agreed with her, and I did go to school right there in Lancaster with the Reverend DeVare. Next time we saw each other, I was dressed in a vest coat and buckle shoes, and she smiled at me and introduced me to her father.

"Everyone presumed that from being sworn enemies, Livia

Jespers and Henry Stanforth—now first in line for a baronetcy—
had reconciled their differences sufficiently that soon enough they
would wed, perhaps as soon as he came down from his studies at
Oxford. Nothing they did or said over the following few years
belied this general presumption.

"Upon Henry Stanforth's reaching his majority, he obtained
the obligatory degree in religion and another supplemental one in
the law, the latter mostly about maritime aspects of the unwieldy
British legal system, since after all it was Lancaster-sur-Mer that we
all resided in, wasn't it? I had received my own little education in
religion, and Henry and I met occasionally in Reverend DeVare's
offices, where we would discuss many and varied topics, and Henry
would expatiate upon aspects of the writings of that arch-Latinist,
Thomas Aquinas, whom he admired greatly.

"It was your mother, in somewhat later days, who told me what
occurred to actively curtail their engagement. Henry, naturally
enough, proposed to her, and Livia demurred. Worse than that, she
said Henry must wait as she felt utterly unready for the state of
wedlock as he described it to her. She told me later that she had
been unprepared to give up her independence. This latter rather
generalized concept, she explained, consisted in her doing more or
less *what* she wanted more or less *when* she wanted, whether that
be her often disorderly chemical studies in the Jesperses' outdoor
laboratory or her studies in natural sciences for which she travelled
far afield throughout the shire, dressed at times no better than a
common yokesman. She also liked to do nothing but read novels for
entire weeks at a time as well as to go barefoot, to swim and muck
about the extensive estuarial basins and tide pools which abound
off Morecambe Bay. She had begun to tutor a group of younger
girls attracted to studying with her, and indeed even emulating her.
Livia was most unwilling to cede these freedoms and benefits to
Henry, or indeed to any man, for the sake of something as abstract
as a name or greater security, especially as that also would entail
housekeeping and having children, both of which failed to excite
her feminine instincts.

"What I am now to tell you I got from Henry and from your
mother both. Finding his affections breached for what Henry could
not understand as very good justification, he flew into a passion—
for his was a most passionate nature, as are many red-haired men—
and decided to do what many spurned men do. Go to sea. Being rich

and noble, he went as a high officer on a large commercial vessel connected with the East Indies Trading Company. He was gone a year and a half, and during that time he often wrote to his family, which hand-forwarded his letters to the Jespers family, hoping to interest Livia in drawing him back home.

"Of foreign lands and peoples, he saw plenty. Henry also had an odd adventure or two, but more of the curious sort than of the daring-deed variety. He returned to Lancaster taller, more sunburned, and handsomer than ever. Richer, too. Also more confident. Once again, he began wooing Livia, and once again she turned him down, saying it was 'for the time being.'

"Once more Henry went to sea, this time as first mate of a somewhat smaller and less prestigious commercial vessel, headed down the Atlantic Seaboard.

"Our British navy ruled the seven seas some twenty years ago as it does now, if with a less sure hand. Following upon a week-long voyage, the decommissioned frigate-turned-trader in which Henry sailed rounded a well-known cape on the north-eastern-most edge of what was then the empire of Brazil. They were hoping for fresh water, provisions, and a bit of rest. Instead, they encountered a harbour-side in flames, and the crews of several apparently piratical three-masters running riot.

"Naturally, as mate, Henry ordered a full retreat. But one of the pirate ships had caught sight of his craft, and sensing booty beyond that of the town, the ship took chase. Back across the Atlantic, Henry's barque sped upon unvarying currents. Pursuing it on those same speedy currents, the sea robbers rushed after. Due to the prevailing westerly winds, this was a more rapid voyage than the previous one, but given their much depleted provisions and much dampened spirits, also one of greater hardships. The crew was first resentful, and then frightened.

"The Gulf of Guinea in western equatorial Africa provided the greatest chance of safety, mostly because the British in the form of both commerce and its navy lay there in strength. Henry had persuaded his captain to aim them into the Bight of Benin, the heart of this power, and they had just done so when a vast gale arose. Their ship was able to outrun the worst of what would prove to be a terrible hurricane, although brushing along one edge of the nearly spherical storm, it took considerable damage to its foremast and rudder. They watched the vessel chasing them begin to spin like a child's top in the ocean roads before it vanished from sight, swept under sea.

"But other continual, if less potent, storms continued to assault them, and Henry's crew was forced to tack northward, ever northward, days at a time, away from safety, if only to escape worse punishment. Along the way, they lost their bowsprit, jib, yardarm, aft mast, and some rigging.

"Finally surcease arrived in the form of a clear, sunny afternoon and a dead calm sea. The exhausted crew scrambled to eat and drink whatever they might rummage from their much reduced stores, and then stumbled into a well-earned and long-delayed slumber. One experienced old salt declared to Henry that this delightful absence of wind was, instead of good, the most negative of indications that they had so far encountered. It needed only a burning red sunrise to portend utter disaster, he said.

"They awakened to just such a fore omened rubescent dawn. Henry had drunk a cup of grog, eaten his heel of bread, and sailed out in the ship's small boat with another deckhand. They were attempting to carpenter more wood to their damaged rudder so they might steer again, when the sky turned greenish grey and the sun vanished. Giant storms loomed on three sides of them, the sea churning up waves half the height of the craft within minutes.

"They abandoned their unfinished task and sought to return to the frigate. His fellow crewman had just clambered up and quickly dropped guy lines to the apperceived safety of the mid-deck, when both the ship and the little boat were struck by the first of what would prove to be three gigantic waves of seawater, what the Asians call Soo-Nah-Mee.

"Henry's smaller craft was instantly swept far from the larger boat by the first huge wave, and so they were able to see it and to hear Henry shout out. After almost two minutes, a second monumentally large wave interspersed itself between his shell and the frigate, and upon this wave, his little cockle rose and twirled madly. When the crew looked for him, it seemed that a mountain of water lay between the two craft. At its far end, the frigate was a league distant, the little boat perilously inclined against the gigantic curve of the third, and by far largest, wave. Then it was gone, out of sight. Henry and his boat lost.

"The first mate had the area searched for two days, but all they could descry was timbers of the little boat and scraps of cloth. So they reported when they returned to port a week afterward.

"Livia blamed herself, naturally, for his death. Her selfishness, her refusal to give up her own capricious wishes and unpredictable delights to his more legitimate requirements weighed upon her heavily. She admitted that her education was somewhat to blame. Having been taught to despise the nobility and to ennoble the common man, she had always thought Henry overprivileged and undercriticised, albeit she confessed to having fulfilled that office for him whenever possible. He had been noble, she told me on more than one occasion. Oh, if only she had been less prejudiced against his class and he were still alive!

"I had received my degree in divinity after some perfunctory further studies at York Minster, so I accepted a role of quite trivial employment about the grounds of the Lancaster Cathedral where Reverend DeVare still lingered, seeking a lucrative deanery, and I did so mostly because Livia resided there. DeVare depended upon me only at certain very unimportant hours. This allowed me much time to pass in Livia's company. She'd begun to shun almost everyone else she knew. Her parents especially became objects of her antipathy, as she partly held their teachings responsible for her prejudgements about Henry.

"A year passed, then half of another year, when one day I told her it was time that I roused myself and sought out a more salubrious life position. I was looking at Kirby as a site to settle in, located up the coast.

"Livia asked why I must have a better position in so frivolous a manner, that I replied equally lightly, 'So I might be able to pay for a house for my wife and children.' She then asked whom I expected to marry, as we both knew there were no feasible contenders for this position. 'I suppose,' I said back, equally flippant, 'it will have to be you.' Her response was, 'I suppose so, as we've scandalized the city quite enough always going about together. But you must understand that should Henry Stanforth not be dead after all and should he return alive, that I will fly to him. Thus, our marriage will be quite breached. That, or else your proposal is unacceptable.'

"I was so surprised by how this insignificant conversation had evolved into one of such utter portentousness and so closely matching my desires—I'd made only the most joking of proposals—

that I instantly agreed to her terms before she changed her mind. I affianced her with a twisted paper ring made from a sermon that I had just crushed in my hands and had been toying with.

"My expectation was that Livia would come to her senses, but she didn't, at least not before the Reverend DeVare performed our marriage ceremony. He it was, now come into his much-vaunted position, who set me up at Kirby-Clark, and then who later early learned and recommended me to the living here in Ravenglass.

"Your mother now also came into her own. For it was ever her belief to ennoble the common man, and I was an almost perfect example of that breed, my family being from fisherfolk and yeomanry for many generations without any possible taint of patrician blood. It was she who insisted we take this vicarage position, even though it would remove her from daily contact from her Aunt Blassage, with whom she was considerably close, and also away from her parents, with whom she had newly reconciled. It was especially hard on her when she received news that her mother was dying, and Livia had to travel by dog cart in poor weather, and indeed arrived home only after her demise.

"Although she was intelligent beyond the ordinary, your mother now became driven by the idea of raising her children as perfectly as was possible. Your food must be the finest. Your bread the whitest. Your clothing the most comfortable and of the best cloth and cut. Also, of course, both of you must be educated at least as well as she had been. Although we had a day servant and a grounds-man, it was your mother who tilled a flower and vegetable garden so that you children would never lack for nutrition and beauty, she who planted and cared for the several fruit trees upon the property, she who wove and sewed for you long after I had gone to sleep, she who ordered you books from Lancaster and Broughton, using her own few extra thruppence for it.

"No wonder then, when you were three and your brother four years and a few months old, a letter arrived for her from Stanforth Manor and my head was whirled into near madness. I had never opened any messages for her before, but this one I fore omened badly. It was a thick packet of many pages, and so I at last opened it, read it for a long time throughout and learned of all I've now told you of what Henry Stanforth had written.

"I was sitting there all amazed when she returned home, with you napping in her arms. She had been to a neighbour's sewing circle where she had gone to learn to embroider so she might ornament you and your brother's jumpers and little vests.

"She put you to bed, then came to where I sat. She calmly carved clean a new taper, replacing the stub my candle had become, and put out her hand for Henry Stanforth's letter, which I held out numbly. She sat, and I looked the other way the entire long while that she read the letter. After another very long time, she asked me what she should do.

"'You must fly to Henry Stanforth at once,' I replied with as much mettle as I might find lurking deep within myself, repeating what she had said to my marriage proposal.

"'Yes,' was all she replied. But she remained awake while I went to bed, even though I slept hardly any at all. Next morning while you still slumbered, I walked her to the Lord Rothbert Inn, where a stage stopped and swept her away from me, off to Lancaster.

"You will recall that time—if you do at all—as the first time your grandmother, my mother, came to stay with us and cared for you and Rudolph. She was all wound up to be sent for, though she never quite understood how it had come about. She quickly made pets of you both and treated you remarkably sweetly, given how hard a life she'd had, and how almost callous she'd been to my brothers."

My father ceased. "That is what I had to tell you, Lillian."

Listening to my father's tale, and especially the last few sentences, I found myself wreathed in torment, my eyes burning with barely suppressed tears.

"But," I said, "our mother came back to us."

"Yes, she came back," he replied, "after a triple fortnight. I never could bring myself to ask her *why* she had done so, nor what had happened between them or how she had decided against Henry and for us. Livia and I became what I believe your compeers refer to as platonic Friends. We no longer shared our bed, nor—in time—our thoughts and feelings. Eventually Henry Stanforth married a younger woman of no great consequence but of his class, and he gave her several boy children. Subsequently, the subject of your mother's great love was never once mentioned in this house, nor I think never outside it either by her."

"But then, something did happen," I told as much as asked my father, "some two years ago that brought about our mother's decline."

"What happened two years ago was that Henry Stanforth

died. A letter came about that happening. It was nothing more complicated. I must suppose that with Henry's death, your mother saw her last opportunity gone. Her decline began. I, of course, had lost her many years before. We seldom spoke, and it was fortunate we had this good-sized house to keep out of each other's way, for I think in those intervening years she had come to hate me as much as she had come to hate herself."

"Noble and self-denying as that decision had been for her—and for you," I assured him. "And now," I remarked, in wonder that such an ordinary seeming family as my own could have such a mysterious and remarkably romantic history, "I also understand why she so hated Rudolph going to sea."

"She died, I think, only so she could never receive news that he and his ship had been lost," my father said.

"This is all very very tragic for you, dear Father. I am grieved for your sake."

"Daughter, I wish it had all been otherwise. But I entered into this marriage with my eyes fully open many years ago. I received no more nor less than I declared myself prepared for," he said staunchly. "I cannot complain. I *dare not* complain. For if I had not the first and the purest love of Livia Jespers, then at least I came to possess for a time some of her secondary love, and for a while, that was more than enough. In addition, I have her beauty and high spirit in your brother and in you."

"Now too," said I, "you have the careful attentions of good Mrs. Cupp."

"Dora Cupp," he muttered, making the three syllables of that simple woman's name sound so—I search for the word and I cannot find it—that I had to wonder for years after that parlay whether that ordinary-seeming woman possessed as exciting and remarkable a history as my previously humdrum sire.

I remain,
Lady Lillian of Ravenglass

To: The Earl of Ravenglass
11 Hanover Square
London, England

2 October, 188—

Dear Papa,
It is All Hallows' Eve, and here in Kent shire they celebrate the unholy day I cannot say how. It is certain to be odd and outlandish, as it seems everything is in this quite gentle part of England that I never knew very well before, and hope to get to know quite well.

It is your own fault. You have no one but yourself to blame. Well, I amend that a bit. My wife, Caroline, or Carrie-Ann, as I now am instructed to call her, pretty much insisted we come here directly from the honeymoon.

I know you would have preferred us to go to Ravenglass, but what are we to do there, the lot of us? Her two brothers must return to school, and her parents must return to their little farm here, and to their circle of friends, a close-knit and most affectionate set, very different than what we knew in Cumbria. Then there were Carrie-Ann's quite rational arguments, which went like this:

"What is Ravenglass like in October and November," asked she one day while we were lolling at the Rye Strand, for we went there almost every blessedly sunny, not too windy day once I had relented and saw all the good to be gotten from it.

"Ravenglass is grey and stormy those months. Rainy and blustery," I was forced to answer.

"Are there many brilliant changes of leaf colour upon the trees about the manor house?" she persisted.

"What can you mean? The leaves turn brown in October and are mostly blown off before the end of the month. Why? What is your home shire like in October and November?"

"Golden-green, pink and pale orange, deep golden, and sometimes even red from maple leaf change. It is a picture book. And it hardly rains at all. But instead it is as fair in October as it was in September. While November does chill and rime all around, that's merely the dew, and it's quite gone by noon. It's all lovely and soft."

Lord Oliver had overheard us and later on said, "Well, if we're not called back to London, by all means let's go to Kent shire. It sounds scads more pleasant than your draughty old manse, Roddy."

He agrees with me that my Carrie-Ann is a most rational and modern young woman, not at all the gorgon of ill temper and caprice you led me to expect of her.

For example, upon our third day at Rye-Strand, I carefully lectured her thusly: "Even though you are my wife, Lord Oliver is the person I am closest to in life. That shall never alter."

"I would not expect it to alter a jot," said she. "I would think the less of you if it did."

"This means," I clarified, "I must pass time with Lord Oliver, not with you."

"That is perfectly clear to me, just as I hope to pass time with my brothers and parents and old friends, and not with you."

"I know him since early youth and owe him all kinds of debts of gratitude."

"Indeed you do, and I heartily thank him for helping you become the lovely Roddy you are become," said she.

And so, Papa, you see that we are in Kent shire. We're all getting along famously, and I like my wife. Perhaps, someday, I'll like her as much as I like Lord Oliver, although she has many years and good deeds to do yet to catch up to him.

By the by, did you want to know if my mater is still sending her letters? I think I saw one forwarded from Rye yesterday, but when I asked Carrie-Ann about it, she simply looked at me and said, "The poor thing!" and swept away off somewhere or other to oversee Cook, who was baking a damson tart from a tree the three of us picked clean yesterday.

Can you picture us? Roddy, Oliver, and Carrie-Ann, most of our bodies whitely netted against yellow-jacket stingers, picking ripe blue plums a few yards from the kitchen? Now, that was an egg tempera panel subject for Mr. Rosetti or Mr. Heuffner to have painted.

Your loving son,
Roddy, Baron of Ravenglass

To: The Honourable Lady Caroline-Ann Augusta
The Glebe, Ravenglass
Broughton, England

3 October 188—

My Dear Lady Caroline-Ann,
Someone, either the knowledgeable poet and critic Matthew Arnold or that tempest in a teapot novelist, Miss Jane Austen, wrote that all stories should end with a marriage or a death? Alas, some stories only reach a climax at marriage. My own, I must say, was one.

After listening to my father's long account of my mother's misfortune in choosing one marriage partner over another, I still believed she had made the right choice, no matter that she ended up concluding exactly the opposite. Yet the moral of my father's tale was not lost upon me. Bloodlines weren't really the issue and ought never to be the deciding factor. If the earl and his wife and their son credited my person with sufficiently established genealogy to mix into their line, who was I to gainsay it? As for myself, unlike my mother, I possessed no true option. Lord Roland had let it known he would propose. The only other possible man I had in any way even considered was his closest friend, Lord Robert, but hadn't he acted from the onset solely as Roland's agent or proxy?

Easter Day in Leeds was a joyous and colourful holiday, especially for one residing in the vicinity of the cathedral or its many annexes and supplemental edifices. Our little women's college was in some minor way so associated, and thus our ordinarily insignificant assembly took its place amidst and enjoyed many of the privileges of the grander festivities.

Lords Roland and Robert somehow found time from their own studies to join us in Leeds and at the cathedral, from Holy Saturday onward, so we were all three gathered again, along with Mrs. Starkweather-Caine and Georgiana Milton, at a particularly gay Paschal Sunday afternoon dinner at the home of a local church authority somehow related to many of his guests.

The day was clear, warm, and cloudless, with a hint of a breeze. We were on our way there, strolling through the grounds of the cathedral, when Lord Roland took my arm and slowly impeded my forward motion. At the same time, I couldn't help but notice Lord Robert surely and rapidly impelled the other women ahead.

"What do you think of our college's new prodigy?" I asked. I had watched Georgiana's first encounter and subsequent observation of the two young men as though they were some subspecies of East Indies caterpillar she must carefully categorize and analyse.

"If you speak of Miss Milton's views as she expresses them, I fear for the reputation of your college," Lord Roland replied.

"Indeed, I'm certain real scholars as yourself and Lord Robert already look down upon us. I don't think anything Miss Milton might say could alter that perception."

"You're quite mistaken. We think of you as the prodigy, and Miss Milton as the…well, the polite term to use is inflexible bluestocking."

"Her stockings are pale lilac and newly bought, of the finest lisle from the continent. My own, by contrast, are…"

"Are encasing, if I might say so, the loveliest legs in Leeds. What I can see of them," he added, making us both laugh. "Well, then, the loveliest ankles."

"I don't think Lord Robert agrees. He has quite taken Miss Milton up."

"If you mean he has lifted her in order that he might then utterly flatten her, I think you are right."

"Then that grimace I see plastered upon his face is not infatuation but…?"

"More likely intimations of homicide, miss. For infatuation, you must concentrate upon the visage before yourself."

With that, the others turned a corner and vanished. We stopped at a convenient bench, where he asked me to sit. He produced a large ring inset with a large, oval, nearly iridescent fire opal he said had been mined from the mountains of the Antipodes, amazingly rare. He fitted the ring to my finger and asked me to be his betrothed, speaking rapidly of all he hoped from our union.

What, Lady Caroline-Anne, should I have responded?

Unlike Livia Jespers, I had no unblemished freedom of action, no choice of suitors, no experimental laboratory, and no gaggle of girls hanging on my every word and deed for emulation's sake.

A year August would be the first anniversary of my mother's death. He asked if I might come out of mourning a few months before, say in June, shortly after we both returned to Ravenglass.

I said I must write home and acquaint my father with the proposition. Lord Roland said he was halfway home already by being in Leeds. He could be all the way there tomorrow night, acquaint my father with my request, and obtain his blessing in person, should I allow it.

I had three months then until the day we had set.

Lord Roland kissed my hands through my lace gloves, and I gave him both cheeks to kiss. I was surprised by how much heat emanated off his body from such close range, and I shivered a little at the prospect of being in such close contact for a longer period with such incipient volcanism.

He then stood us up and walked us to where the others had stopped. It was a cool place, roofed by a semi-dome and surrounded a busily plashing fountain, centre-pieced by a large, doubtless mythical sea monster, double-netted by two stalwart tritons with Herculean muscles and especially loving expressions upon their fine faces. I pondered for a few seconds if the story it alluded to was one I'd read of a girl metamorphosed by a jealous goddess into a beast until she might be snared and converted by the affection of another deity.

Lord Robert had evidently been aware beforehand that the proposal would take place when it did, and upon seeing us arrive, his face was as handsomely gratified as that of his friend. Miss Milton's large eyes promptly noted the new jewel upon my finger, but she only said to us, "And there, Lord Robert, is an instance of what I meant. Had the sculptor been a woman, the ensnarers would be lovely nereids."

"There *are* no women sculptors, Miss Milton," he argued.

"That's my point exactly." She lifted her skirts and flounced off across the lawn, so that Miss Starkweather-Caine must hurry to catch up.

Later that evening at the college, as the other young ladies went out of their way over my new bauble, Miss Milton stood aside.

"Won't you come at least and look at the sigil of my impending bondage?" I quipped.

She did so, once the others had gone off, and said in a low voice, "Those two young men are exceeding rich, exceeding handsome, and exceeding ambitious."

"Then why not set your cap for Lord Robert? I will be sisterly and aid you."

"Not in a million years!" she declared. "That one is not for the plucking. His heart is already given to another for good."

"Have you a suspicion of who it is?" I asked, colouring a little for, of course I suspected it was me.

"No suspicion at all. But whoever it is, the connexion is unsanctifiable, I do believe," she added, astonishing me. Then when I was about to ask why she thought this, Georgiana Milton added words I would remember for years, "And because he is so head over heels, the fool, the connexion is certain at last to undo Lord Robert."

"I hope not, as he is my friend," I pleaded.

She had said enough and went back to silently admiring my engagement ring, reflecting merely that "Lord Roland certainly knows how to achieve an effect!"

❖

I now pass on to our marriage night. I don't know what you were told, hinted about, or lectured about for this supposedly all-important event, Lady Caroline-Ann. The young ladies at our college had varied discussions at which rumours and innuendoes of all sorts were tossed around the chamber like so many shuttlecocks, all of them about as insubstantial as that feathered object. My mother, however, had said nothing at all to me, and it had been her place to do so. Lord Roland's mother, as I have described her, was hardly to be pursued about the subject. Only dear old Dora Cupp said what turned out to be relevant words: "Don't over-worry yourself, my dear. It'll all be over before you know it."

We were wed in the chapel of Ravenglass. Pastor Rose was somehow not embarrassed to officiate. Lord Robert of Blackburn stood as the groom's man, and—because she had specifically requested it, to my surprise—Georgiana Milton stood next me as bride's maid. The foreman's wife was my matron of honour. My new in-laws, Lady Bella and the earl himself, were in attendance, naturally, she in her mobile wooden chair, he apart from us all with his usual London lord and lady; the brace of them changed individually, if rather closely following the type. Also in attendance, either inside or outside the church, and later in the great hall of the manor house, was fairly much everyone I knew or half knew in the town, manse, or shire. It was in the truest sense a popular marriage. Before the marriage feast, I'd been quite unaware of how politically apropos a union this would be, a real triumph for the Ravenglass family.

Only Matthew, the young, mute carpenter whom I thought my dear friend, never made an appearance, and I couldn't get a satisfactory answer from anyone I knew for why he was not present.

Possibly because the feasting and toasts and then dancing in the large ball room went on at such length, we didn't go up to bed until two hours after midnight, applauded by what remained of the group, mostly the younger people.

Earlier in the day, I had transferred to the manor house what few possessions I had then, including of course my "enormous box" which looked quite insubstantial in the great bedchamber. My suite of rooms was located on the lower floor of the new wing the earl had built not many years before, and it consisted of my sizable bed's room, with its larger sitting room, dressing chamber, and a maid's chamber. Huge windows from the first two looked out onto the manse's lawns and gardens. My husband's suite was across the wide corridor and was as large as mine, with one further chamber—a library. Next to his were guest suites, including the one where Lord Robert had become used to staying. The earl and his London guests usually resided in identically sized, if more richly furbished, rooms on the floor above us, while Bella remained in those much more bare-boned upper rooms of the oldest wing where I'd last seen her, and where the wider doorways more easily accommodated her mobile chair.

As he kissed my cheeks and said goodnight just inside the threshold of my rooms, Lord Roland said, "No more for you today, my dear. You have had quite enough excitements for one young lady."

I was most grateful to be left without any further duties, and indeed fell to sleep almost before I was fully dressed in my night clothing.

The following day was another chain of celebrations. A wedding breakfast, allegedly *en famille*, lasted until well into luncheon time. This had been especially scheduled so the earl's London friends might at closer breadth look upon me, feel the size and fineness of my hands and face, and I suppose also subtly test my knowledge, which was an inane exercise at best. They knew little enough, and I not a great deal more.

One particular silly moment had gone thusly: Countess So and So asked me had I learned any foreign language. Fluent written and spoken French, I answered, some spoken and written Italian, a little

Latin, and some Greek. "My dear," said she, "if that's all crammed into that little head of yours, where can there be room for truly important things like rank and precedence?"

At last Lord Robert had had enough of them and began speaking of Parisian poetry and German plays and Italian customs in such an overly admiring manner, they found him to be "shockingly modern and really radical!"

Once the "fogies" were all fled, we three younger people laughed at them and took a long walk out on the lawns. I sat and watched the young men at lawn tennis, admiring their figures.

That night was another long dinner, this one for distinguished local and shire folk, all of whom simply had to come pay their respects, this time free of their inferiors. Among the former was my father, accompanied by Mrs. Cupp and, of course, Pastor Rose, who after he had kissed my hand, said, "I do hope you understand, that when we first met I didn't think it at all an aspersion to *aspire*."

That made me laugh, and Georgiana, who was still with us and who had overheard, took aim at the pastor and asked if he had ever thought it an aspersion to *aspire* to pottery. He seemed eager to please her, yet rather dumbfounded how to reply. Somewhat later on, as he was making a formal departure, I whispered to him, "That young woman has seventeen thousand pounds per annum already with a great deal more to come." At which he gawked at me and uttered in disbelief, "Do you meant to say it's all from earthenware cups and such?"

That night we didn't attain our beds until an hour after midnight, and I was kissed and once more chastely sent to sleep.

Four more days passed as filled with activities: impromptu parties, a yachting excursion, pick-nicks upon the cliffs. Every night we must dine with someone—Foreman Rocksmith and his wife (a pleasure for me to repay their hospitality), Lord Robert's family "visiting in the neighbourhood," more friends of the earl, and even some rather dour and elderly persons somehow related to my mother-in-law, Bella, were unearthed and dragooned to supper. Bella looked on in a kind of puzzlement, gnawing at intermittent times at a duck leg, and splashing about her dining place the major part of her raspberry trifle. Remembering her kindness to me from old, and noting Lord Roland's discomfiture around her, I had my own chair and a small table moved next to hers and kept her company throughout the meal whenever possible, trying to include her in the younger peoples' conversation.

Before she left, she took my hand in her own by then quite skeletal ones and simply ogled me for a long time before suddenly spinning about and flying out of the dining hall, her chair making its usual racket. Before we said good night at our chamber doors that night, Lord Roland engaged me in conversation, saying, "You take upon yourself more and more, even when it is so very difficult."

I wondered if he were warning me away from his mother or meant to chastise me, and I tried to not too hotly reply. "She is ill. It is not so difficult to be kind to her. Surely you recall how long ill my own mother was? It seems the least I can do, as none of us seem able to do much to offer her a moment's surcease."

"Whyever you do it, it is superbly kind of you. And your grace in doing it makes us admire you all the more."

That was better. I changed clothing for sleep and let my maid take down my hair, thinking I would like it here in Ravenglass Manor very much. The summer was soft, the afternoon rains quickly depleted, the terraces were dry again before one needed them, the company was interesting, even if Georgiana Milton had left to go back to the North country—it is a place not a direction and tomorrow my husband and his friend would be off again to London.

Earlier in the day, I had received a letter from abroad, brought from the vicarage, written by my brother Rudolph to my father, reporting aspects of his situation in his new life on the sea. The fellow who brought it, Homer Eagles, had been a schoolmate of both myself and Rudolph in earlier days at the manor's cottage school. When Homer made his delivery, I took him aside and asked him to join me in a side parlour, having cold meats and tea brought to him, while I read the letter. He'd apprenticed to the cloth trade, and he was only just on his way to Lancaster to take up his craft in a thriving concern from which it was believed he would make his fortune. Homer and I reminisced about our schoolteacher and our simple ways of having fun back then.

"Those remain fond days for me to look back on," I mused. "My brother too thinks on them fondly."

"Does he now? I thought it was unusual him going off to sea when he never much cared for that life as a lad."

I'd not heard this before, and Homer had no real details for me to batten upon. Instead, he said, "You have risen highest among us, but so were you fore destined from a very young age. We knew it then. Remember how we boys parried who would carry your book sack and hold your other hand on icy morns? Both myself and Eldon Creff said, 'Some day she shall be lady of the manor.' And look, it's come to pass."

"Never too much lady of the manor that I shall not have time for old friends like Homer and Eldon. My rank and my means are ever open to you, as sure you must know by now."

"And so I told Eldon it would be when he stopped me in my path here and said he thought otherwise."

"You must tell Eldon, whom I recall as being particularly partial to sweet butter-scones, our cook here bakes them very well and ices them with jam. Eldon is welcome to come and partake of them with this manor lady."

Such pleasant memories of the past day were flitting in and out of my sleepy thoughts, my candles but tiny guttering things, when I was astonished by a knocking at my bedroom door. Before anyone could answer—I could hear my poor maid not even stir in her sleep—the door was thrown open, and I was barely able to make out a tall figure rush toward me, his approach scattering what insignificant candlelight remained in the room and casting us into darkness.

"My dear!" he uttered hoarsely, and before I could sit up or respond, he threw himself bodily at me.

I was so astonished, I almost asked what had gone wrong. But he was atop me, and he was so very hot a personage so very noticeably without any clothing, that I grasped in a second what was about to happen.

Roland muttered words I could not make out. Were they endearments, enchantments, imprecations? All the while he covered me with his burning face and flaming limbs, and I felt at that moment I must die of confusion. Instead, he pulled away the bedclothes and my night shift, and before I knew what was happening, he had pierced me. This new sensation, a combination of pressure from being pinned to the mattress by this unstoppably hard and heavy body as much as the hot specific pain below, gave way to stranger new sensations as his mouth covered my face and ears and hair, and he undulated against me with such force I thought I would split in two. I was about to try to push him off or at least lean him to one side, when he suddenly stopped all motion. He gasped as though breathless, the water of his eyes now visible in the little light of the room, before his head fell forward on to the pillow by the side of my neck.

He lay there so long, his body heaving, his hidden head panting the way I recalled over-ridden steeds doing, that I must wonder— now what?

At last he lifted his face over mine and kissed my forehead. "You are an angel," said he in that same hoarse voice. Then in one movement, he was outside of my body again, off my body, and thence off the bed altogether. I saw or heard him stop only long enough to find and pull on his over-robe, and he was out of the chamber.

I lay there I don't know how long in shock, before I noted a small candlelight and my young maid standing there sleepily, holding out a cloth and saying within a yawn, "You'll be needing to wash somewhat now, my lady."

She washed me very gently, and put on me a soothing unguent she'd had earlier set aside especially for this purpose, but I couldn't bear to look at her ministrations. Soon she was done, and I was once more fully clothed, the blankets were once more placed gently over me, I asked for extra pillows, which I placed atop my midsection, a defence too late, and minutes after, I could hear my sleepy maid abed and snoring.

I remained awake far longer, I can assure you, until in fact, I noticed dawn light. But as Mrs. Cupp had said, it had all been over quickly, and now I was a wife.

I slept late and didn't even hear Lords Roland and Robert as they set off for the south.

Lillian

To: The Very Reverend Horace Jasper Quill
The British Church at Campofieri
Town of Fiesoli
Province of Toscana

4 October 188—

Sir,

We are in Italy. The road from Innsbruck across the Brenner Pass took us into Bolzano. We remained one night there amid a crowd of railroad travellers. It then dropped down the Alps by narrow gauge rail hundreds of feet at a time to the old city of Trent, where we rest for this day and possibly another.

The lady wishes to see Lake Garda. And so we shall be delayed by tourism. I cannot say how long, one day or several more.

Several incidents occurred I thought worthy of your knowing. But first, let me write what you already know, which is that the lady is more remarkable the better I get to know her. I've already written you of several incidences of her liberality, concern, compassion, and goodness to others in the past. She is a mothering angel to the young Greek men. She is helpful to strangers when she understands that it will not endanger us.

But you already know this, don't you, sir? It had been your privilege to know of her from your friend before I did.

I am reconciled to what happened in that previous train regarding the gaming, and I am heartened and thankful for your carefully chosen words. As for the lady, the very next morning after our conversation and my revelation that I was a foundling, she took me aside and said to me, "Although we are yet strangers, my unusual history means I have learned and experienced much in this world, sir. Trust me as you would a relation with your best interests at heart, and I shall endeavour to be of good use to you. Should you ever decide to express to me what specifically ails you."

I nearly wept at her words and said that while I was not yet comfortable enough to be quite so candid as she had asked, I would like to be, her words and directness of intention had already helped me to see my path more clearly.

So yes, I do understand that I have friends all about me, as you have kindly written to me, friends I may turn to when those temptations I despise and abhor arise try to pull me down.

Now to these small, yet, I think, important incidents that I mentioned. As you know, I handle our passports and visas from one station to another. The ladies remain where they are and all manner of official customs, visas and such requirements, I manage completely for them. Now that the young Greeks are with me, I have also taken to handling their border-crossing papers.

You may imagine then, how surprised I was when the lady's maid came to me during our traversal of the Brenner Pass, and clandestinely handed me another passport, asking for the one I'd been given to be given back to her. I naturally enough noted from its colour that this one was Italian, not French, and the name given was not that one that we, or any other customs inspector, had been given.

I was most surprised as you may imagine and expressed this sentiment. The young woman took my hand in her tiny gloved one, lifted it to my throat, and said, "While you slept, I saw this scar almost the size of a man's hand. Would you like to explain to my lady how exactly it is that you have obtained this atrocious scar?"

The bold thing. I must admit, I blanched at her words, but I have a story for it. I told her this scar is a memento of an illegal duel I engaged in while a student in Germany and is due to a piece of youthful foolishness on my part. Of its existence, I am neither proud nor ashamed. Yet I immediately understood the thrust of her question. Both of us have had surreptitious, possibly scurrilous moments of our history we would prefer were not broadcast, never mind made known to the lady, nor to the Greeks, lest they lead to other, far more insalubrious questions.

Therefore, I was forced to say to her, "Your passport is Italian. Your name is Henrietta Acropilla, born in Bergamo, Italy. Exactly as it is written here. Of you, I know nothing else."

She dropped a curtsey. "Thank, you, sir. You are a gentleman of great common sense," said she, and she flounced away with her French passport in hand, leaving me with the Italian one. I doubt I shall ever see that other passport again anytime soon.

The truth of how I received that scar is quite different. This will doubtless surprise you. As I have written to you before, when Mr. Undershot took me in at the age of six and a half years old, I was part of another family, very poor, living in a ghastly slum of London. Our father was a sot and a bully who abused our mother and us small boys. He abandoned us when our existence interfered with his drunken pleasure, which was often enough. Once our mother died, he never trod near to us again. Before my father left, however, he gave me that scar as a final remembrance. He used a shard of a broken gin bottle to do so while deeply drunk. It was remarked that it was a wonder I did not perish from the wound. Two medical students roomed nearby, and I was carried to them and cared by them. It is one of the few memories I have of that other life. What other ones I have are too painful to recall, or to relate. Perhaps when we meet in person...

The second occurrence of note took place earlier that day, in Innsbruck, the morning we were to entrain after being so long detained by weather.

Since the repulsive episode upon the private car of the train, I found I must be out of doors, engaged in exercise, in fact, tiring myself with strenuous physical exercise as much as I could, if only to be able to catch a few moments sleep at bedtime, so much does that event prey on my mind. Therefore, while the ladies and the Greeks were engaged in breaking fast and packing their bags and boxes, I flogged myself into the snow-drifted street atop staggering snowshoes, and I trod that little town from one end to the other.

It was during this early morning tramp of mine that I couldn't help but notice a young man, especially as we were alone on the snow-bound street. I don't know what it was about him, possibly his raven hair, his blazing eyes, his intensity, his—I almost wrote "dissoluteness," but then I'm the dissolute one, aren't I? Something told me he was not German nor Austrian nor even, given the blazing eyes, Italian, but instead, British as I am myself. And yes, he was dissolute. But he was quite pleased about being so. And also that he was—how may I write this so you don't think me gone mad—that he was someone I *must know*, and *shall know*, for better or worse, I know not which.

All this, mind you, in a half a minute as we passed each

other with barely a greeting on the frigid, early morning, snow-crusted street.

Yet the memory of that young man who was so pleased with himself also preys upon my mind. It truly does.

Your friend and Servant
Stephen Undershot

To: The Honourable Lady Caroline-Ann Augusta
The Glebe, Ravenglass
Broughton, England

4 October 188—

My Dear Lady Caroline-Ann,
    We are arrived in a beautiful spot, and I would like to share
it with you. Far-off mountains ring us with their frozen majesty.
Closer by, somewhat lower, level peaks are lined and topped with
towering pine trees. All around us they drop in picturesque ravines
and crests, folds of the many coloured leaf-strewn earth, down to a
lake so long and blue and so heavenly! The people here seem not
as though they live in the last decades of the nineteenth century
but instead, as they have always lived, perhaps a thousand years or
more.
    Their dress is bright, typical, yet useful, too, and apt somehow.
Their colouring should be one thing from their nationality, and yet
it's more Northern, fresher, brighter, and cooler. Their pleasures
are simple, and I have with only the greatest difficulty found an
international bookseller who had upon his shelves a Charles Reade
novel I have never read and two more English volumes, one of
shorter stories and a novel promisingly titled *A Pair of Blue Eyes*,
both by an author I'd never heard of named Thomas Hardy. For
my male companion, and to keep him from brooding overmuch,
I purchased a highly recommended American volume all about
traversing their immense Mississippi River!
    This touristic preface does not serve, I see now, to divert you
one bit, I think, from the rather bleak content of my last letter.
Indeed, perhaps you ought to get your own bookseller to find you
some work by Mr. Hardy rather than read the rest of this letter.
    And yet, I insist you read on. I always insist on that since, Lady
Caroline-Ann, a little knowledge, as Mr. Pope says, is a dangerous
thing. Fuller knowledge, on the other hand...
    Lords Roland and Robert returned once more to Ravenglass
and to me after a fortnight in Leeds. The summer continued warm
and calm, more lovely than I ever recalled it. Naturally I stayed
awake the night of his return, awaiting a fresh onslaught from my
husband. It did not happen, and I would come to understand it
would not until the night before he left again, as though he couldn't

face me the following morning—as I would not have been able to face him either.

I obtained a quantity of the ointment my maid had used upon me that first time, and I put it upon myself anyway every night he was there as a sort of prescriptive assurance. The pain of that first occurrence had been memorable. It never was again, although the suddenness and the shock would never let me remain at rest, at least not while he was inside the house.

During daylight hours, no lover could be more gentle, more attentive, sweeter, more accommodating. It must be churlish of me to even...nevertheless, I was glad when it was the hottest days of early August and I had no "visitor" that month. I think you must know I mean—the sanguine visitor who comes every month to girls and young ladies, no matter what. Unless...

My maid, though an ignorant girl, noticed first and pointed it out to me, then spread the word about the house servants. And still I had no visitor. And Lords Roland and Robert would come and go, a week at the manor and then a fortnight gone, a week here, another fortnight gone.

It was on one occasion when they had returned and been in their rooms but only a half hour, surely barely time enough to change clothing for a late supper, as I was doing, when there was a knock at my door, and my maid let in Lord Roland, who was terrifically excited. Lord Robert followed, and they rushed and lifted me up and twirled me about in mid-air and took turns kissing my cheeks and asking were it true, were it true, until I must say, yes it was true. I was *enceinte*, with child!

The night was a celebration, nearly a carousal. The next night the foreman and his wife were invited. Then my father and Mrs. Cupp, and Matty must come for dinner. Mute Matty the carpenter had returned to our lands and meanwhile been doing wonders about the manor, first out of doors, then downstairs, and little by little, everywhere that he stepped or happened to look, amendments and improvements sprang up like mushrooms after him.

That particular celebratory visit saw no more past-midnight visits with me frightened out of my wits as he leapt upon me like some demon. No, Lord Roland paid me only afternoon and sunset visits, and he was the charming and amusing husband I married in the vicarage chapel. So I learned to further cherish the child that grew so very slowly within me, for its protecting me from him.

When the summer turned to autumn, my husband and his friend must, I knew, return to their classes for the final term baccalaureate, so I saw him less and even came to look forward to their infrequent visits and their gifts, for now they both brought gifts in large number for the mother and the child.

I had not thought and had never cared whether the child be girl or boy. I knew an heir was wanted. But we were freshly wed and young, and surely an heir could be had the second or third time should the first child be a girl.

But I quickly noticed two things. One was the growing speculation about the lower portions of the house as to which gender I was carrying. Some said carrying high was for a boy, carrying low for a girl. But which was I doing? Some said one, others the other. Some servants below stairs told my maid of various prescriptions for discovering the gender of the child. These included floating an uncooked egg in the water I had bathed in or weighing my discharge when I made water to see if it was heavy or light. All great sillinesses, I thought. Next, they would slaughter a squab and consult its entrails!

The second noticeable thing was less silly. It concerned the gifts being brought to the child-to-be-born from London. While Lord Robert's were those that any infant might like—a rattle, a spinning mirror—those my husband brought tended to be what a male infant would prefer. Once or twice when he was being especially tender with me, I attempted to discover his feelings, and if he so much more preferred my having a boy. I did this, I thought subtly, yet with no dishonesty, and had just about persuaded myself he would not care either way when I added, "I think the Lady Bella would be happy to hear a baby's gurgles, whichever it may be?"

Lord Roland startled as though he'd heard a revolver shot go off. His head swung back a moment toward the wing of the house his mother kept to, as though she had inched forward in her chair perceptibly at my words, and he had heard that forward motion. Very quietly, he said, "I should not like it all if she had *any part* of an innocent babe. Not with *her* accumulation of corruption!" The last phrase he said so cold-bloodedly I must shiver.

I shall not fill your mind with the travails nor with the benefits of lying-in, nor of carrying a child for the first time. I will only repeat what my little maid said to me a week before I was to give birth: that country women ate clay and even at times dirt to harden their lower parts, some even laundry starch, so the child might come out more easily. She had gotten me some very clean variety of the latter stuff and had begun slipping it into my broth, where I somehow did not notice it.

It was still a wintry cold late March when Lords Robert and Roland returned to Ravenglass, their baccalaureates won, their wanderings done for the time being. With them arrived a young doctor, a friend of theirs from school who would attend me at labour. In vain did I explain how our old Doctor Tobbler, who had cared for me since I was a child, had been to see me or I gone to see him almost every Monday week, and what his words and prognostications were. For them he was "a fogey. Centuries behind in medicine and surgery. Doctor Eben Sharpless is your man. Up to date as yesterday's newssheet." Nor were they happy to know that a midwife had been arranged. "They are septic old hags and potion-making witches," Lord Roland declared. "I'll not have one around to infect my issue."

And so Eben Sharpless it was to be. Even so, I arranged to have the midwife come stay nearby in the maid's room. And Old Doctor Tobbler was to be notified by boy messenger as soon as my contractions began. Their friend, the doctor, was even more adjacent. He moved into rooms next to Lord Robert's, and the three of them went riding and were daily to be found at archery and playing tennis and at the billiards table. He was a nice enough looking fellow, easy to like, despite an impediment of speech which made him pronounce oddly those words with the letter "s" in them. He did keep the others good company, so I didn't much mind.

One thing Dr. Sharpless was especially current on was the use of palliatives. He had studied dentistry, and he had learned both mesmeric techniques and those entailing the use of a chemical extract, either or both of which, when employed upon a young person such as myself, would remove all pain and memory of hardship during childbirth, he said. Indeed, they might even render me for a time without consciousness. This, all three young men assured me, was the preferred manner by which all the best ladies in London all now underwent their final lying-in, and had been approved by the highest echelons of society.

That will have to stand in for any tales of the childbirth I might have otherwise had. Since I was both mesmerized and then, when that method seemed not to be operating sufficiently to keep me from making noise, I was anesthetized, using Eben Sharpless's chemical means, the formula for which was never given me and which may have been similar to what Lady Bella ingested at such length.

The child was born. I was given her to hold. She was tiny and very red faced with tiny hard little limbs, and she yawned and went promptly to sleep. After a short while, I too slept.

Lord Robert came to me just before then, I think. I am not certain as all of it is rather a muddle due to the medicines which he admitted Sharpless had construed to be a little unbalanced. But my friend said soothing words to me, and perhaps he may have explained where my own husband had gone and why he had not come to me. That I don't actually recall.

It was another very long time before I awoke fully. Then I recalled that there had been a period, perhaps short or longer, I couldn't yet know, when I lay in a state not quite deeply asleep and not quite awake. People had been in my sitting room, nearby. There had been arguments among men's voices. One had exclaimed loudly, almost violently. Had I been so ill, then, that I could not recall? And after that was naught but a long and brooding silence from them all. But now it was dawn, and the weather had broken. I parted my bedcurtains and saw that a slight rime all-round the panes of windows was visibly melting before the assault of sunlight. My little maid lay asleep in a large chair that had been carried in to be near my bed. Blankets fondled her. Through the thrown-open doors of the sitting room, I could make out a man's figure upon the divan, also asleep upon pillows wrapped in blankets. Dark haired. Yet not Lord Robert. Was that Doctor Sharpless?

I sat up and even attempted to move a blanket. I said something in a voice so hoarse I could not recognize it. A cup of water was by the bedtable. I had turned myself half around in bed to reach it when my maid awakened and instantly so did the young doctor. He rushed in to stand behind her.

"My lady," said she, "how do you do?"

I had sipped and thus got back my voice, although it was a very little one.

"I feel I have slept weeks."

"Almost," the doctor said. "Five days."

"Then who has suckled the babe?" asked I, expecting to hear some local girl had been brought in to do it, as was the common usage.

My maid burst into tears. The young doctor came closer and knelt by the bed. "My Lady Lillian. I regret to inform you that all our labour, all *your* labour, was in vain. The infant was," he said, letting go a sob, "alas, defunct before it could suckle."

I looked at my maid. The babe had been healthy in my arms. What had happened meanwhile? Or had I been so ill myself I could not know? No. I knew. The baby had been healthy. How its little arms and legs had moved about, how its little red face had seized up like a closed hand as it had yawned.

"She is gone, my lady. We buried her two days ago," my maid added and burst into fresh tears.

I lay back upon my bed and felt a chill that no blanket added on top would ever bring warmth to. They began speaking together again, and then Lords Roland and Robert were called in, and all became a great tizzy about me, and their great joy at my recovery, and their unhappiness at our loss.

Had I suspected then what I know now, I would have fled Ravenglass at that moment, even if I must perish doing so.

Ever yours,
Lady Lillian of Ravenglass

5 Octobre 188—

We haf him see. The bad pretti homme of his L-ship.
It was unwis of him, of u, of his L-ship, too. I preten I
kno not, but I kno. The distinse must b kept grater. The big
one he suspiches me. Et not so good is.
Mor care, I beg thee.
Henriette

To: The Honourable Lady Caroline-Ann Augusta
The Glebe, Ravenglass
Broughton, England

7 October 188—

My Dear Lady Caroline-Ann,
Are you even there? I sometimes wonder. At times, indeed, I wonder if you ever received even one of these letters I've sent. I wonder if, instead, they have gone directly into the hands of my husband or one of his henchmen. Yes, my dear, I fear at least one of his men follows us still. I don't know how many others. But I believe it is the very same one I've mentioned before, the darkly handsome younger one who is the earl's special favourite.

I know this because he has been seen again very recently. First, on the railroad car taking us down the—— Pass, and after that he was seen waiting outside yet another train station when we dropped down to yet another plateau from a sublime mountain lake that we visited. My little travelling maid had previously recognized him and blurted out that information. So she and the two Greek young men travelled ahead of us in a front car, in case he might be waiting for us at the rather small railroad station. He was indeed espied there trying not to be too obviously curious. Theocrakis was sent back to tell me. I was heavily veiled and given a walking stick, and I affected a great hobble and a cracked voice, as though I were twenty-five years older. My companions were put behind me but out of sight, the two young Greeks placed on either side of me, and all three of us together exited the train, arguing in voluble Greek until we had gotten into our waiting carriage to take us to our hotel.

He tipped his cap at us—he had met the Greeks before— and kept looking behind us for some others. Henriette and my secure gentleman exited behind us and took their own taxi. He was disappointed, my husband's man, not to catch me so easily. But then he must think all of us terribly stupid.

We are not. I certainly could no longer afford to be unobservant, not after the following incidents I am about to report happened when I was first at Ravenglass Manor, as I have previously related. Where was I? Ah, yes, the baby. Hannah, I called her, for she had lived long enough at least to be named. I kept her name and her existence thereafter close in my heart, although I could never know whether she'd been secreted away or somehow or other made to die and had been put into that little coffin they all reported burying at the churchyard. In later days, I would ask of the gardener Samson who did the burying how sad an occasion it was.

He said the coffin was light enough for him to carry alone, but unquestionably contained some object or other that thumped about a bit when he carried it. That news stopped me cold, I can tell you, Lady. Even so, for years afterward, I would look at little girls when I went all about the shire on my charity visits and whenever any one of them was however many years old Hannah would be, I would observe her carefully to see if she resembled my father, or my mother, or Rudolph even. Never did I stare at them more if they looked like him, naturally. He might have sired bastards all over the countryside. Perhaps whether Hannah lived and was sent away or died is a mystery that will never be solved.

At any rate, my husband returned to Ravenglass Manor as soon as he was well and in no time at all, following the usual night-terror which resumed at the very end of each of his visits, I at last found myself with child again. This time it all occurred differently. Whatever ill omens had attended my first carrying seemed now blown apart like clouds on a June afternoon. I can't say why exactly, but they were. As though little Hannah's having come and gone had somehow cleared the air. I know that makes little sense, and yet I know no other way to phrase it.

For example, on the first afternoon in my second third, when I was walking with Lords Roland and Robert, we had gone far, despite my condition, as Dr. Sharpless's new regimen for healthy lyings-in required a deal of exercise. We had almost achieved the village of Ulverston, in fact, when we came upon a deep glade of tilled land and a gathering of local people. It was the season of the first reaping, and they were all gathered there for that, but they also had massed around a certain hay wagon. From our vantage point as we descended by rough path, we might view the entire narrow vale and clearly make out the great crowd around someone standing upon the back steps of that vehicle, a person speaking.

As we approached more closely, Evelyne and Chesley Dribb, a young couple that farmed for us but had temporarily hired out to this neighbour of ours for his bean and barley harvest, came to meet us carrying a half flagon of milk, refreshment for which I was in need. Evelyne took me aside, and when I asked who was speaking, some politician or divine, she said, "Neither, my lady, nor no Methodist either. 'Tis an American Spiritualist who has been going about the countryside prophesying."

My gentlemen escorts naturally scoffed, calling it a "typical rural folly," and they sought out ale they might purchase as well as a place for us all to rest. Chesley saw to that. But I followed Evelyne over to the wagon and there I sat a bit and heard the American speak.

I'd never seen one before, and because of Mr. Cooper's novels, I expected this one to be in buckskins with feathers in his hair and bear grease across his face in arcane signs. Instead, he was tall, thin, and well dressed in everyday British apparel, with a larger brimmed hat than normal, I suppose, against the summer sun and wearing stronger shoes, with hobnails in the heels for his great perambulations. His voice was loud and strangely high in pitch, and he wasn't deafening like many of our British orators, but spoke in a normal voice and yet was able somehow to be heard by listeners sitting forty yards off.

"Today is tomorrow's yesterday," I recalled him saying. "Yesterday means nothing. It is gone. Tomorrow is equally nothing. It has not yet come. Only now and today counts for aught. Or should." I could see folks shaking their heads in agreement, and Lord Robert waving a hand at the words as though brushing off flying insects, though I saw none nor heard any.

"God's gift, people," said the American, "is to dream tomorrow today. I do that. I prophesy thereby."

"Will this year's crop be a good one?" one man called out.

"That ye can see with ye own eyes. Ask me a hard question?"

"Shall you be gaoled for false omens?" Lord Roland shouted.

The American stopped and stared at the gentry, then at me. "Her Majesty's gaol awaits one of us here today. But not I, sir."

Lord Roland was loudly wondering if that was an insult worth replying to, and precisely in what manner, when the American pointed at me and shouted, "He is a jolly lad, healthy and fat. Best fortune to him and to you, fortunate lady."

"Did you hear, Robert?" Lord Roland said, amazed. "He prophesied a healthy heir for me."

In seconds, I was gathered up and congratulated by those about me. When we looked up, the American had vanished.

A few days later, I was walking through the Italian garden the old earl had let the care of go too long. Lord Robert had found and brought me from London-town a fine-looking Florentine folio upon the subject of gardens in that style, written by the architect Vitruvius, newly rendered into the Italian language. I was reading it, showing it to our new gardener, who proved more open to fresh ideas than his predecessor had been. I had just pointed to those symmetrical areas which should be defined by four cypress trees at each side, not the scattered about two presently in place, when four women from the village walked by, taking a side path to the vicarage which some old Lord R. had allowed some free use of.

Among their number was Mrs. Cupp, returning home, as well as the three young Creswell sisters, all still maidens at the time. I waved them closer, and Samson opened the double gateway from the path, so they might enter the derelict garden and have a seat upon one of the two, facing, somewhat age-worn marble benches the earl had come upon while on his grand tour of Italy forty years before. The ladies were grateful for the rest and for the spring water. To a woman they all marvelled at my appearance. Mrs. Cupp said for all of them, "My dear, you look today fresher and younger than ever. Your interesting condition quite agrees with you. I've no doubt..." Hearing her friends murmur assent, she changed it. "*We've* no doubt, an easy birth of a needed heir."

It was then, of course, that I first noticed Miss Adelaide Creswell, who, as I earlier pointed out to you, would become my friend. While her sisters parroted their elder, Miss Adelaide changed the topic rather suddenly to the folio that lay open upon a small folding table. She had glanced at it as they'd entered and spread their gowns to sit, and now she asked me several pertinent questions about both the author and the garden to be. If I had any question as to her intelligence, she quashed that by saying, "Our Aunt Creswell keeps in her sun room a bush of rosemary brought all the way from Sorrento, a seaside town outside Naples. We've already taken cuttings from it, and I'm certain she would be happy to offer you some to replace this less authentic sort now planted."

I digress. You will learn more of Miss Creswell at a later juncture.

Meanwhile, my health continued reasonably well. My husband's college friend, Dr. Sharpless, now licensed to practice, kept at me constantly to walk and even to dance. He had moved back into his earlier kept rooms across the hallway where he whiled away those hours he was not annoying me with new regimens by reading very old books—by no means all of them on medicine—and by playing not too poorly upon a very ancient spinet some of Mr. Handel's suites and those of the old German master, Sebastian Bach, newly discovered by Mr. Mendelssohn. To those gentleman's *allemandes* and *courantes, passepieds* and *sarabandes*, I would step and twirl in my own fanciful imaginings of how our ancestors danced a hundred years before. All the while under his care, I gained weight. I thought it was too much, but I slept like a babe, ten hours at a time at night, and at least two more during daylight hours.

All the more of a surprise then, when I felt myself shaken awake one night, for it must take a great deal of shaking to awaken me. No candle was lit, but then I espied a very small one and next to it the familiar face of mute Matthew. Before I could utter a word, he had gently placed his softly gloved hand over my mouth and he enjoined me by gesture not to speak.

My silence obtained, he then attempted to have me understand him, but I was too sleepy and could not. I kept turning to my pillow to sleep again, while he continually jerked me back to consciousness.

"Awaken my maid," I dismissed him. But he would not hear of it and kept shaking his head no. "Then leave me be," said I. "Unless... is it Lady Bella?"

Again he shook his head and I noticed, now that I was more awake, that he seemed to be wearing some kind of actors' paint upon his cheeks and brow.

Finally, and I knew this must have cost him dearly, as it came out so distorted from not speaking so long, Matthew managed to utter very hoarsely the word, "Urrrrll!"

"The earl?! Is he taken ill?" He nodded yes. "Then why not waken the others?"

He shook his head to this. "D-D-D-Dare not!" he uttered, the second words torn from him in over twelve years.

Now I truly sat up. "Pleeeeeeeeees...miss!" Two more words newly uttered, and he began to tremble all over.

He wouldn't allow me to waken my maid, and re-enjoined my utter silence by more gestures. He had warm garments ready for me to put over my bedclothes, and he led me silently out, me gripping his arm through his shirt all the while. No lamps were lit, and we sped through my corridor and into the centre, or older house, in the very greatest darkness, only gaining a bit of starlight from quickly passed windows.

From the great hall, Matthew led me up into the older annex, much unused of late, I believed. By much turning and rising, we arrived in chambers that I could not tell you where they were exactly, except perhaps atop the first manor house built here and, I'd thought, long fallen into desuetude.

All the corridors had been dark, and I was cleaving closely against Matthew as we attained a closed door, around and behind which I could see candlelight was burning, the first in the great house aside from what we carried that night.

"In there?" I asked. Matthew nodded yes. "Then open it." But he could not or would not. Instead, he cowered behind me into the darkened corridor. I pushed the door ajar and stepped in. At first, I was blinded, then the light gradually was less dazzling, and I could make out my surroundings.

I felt myself to have stumbled into some sort of theatrical behind-scene, it was so garish with stage décor of a movable sort— here a half-wall of painted trees, lying next to it another pictured wall of a castle moat and bridge, abutted by another half-wall painting of a crowd of people, depicted cheering before old-time wooden houses. The lamps that lit us were tall, like those carried by footmen through the streets many years ago, broad at their top and flaring forth pale colours. These were induced by tinted mica panes of windows before the candlelight, some vermillion, others cobalt, yet others glaucous-green, all of it again just like that upon a theatre stage.

On the floor, almost at my feet, lay a woman, fallen and oddly turned, her skirts thrown over her upper body, baring her legs and nether regions. My heart burned as I wondered if my errand wasn't a matter of a sick lord, but instead of a plaything of that lord, which my poor Matthew had happened upon, in this bizarre Play chamber.

I whispered Matthew's name, and he was in the room with me, the door quietly shut behind, and in his hand a flask of brandy he urged me to take.

"But where is the earl?" I asked.

He pointed at the figure upon the floor, and then pulled me over to it. As I dropped to my knees, dragged there by his panicked force, he lifted the skirts away, and I could then make out the rouged and powdered face of the Earl of Ravenglass, his cosmeticized eyes facing straight ahead, his ruby-coloured lips agape, and none of his white powdered cheeks in motion. I was astonished, and I was utterly repulsed by what I beheld, but even more was I concerned for him, for Matthew, for all of us. I placed my ear to the earl's mouth but could hear no breath. I placed my fingers beneath his hairy nostrils but could feel no respiration. I put my fingers athwart that part of his neck where Dr. Sharpless had shown me lay the carotid artery, bringing blood from heart to brain, but there was no throbbing, not the minutest pulsation.

Matthew continually tried pushing the brandy into my hand to revive the earl, but I turned it away. "Fetch me a hand mirror! Quickly."

He brought it and I held it under the hirsute nose a long time, but no mist ever frosted it.

"Look!" I pointed it out to Matthew. "He does not breathe. Feel." I grabbed his hand and placed it, shaking, upon the bare, fat, nipple-painted breast. "No beat of his heart. He is dead."

"D-D-D-Dead?" He croaked at me. Another word spoken.

"Quite dead. A fit of the heart, I fear." And looking at the froth that had gathered upon the lower lip of that awful, painted mouth, I added, "Or a stroke of the brain. He's quite dead, I'm afraid, dear Matthew."

Matthew fell back sitting upon the floor, weeping.

I pitied him then, but even so I must wonder so very much about what it was that I beheld around myself. What was this chamber? Why was the earl dressed in this fashion? Why, as I looked upon Matthew, was he dressed as he was, in tight pantaloons and tight vest jacket with blouson sleeves and a little peaked cap? What show, what play, what...

As I drew down the skirts, I couldn't help but see the earl was unclothed beneath, bare beneath both bodice and skirt. I righted these and then had a thought. "You must tell Trithers!"

Matthew leapt up and back to his feet and would have rushed out the door had I not stopped him.

"Why not? What were you doing here, you and he? In this chamber! Matthew, look at me and tell me."

He could not look at me, but allowed himself to be restrained.

At last he uttered with great contempt, "J-J-J-Jockey and mmmmmilkmaid!" and he must turn away directly after he said them.

"Jockey and milkmaid?" I wondered, and then it all came rushing to me, came with the burning flush of my entire person. The game *en travesti* was not for any play's sake, for if so, then why would the earl wear no underclothing, and why would Matthew's flies be undone? Dizziness swept me head to foot, but I resisted its pull, for I knew I had to do something to repair this.

"Matthew," said I, then, "Look at me! Matthew? We must get his lordship and yourself into proper clothing. Quickly! We must endeavour to move him out of this room to another spot downstairs so that not one hint of what happened in this room is known to any but us. Do you understand?"

"J-J-J-Jockey and mmmmmmilkmaid!" he repeated in disgust, trembling still.

"Matthew. This you must do if you loved him."

"No, m-m-miss! Never!"

Even so he vanished into another section behind some other scrims and came out holding what looked like the earl's at-home clothing.

Slowly, very carefully, we removed the milkmaid's costume from off the fat, dead nobleman and carefully replaced it with his own discarded undergarments, trousers, shirt, cravat, vest, and jacket. I found a vial of rosewater and mixed it with some brandy to remove the powder and lip paint, though some must remain. Once he was dressed, lifted onto a chair, and left there, he merely looked like a vain, defunct lord. Next, Matthew must return to his own clothing. He did all of this occasionally breaking out into sobs, from which I somehow gathered this was only the concluding, perhaps culminating fantastic pairings the earl had devised and the two of them had enacted over the past few months. It explained Matthew's special place among those working in the house, his coming and going at will, and the constant gifts of fine clothing to him.

I used water and brandy to wash what paint was upon Matthew's face. He appeared so heartbroken, so entirely despondent a being, that I took a minute to kiss his lips and hold him very close to me. "You must never speak a word of this to anyone. Not ever." I felt him flinch away, but I held on tightly. "I vow never to do so. I vow it, Matthew. Now think upon it. It is not all evil! One horrible shock muted your voice years ago. This new shock gives you your speech back. I feel that God is nearby, Matthew. Looking over you—over us. I sense it strongly."

He held me as though we were drowning and I had to at last pull free.

"We must get him down to his rooms," I said.

Descending with the corpse between us was no easy matter, for the earl had lived well and had missed few meals. In this regard, Matthew's strength did us well. He held the shoulders and head, I the feet, and we barely even made any knocks or resounds as we went down the now endlessly dark and twisting corridors and stairways. I thought for a brief moment the door to Lady Bella's wing was ajar as we passed. Indeed, I actually sensed her watching the three of us go past, but she never uttered a sound, not a hoarse breath, if she was there, and I could not stop to be certain.

We managed the body as far as my husband's library, and there we placed him into a reading chair with a copy of Livy's history in his hand. We quietly pushed over the chair so that he sprawled as though naturally falling upon the Turkish carpet, striking his head upon a lion's claw foot of the large *escritoire*. Our work done, Matthew stood stock-still in renewed horror.

I left him there, rushed into my sitting room, and found my purse of coins. I thrust it deep into Matthew's trouser pockets. "We do not know the future. You may require this," said I, and then I directed him upstairs to his bed-chamber.

Once I could no longer hear his mouse-soft step or believe I could descry the murk of his candle, I rushed into the hallway screeching like Mrs. Kean had done as that lady in Shakespeare's Scottish play.

When first Trithers and then momentarily later Dr. Sharpless came out of their rooms, I half fainted, and then managed to confusedly say I'd been awakened by a noise and had run to the library.

They rushed in and found the earl. I composed myself a few minutes, and joined them. Trithers was on the floor, his lord's hand in his, sobbing. The young doctor was sitting in the corpse's recently vacated chair, examining the fallen book. Cool as glass he turned and said to me, "*Ab Urbe Condite!* Imagine! All this while I took him for a Tacitus man."

Lady Lillian of Ravenglass

To: The Very Reverend Jasper Horace Quill
The British Church at Campofieri
Town of Fiesoli
Province of Toscana

8 October 188—

Sir,

First things first: The lady is well. There are some minor adversities, but as you assured me more than once, the lady thrives upon them. At this hour, all of our little party sleep but me. Gone is the nervous condition that followed close upon my falling into the temptation of card-play. Now I am weary, and I will doubtless sleep deeply once this missive is sealed and left at the front desk.

Since it is germane to the lady and to yourself, sir, you ought to know that we are followed and have been, I must assume almost from the beginning despite so very many precautions. Or we are followed anew, the trail somehow picked up.

Our hunter was recognized by the chambermaid. She knew him in England, and her surprise at seeing him was so great she cried out and hid herself. He, however, does not seem to recognize her beyond her type. Perhaps that is the failure of lady-killers, for I do think him to be of that sort.

We eluded him here in Bolzano through wisdom, precautions taken, the use of the Greeks, and the very great aid of the lady herself. But why is he here? What does he hope to achieve? What did I write you recently, that I somehow recognized him? I have now seen him up close for the second time. The first, it turns out, was in Innsbruck, when I came upon him in the snow early one morning less than a week ago. He seems not as strong as myself. Rather slender, wide-browed, with a small, fine, straight nose and dark eyes that three volume novels for women refer to as "melting." He is typically pretty and very much how your friend explained how our nemesis's usual sort of young attendant would look. He dressed carefully, not too expensively to stand out, however, also without a hint of shabbiness. He affected a most *soigné* air as he lolled at the terminus seeking us out. But his eyes were quite amazingly alive.

We glided by, the lady over-dressed as an old grandmother,

loudly bewailing her young Greek kin. The chambermaid was in charade, with tinted charcoal glasses she had obtained at Lake Garda and scarves about her throat, her irrepressible hair kept in a sort of turban hat, wearing one of her lady's frocked coats from her neck to toes. She resembled nothing more than a sanatorium patient, perhaps on her last holiday, and I was her all-caring partner. The vain fool didn't guess a thing. But we got a very good look at him, I can assure you, as the little minx stopped in her tracks not far from where he loitered and there she had to rewind her scarves with my assistance.

Of course, by then the trio, including the lady, were ahead of us and already within a vehicle. They arrived at our lodging by one cab, we by another, somewhat later. We have obtained an entire floor of the small *pensione*, and after we had unpacked, we gathered in the *sala de cena* for a meal of risotto and veal. All very tasty. We all were in high spirits for our little game of fooling his spy.

Still, it means we must travel about town and entrain again only once his whereabouts have been accounted for. This is an annoyance. For while there are trains further south and coaches aplenty, they are bound to be small and easily watched.

It is more than I like to have to do, and I am more than a little annoyed by the superior air he assumed while lazing against the advertising placard, as though he hadn't a care in the world, the swine! I would dearly liked to have wiped that smirk off him.

You will have noticed that I go off constantly in wrong directions and wrong-headedness. This is indeed a problem, both in my letter and in my mind. For I am now sorely distracted at a time when I ought to be most fully concentrated.

The culprit is, I'm afraid to write it, my other ruling passion, which suddenly reared its own very hideous head just last night. It was after we had eaten and I decided I needed a breath of fresh air. Our *pensione* is centrally located, and I found myself perambulating about the centre of the town and into an *enoteca* where I imbibed a glass of Barolo wine with a dry but very delicious rusk-like biscuit.

It was later than I expected, and the streets were suddenly quite vacant. I began to hurry back to the lodgings when all of a sudden, my nostrils were assailed by that unmistakable fragrance, that distillation of all Eastern perfumes, that *houri* of aromas. It was barely a whiff that I caught, yet it was instantly recognizable. Who would know better than I, who spent better than a year in the sinuous clutches of its soft, yet all-powerful grip?

At first it was curiosity. Where, thought I, in a moderately small-sized Italian town would a person find the contacts, indeed the wherewithal, to locate whoever would possess opium, never mind to become its devotee? That was followed by a thought I'd never before had. Was the marvellous soporific even outlawed in this land in which we now sojourned? For some reason, I felt it was not, and worse, that it might be rather easily obtainable. Perhaps even a so-called "parlour" for its delectation by aficionados might exist somewhere nearby.

Whom might I stop to ask? There were so few strangers on the street, and those few seemed intent upon returning home. None even dared look me in the eye.

I continued to follow its dissipating aroma, and had just picked it up again when a middle-aged gentleman with a beard passed me by and sniffed and also recognized it.

"L'Opia," said he, smiling to himself. And when he saw me, he added in German, "Not a very good quality."

"And where," asked I back, "might one find some of better quality?"

"*Nicht hier. Aber im Venedig!*"

And so I learned that not here, but in Venice I might find some. He then named streets for me, not far from what used to be exclusively the Hebraic settlement, in an area known as *Il Ghetto Ebriaco*, where I should find what I sought. So now I know where to go. God help me! I must resist the urge?

Your troubled friend,
Stephen Undershot

To: The Earl of Ravenglass
11 Hanover Square
London, England

8 October 188—

Dear Sir,

I would much prefer addressing you as Papa as in the past. But your last letter was of such a fiery temper, that I must say we all—myself, Carrie-Ann, and Lord Olivier—were quite shocked to read. Thus, the appellation applied as well as the formality I am saddened to feel forced to use, sir.

I know very well I had written in the past that I would accept orders to return to London and to your offices, and so would have Lord Olivier. But that was before, and is all now changed. You have received the letter in which Lord Oliver resigned his after all, unofficial, position. This letter now constitutes my own withdrawal from the similar post.

You don't at all "need" either of us there. You never really ever "needed" us. We have all come to believe you merely "needed" people about you whom you believed you might trust implicitly, who would take your merest whims and desires as absolute and unswerving law.

We cannot assure you of any such obedience. So it is best that you are surrounded only by those about whom you can be assured. Those are who you "need." Not people who have been educated to think, to question, to doubt, really, if truth be told, what exactly you have done vis-à-vis my mother—among other mysteries.

Your son,
Roderick of Ravenglass

• 146 •

FELICE PICANO

8 Octobre

Who is dis MacIlhenny? Can be trusted? You writ he is "scurrilous." Dat maters nott.
Can be trusted essplicit? No mater wat or who?
Dis other on my nerves now is.

To: The Honourable Lady Caroline-Ann Augusta
The Glebe, Ravenglass
Broughton, England

11 October 188—

My Dear Lady Caroline-Ann,
 I hope you do not have to learn as quickly or harshly as I did what a strange and really quite awe-filled place the world is. But I fear you probably shall learn. Just as when I thought I had learned from the old earl's death the ultimate in disgrace, I came to slowly discover it was the mere symptom of an elementary unsoundness that has poisoned my husband's family, perhaps for untold generations.
 Lady Bella did not attend her husband's obsequies. No one expected her to do so. Reverend Rose gave the elegy. My father was now grown quite weak and even distracted. It would only be a short time before he would have to give up the vicarage and naturally too the living that went with it. But with his daughter now so well wed, he was at least assured of a secure retirement.
 At the manor house, the dowager's wheelchair turned so often now and in such unending, clamorous circles above the heads of servants working in and about her wing day and night, until finally, even before my husband returned to bury his father, I was approached by the head butler, Trithers. He was rather timidly heading a delegation of the downstairs folk to ask me to "speak a bit with her ladyship."
 Since my marriage, Lady Bella had fled whenever I had come near her, and I could usually not find her. From this, I had concluded that what little friendship we had possessed when I was a girl had vanished.
 So this time, I had some of the maids fit out a double chamber as a drawing room and bedroom for me close to those chambers Lady Bella was believed to live in. I prepared for myself waxed cotton earplugs to be able to endure the commotion she was certain to make in her attempt to drive me away, rather like Ulysses's crew protecting themselves from the Sirens.
 I was nearly ready anyway, as I mentioned in my last letter, to give birth to your husband, and so I was hardly stomping about the heather as I had been doing of late, despite Dr. Sharpless's theories

of much needed exercise. Thus, I had more sedentary pursuits arranged for me: a portable shelf of three-volume novels—including Mr. Currer Bell's *Jane Eyre*, a little, well-stocked *escritoire* for me to catch up on my letter writing to my friends from the women's college, and my latest sewing-frames, all brought along with me as though I were on a jaunt to the countryside, and not merely in another, albeit distant, sector of my own house.

It was a full day and night before Lady Bella dared approach, and only when the fire had gone out at half six of the morning. I'd awakened to drink water, and I saw her movable wooden chair and figure dimly in the doorway.

"I wish you would step in for a daytime visit," said I, very softly, so as not to frighten her. "I recall that you were once fond of me."

From bed, I slipped out, and began washing my face and hands. She slid up behind me almost noiselessly, which meant she made noise only when she wished to do so.

"Yes, but then you were not then one of *them*!" Bella hissed.

"Nor am I now one of *them*. As you very well know, I am myself and no one else's retainer."

"Yet *he* put a loaf in your oven. See it rising high!"

"It is a wife's duty and a responsibility to bear her husband's young and a lady of the blood's duty to bear a son and heir. I have taken on this role by myself." I hoped to thus clarify my position to her.

"*He* returns soon."

Lady Bella's particular use of the word "he" was so much as I recalled her referring to the earl before, that I answered, "As you very well know, Lady, *he* is dead. You witnessed us carrying down his body," I added, lest she think to use it against me. "Your son, however, returns to bury his father tomorrow."

She did not respond. All washed, I turned to her very slowly, as one does when one wishes not to spook an animal. I sat down, and she looked at me closely.

"You seem mostly yourself," she at last observed. "But then I well know that this is one of the most self-deceptive stages of them all."

I decided not to address this ambiguity but instead asked, "You knew about his lordship and his theatre up the stairs?"

When she continued to glare at me, I said, "Yes, of course, you knew. I insult you by even asking. And you knew of all his other indecencies in London-town and here, with those couples he would bring to visit. And I must suppose other indecencies too."

"I knew. You did *not* know. And *you* were *most* put out!" she said with tangible pleasure in her voice.

"I *was* put out. But really, Lady, only because a dear friend of mine was so implicated and so abused in the process. He's a simple lad and only aims to please. He would never have initiated or…" I could not continue but instead began to choke up.

For the truth of it all was Matthew had left the manor and the area and possibly the shire itself by dusk of the day following his master's death, and I had no idea where he'd gone nor when he would return, although I made certain to put out various extremely discreet inquiries. I did know how much Matthew had always esteemed myself, and for me to have been the observer, even if after the fact, of their disastrous final tryst *en travesti* must surely have been of the most intense mortification to him, no matter how much I might gloss it over.

"We are *all* abused," said Lady Bella. "*All* of us every day, even though *you* don't yet admit it."

What might I reply to that? Instead, she went on. "Now *he* returns, and so long as you deliver a healthy boy you are yourself, for a while, quite safe. But not I. Not I!" Her last words were almost a wail.

I fell over nearly onto her lap and took her wringing hands in mine and stilled the strange sounds her bones made rubbing against each other.

"Do not worry yourself, Lady! He is your son and he will honour you!"

She laughed. "Honour me? He thinks me a harridan from hell, as did his father. He will rid himself of me as soon as he may do so with the least bother to himself."

I tried to allay her fear, but she would not listen, though she tried to lift me back up on my feet, and I did succeed in returning to my chair. Just then, a maid came to clean the fire and reset it, and we sat there, in the servant's eyes at least, Lady Bella and myself, a *tableau vivant* of affectionate mother-in-law and daughter-in-law, as prim and proper as any litho printed in *Household Words*.

Once the fire was going strong, our tea was poured, and buttery, still warm scones were laid out for us. I watched with fascination as Lady Bella crumbled one almost entirely to eat but four crumbs.

The moment the young maid was gone, Bella reached for my petticoats under my wrapper and held on firmly.

"In your greatest extremity," she declared, "and it shall arrive one day, go to my sewing box. Remember! When all seems lost. When the despair I know daily has come to you at long last, go to my sewing-box!" She was silent again, and though I tried to engage her in conversation again, she merely brushed me off, waving her hands in the air. At last the warmth of the fire and the satiation from the *petit déjeuner* overwhelmed me, and I'm afraid I fell asleep where I sat. Lady Bella may have watched over me some minutes, but she was gone by the time the young maid returned with warm rashers, toasted bread, and eggs. I greedily ate it all myself.

This was to be our very last conversation, although I believe not quite our final *communication*. That would take a strange form much later.

My husband and Lord Robert rode into the manor gateway that night at nearly nine of the clock, and they took turns consoling me, having known from Sharpless's correspondence that I had discovered the body and "received a possibly great shock!" Roland was never so kind as he was then. He was an angel of breeding and consideration, and it was a good thing it was a warmish day for the funeral so I might sit in an open chaise and slowly ride behind the horse-drawn hearse in Ravenglass's stately cortege. It was attended by half the county, whether on horse, carriage, or on foot, and if it had been any weather out but fair, he would have insisted I stay at home.

I searched for Matty in the next day and more, but alas saw him not.

The next day, your husband was born. I awoke with a twitch and felt myself wet. I called a maid, who called the doctor, sleeping four doors down the corridor, and in a matter of some ninety painful but blessedly brief minutes, I was holding the swaddled Roderick, who was already manifesting his usual good and easy nature by quickly feeding himself and then sleeping.

Your father-in-law was ecstatic. I never saw the man so happy, so beautiful, so soft. Alas, never so again. He only left my side when the doctor and Lord Robert both were there to replace him. For his part, Lord Robert was as happy as any husband would be, and outlined my boy's future so thoroughly, I must wonder had the two of them pondered long and then written it down somewhere.

We all wore funeral black at Roderick's christening, and this rite, short and simple, was the last of God's ceremonies my own father ever performed as vicar. Afterward, at our large hall celebratory dinner, in the presence of dozens of witnesses, Lord Roland thanked the vicar for all his good offices over the years. He alluded to his ill health and age, and he spoke of a cottage not far from Ulverston that he'd had especially prepared for a couple such as Mrs. Cupp and my father now formed. Roland said it was theirs with a stipulated income so long as both lived. And thus, my dear father, never a large influence in my life, became even less so. Perhaps at the very moment I most needed him.

Roland made no reference in the speech at all to his own sire, nor to his mother. Once, after a month of him remaining at the manor with Lord Robert coming and going frequently, he said at tea in which I was entertaining a half dozen townswomen come to see the baby, "You are unequivocally kind, my dear Lillian. Do not think that your less public works of charity to the unfortunate are unknown to me. Only," and here he seemed to hesitate, "I wish you realize that some of those most near to us are perhaps excessively troubled and should only be visited when you are quite by yourself."

The other guests were out of hearing at the moment, and I took his meaning at once to say I should not bring the baby to Lady Bella. Without constraint, I rather hotly replied, "Is she not even to *see* her grandson?"

"Believe me, *she* has seen him more than once, already," he replied, cool as ever. "I have lived in this great pile of stone and brick since I was a little boy, and I know it inside out. I am able to see her going about her stealthy ways when others cannot and must rely upon her sounds alone to know her whereabouts. She has *seen* him quite well already, and from close up!"

Before I might protest, he added, "If I deem it advisable, I will bring the boy to her, but only *then* may he go. For she is not herself all the time, as I'm certain you recognize. She may do some *inadvertent* harm to the child and reproach herself forever. I am confident you would not wish that added misfortune. Promise me."

Thus he made me agree to his terms.

I did so in part because I was happy. So happy, that before I knew he was to leave for London, the baby now healthily safe and Dr. Sharpless still at my beck and call, I made a tiny reference to Roland's previous nightly visits to me before he usually went away.

"You need not worry, my dearest," he answered. "We need not fall back into that sort of situation ever again. It was necessary at the time, but I well realized how extremely difficult for yourself to bear." Roland kissed my hand, allegedly reassuring me.

I didn't know it then, but he had just informed me we two would never again have intimate relations as man and wife. He had not asked me. He had simply told me, as if he had told me he'd let go of the older gardener's boy.

At the time, I suppose I was somewhat relieved.

The following months of *post-partum* passed much more dreamlike than the previous period of my carrying Roderick. The only blot upon that otherwise happy time was seeing my father and Mrs. Cupp off to their new home and having to welcome in their place the new vicar, Mr. Rose, and his new wife, Althea.

How it was that he acquired her so abruptly is owing of course to her being the eldest of the three Creswell sisters, and thus among the most eligible of the female sub-gentry in the shire. Indeed, while my Miss Creswell was sharp faced and even more sharp-minded, her elder two siblings were remarkably agreeable, quite round-faced, and most tranquil in their natures. Althea especially, in her younger sister's estimation, was "a great cud-cow." But she was handsome enough for her new position in life and was soon with child, a circumstance she continued seemingly unabated for the following twelve years, which suggests she was handsome enough in various other positions as well.

But wait! I miswrote. There was a second blot on that period: Lady Bella. She returned to her peripatetic ways about the manor house and could be heard at all hours coming and going in her unoiled mobile wooden chair. She kept mostly to her wing, but more often she might be heard rolling throughout the many empty second- and third-floor rooms and echoing corridors at the most peculiar hours. Never when Lords Roland and Robert were at the house, of course, but otherwise daily, or rather nightly. All of us had waxed cotton in our ears, save Roddy, who slept and ate all the day and night through.

In vain did I once more attempt to approach her as I had the previous time by setting myself up in her wing for a few days. She never came to me again. Nor did it make any difference that she no longer was near her food when it was presented. She seemed never to eat anymore. Food in tiny amounts did vanish from the house if forgotten and left out on a sideboard, but in such increasingly small amounts that it might have been caused as easily by local vermin as by Lady Bella.

In the middle of one afternoon's entertainment in our second parlour, my visitors being Althea *née* Creswell, her vicar husband and two sisters, and also the doctor's elderly wife, all conversation ceased suddenly, as we began hearing the ominous creaking that approached interminably yet never came any closer.

Servants, as usual, rushed out of the room and tried to accost Bella with their usual lack of success. Our conversation in the parlour meanwhile faltered, until I had had enough—in my role as lady of the manor—and spoke quite loudly over the noise as though it did not exist. Then all joined in, sometimes nearly shouting so they might be heard. We then laughed at ourselves after, when her noise had ceased or had become too distant for us to make out. And so I was powerless to stop the word that Lady Bella had further deteriorated in health and was so insane we now ignored her. This was sad to me, but what could I do to counteract it?

I doubted both, believing her to be, if nothing else, a staunch western British woman and thus a hardy survivor.

All the more of a shock to me when quite late one night some six months later, Trithers tapped upon my chamber door just as I had dismissed my maid and was preparing to go to bed. I had been up late, enjoying the balmy weather outside our windows and thinking of this last day of Lord Robert's latest visit. He'd been seen off after afternoon tea *sans* his great friend my husband, who was "stuck like a mouse in a jampot," according to Lord Robert, in London, with his father's unfinished business in Parliament, and thus ensconced at Hanover Square in London. I always enjoyed Robert's solitary visits, and I even a little flirted with him, because, as you may have already guessed from these letters, and as I am willing to now own to, I was a little bit in love with him myself. And as I never heard of Robert speaking to other women, I felt confident in being the single female personage in his life.

Our other "boarder" at Ravenglass, Dr. Sharpless, had just— and for good—left the manor house a few days before, and I had realized with some surprise two matters. First, that I missed his company, solipsistic though he was most times, and second, that he was a good man and fair medico and had become a friend to me. He parted with a gift of a thin golden chain, an heirloom of delicate tracery from India, last worn by his great aunt, said he, which he wished I would wear. I didn't dare to do so, not until years later, when it became all too evident that Lord Roland never looked at me long enough nor closely enough to even bother to note my apparel nor any of my jewelled ornamentation to ask where it had come from.

I remember that night especially well, therefore, being left to myself at last, and especially because of a sudden had arrived that fresh yet chemically peculiar aroma in the air that portends an onslaught of rain storm. Later on, I would learn that the release of the gaseous substance, ozone, into the atmosphere is an actual scientific phenomenon. It invariably precedes thunder and lightning, and this instance would prove no different. The sky tore open, brightening the rooms about me like it was mid-day. The wind rose on an instant. Two of the six tall double casements in my sitting room abruptly flapped shut. Thunder resounded with a high, sharp volley. Just then, Trithers stepped in to where I sat near the dying fire, clad closely about in my bedtime wrapper. He apologized and fiddled a bit with his buttons, not daring to look me in the face.

I asked what matter it could be at this late hour when all of us ought to be abed, and he at last got out, "It's her ladyship, my lady. She's not been heard of going about in her chair."

"Let's thank our stars for that, Trithers. Although with this pandemonium, how could we know it?"

"Yes, ma'am. Only she's not been heard of gone all day now." And before I could interpret this statement, he added, "She's never done *that* before."

Before I might interpolate that she might, finally, have fallen to sleep, Trithers continued. "And worse is to come, for Maisey Cregg thinks she heard a crash."

"A crash?"

"This morning, perhaps, or during the night when she got out of bed to use her chamber pot. Maisey thought the crash came from below the servants' upstairs hall."

"And no one has gone near the Lady Bella's rooms of late?" I asked, already knowing the answer. No one but me would risk going near.

"Jardin and myself," he said, mentioning a stout Franco-Swiss footman recently hired by my husband to be my especial guard, "have thought to go there now when no one is awake, in the event the lady acts unusually. We had very much hoped, my lady, that you would accompany us."

"Lady Bella always acts unusually," I said, meaning to be amusing. "I will come to give your curiosity a more official air?" asked I.

"Something like," he admitted sheepishly. "Or to help calm her. We've got two whale oil lamps for light," he said, I suppose as further inducement. The manor house had just been introduced to this domestic improvement. Oil was far brighter than candles, steadier in illumination, and was protected by a glass bowl, so it did not extinguish quite so easily.

Thunder and lightning now smashed down around us, making even those illuminations momentarily superfluous.

I was not at the time in the least bit sleepy. So I belted my wrapper and slipped on my hardier night-shoes.

Outside, in the corridor, M. Jardin looked refreshingly large and quite awake as myself. Trithers took one of the large, round-bulbed lamps and led the procession from my wing across the large central hall to the older part of the house. The Swiss followed with a second large oil lamp. I could not naturally help but remember the last time I had made such a post-midnight foray, along with dear Once-Mute Matthew, nor what I'd come upon then, and I shivered a bit.

Thunder and lightning surrounded the house, the bolts striking quite nearby, and now I found myself more irritated than frightened. It seemed so much like a scene from some old tingler like *The Mysteries of Udolpho* that had kept awake some of my fellow collegians at the women's school in Leeds, and I almost guffawed at the very staginess of it all.

Her large, high-ceilinged, mostly bare rooms were quite empty and sparer of furnishings than I recalled them. I found myself peering at the elaborate ceiling mouldings and crown mouldings from the previous century, thinking how handsomely "Adam" they were. Beidermeier was now all the rage, yet the current Germanic moulding designs were rather banal to my taste. I thought these older ones much handsomer. As we wandered onward, room after room, I found myself thinking what an ample, attractive art gallery this might make; or even a winter garden, as was becoming common in the United States of America; or even some sort of school rooms for selected local children. Of course, now they were large, echoing, and useless, except to house a prematurely aged, drugged, supremely unhappy woman.

We did not find Lady Bella, and I must ask Trithers again and again where the maid had heard the crash and where that would be exactly downstairs, within these rooms. It took some doing, and he must go back up to the servants' rooms, and walk it off, measuring the distance. Left alone with Jardin, I practised my French with him, and had him lift the whale oil lamp so I could better see details.

I had decided a private painting and sculpture gallery put exactly here might be just the thing that Ravenglass Manor required to give it an air of modern distinction, apt for my own pleasure as well as my husband's ambitions.

Both of us heard noise coming from the great hall, and Jardin stoutly declared he would go investigate, leaving me alone with the lamp. After he was gone a few minutes, I thought I heard a much fainter sound coming from much closer. I needed to wait until the thunder was sallying itself farther away from the house until I could be certain. But then I did hear it, and it sounded very thinly, yet distinctly like a sort of thin slap of something metal upon wood.

The panels of this room had been painted *trompe l'oeil* in the fashion of Louis XVI to resemble doors and windows, and I suspected one of them might be an actual door. Indeed, two on each longer side opened into long, narrow closets stuffed with draperies and extra chairs. But behind the fourth door, I could hear the nearly inaudible tapping, and I began to softly speak. "Lady Bella? My lady? Is that you?"

This door opened inward like all the other closets, but this one seemed to have some obstacle keeping me from opening it more than an inch or two. I set the oil lamp on the floor and knelt, trying to peer inside. I swore I saw cloth and hair. I felt in with my hand, and it was hair! I retreated sharply, then did it again, for now I felt certain Lady Bella had fled into the closet, hiding from some danger, and there she had somehow fallen over and now lay unable to move or get up, except to very lightly tap out her distress.

Although I held my breath as I did so, I reached my hand back into the darkness and felt about and reached her bony shoulder and gave it as hard as shove as I dared.

It was enough. The door now opened inward, and the lamp revealed the truth. The movable chair was still in place, albeit at a severe angle, but the lady had fallen forward. I reached down and, as

Dr. Sharpless had showed me, I felt for her heart's pulse at her neck. I could find none. Alone, I drew her body out of the closet, and she half turned over.

In the light of the spermaceti lamp, she was unquestionably dead and quite stiff in her morbidity. I was less aghast than I might have been earlier in my life, or even earlier that year. Her eyes were half lidded ajar, her mouth closed, and her face almost unrecognizable, it seemed so peaceful. I realized then I'd never seen her quite so serene. I felt and listened for her heart pulse at her icy breast. And again at her frozen wrist. None existed.

But then where had the tapping come from? I could only think dead fingers do not snap against wood, then I recalled the noise had sounded like metal, and I looked for her malachite locket. Had it been torn off the gold chains around her neck in her fall, two ends of which now dangled, broken asunder?

Precita! I opened fully the closet door and searched under and around old statuary until I found where the locket had landed. I wondered if Bella hadn't realized what was happening, and in her last exertion of bodily strength had torn off the locket hoping it would fall, smash open, and let her pet free?

With my approach, the locket stopped moving. I pulled it out into the larger room and into the full light of the oil lamp. I held the locket against my arm, and it was unquestionably full of something alive. I'd last seen the tarantula years ago, and now I was deadly affrighted. What if, with the thunder, it attacked me or crawled all over me? Would I leap up and stomp it to death? I was afraid I might.

I decided to calm it. I took up the locket and held it against my own breast for some minutes as Bella had done for so many years. I sensed the upset creature calming with this familiar warmth and perhaps it even heard my heart beat as it had heard hers for so long a time. Then, when I could wait no longer, I quickly placed the locket upon the floorboards in front of where I sat, and snapped open the lid.

Precita uncurled herself from the locket, larger and even more astonishing to look at than before. I moved back instinctively, but the spider merely stood where it was. I could see its antennae and palps moving in the air before its little high head and many eyes. She sighted me clearly, then turned, and went directly to where her mistress lay. She leapt onto her head as she had done in life and clambered about as she always done and then tried to settle herself. But she felt no warmth of circulating blood, and after a while, she dropped off onto the floor again, and went around in circles, as though bewildered.

I know I could never wear Precita as had Lady Bella for so long, nor even keep her as a pet somewhere as she had, and yet I felt sad for the abandoned, the utterly blameless creature. The wind was playing with a window sash and the night air rushed in. Precita scuttled toward the new sounds and aromas, then stopped, as though puzzled.

"Though your mistress has died," said I, "there is no reason why you must follow her in death as do the wives of the Hindus. You are unique and uniquely you must live—at least throughout this summer, for who knows if you can abide the English winter."

My skin crawled to do it, but I put out one arm, and Precita leapt onto it after only a second. Before I could do anything, she walked up to my head, where she nestled into my hair. This was the touchiest part of all; I commanded myself to not shudder or shiver. Carefully I stood myself up and walked to the window. I further opened the sash and let the night sounds and airs waft over my head, and also, I hoped, waft over Precita.

Where I got the courage, I cannot say, but I lifted my hand to my hair and felt for Precita. Rather than her biting me, she stepped onto my hand, just as I'd hoped she would. I held her before me for a moment, so we might look at each other once more, then I reached out to a branch of a bush. She put a tentative foot upon it from the security of my fingers, then another, and, in an instant, she was gone, her whiteness but a blur in the upper twigs.

Jardin and Trithers arrived together into the room. I could hear them behind me. I searched the dark foliage for Precita but could no longer see her, and so I turned away and shut the window, without ever explaining what I had been doing.

"Your lady is there!" said I, pointing to the heap of body and clothing upon the floor. Thinking of her pain and suffering, her fears and terrors, I'm afraid my voice broke. "She has finally chaired herself off to Heaven above. Look at her face, if you do not believe me."

The big Swiss fell to his knees, crossing himself with his hands over his chest and face, muttering prayers. Trithers soon joined him mutely, and I must suppose, more Protestantly.

No sooner had they removed feather-light Lady Bella down the stairs to lay her atop sheets upon the great table in the great hall until others would waken and care for her than I dismissed them to bed. I had a fire made up for myself, and I sat in the great inglenook settee, keeping warm while I kept watch over my mother-in-law's corpse. Throughout that night, I recalled all she had said to me in life. It wasn't very much as conversation went, perhaps two dozen sentences in all, and then I reminded myself of all I had learned outright or had gathered from her and from others of Lady Bella's life at Ravenglass. Through my confusion, I sensed that unless I was more adroit and more intelligent, I would end up as sadly as she.

Sometime toward morning, when the lightning was but tiny flickerings upon the distant southern hilltops, I determined that no matter what occurred between me and my husband, I would never allow myself to become as she had. It was a promise at times most difficult to keep.

Sometime after dawn, Trithers brought in the whole houseful of staff, from his wife to the lowest gardener's rake-up lad, and they all stepped into the great hall and paid their respects to Lady Bella. Then, one by one, they came to where I still sat and each bowed or curtseyed and kissed my hand, and I said to each their name, adding, "I am your mistress now. I hope we shall be friends." And each one said, "Yes, my lady. Thank you, my lady."

I know that over the subsequent years, He suborned more than one of that staff, exploiting their weaknesses and using his wealth and his power and even at times his perversions. But I am gone, I am free, and he is alone and not.

Which of us won in the end, Lady? Can you make answer? He? Or I?

Lillian

12 Octobre, 188—

We past him by. He hid not himself. They both laf—he is so eesy ful. As bal masque wer we drest.
Again. Grater care, I beg thee.
Henriette

To: The Earl of Ravenglass
11 Hanover Square
London, England

13 October 188—

Dear Sir,

I am gladdened. Carrie-Ann and Lord Oliver are also gladdened to read in your last missive that you are in *not* such a high dudgeon as previously, and that our decision to come to Ravenglass has met with your approval.

We discovered upon our arrival that the house, the grounds, the entire area, in fact, was in perfect operating order. This was no surprise, for it has always been true whether you, sir, were present or not. The heads of staff came to meet Carrie-Ann with such dignity and respect, and reported to us upon all matters appertaining to their own various demesnes, that later on that day, my wife remarked how excellent an estate keeper her predecessor must have been, and what a very great shame it was that she had not been appreciated. Lord Oliver was gratified by the very modern menu of repasts served by the kitchen. He has become quite obsessed with "physical culture," as he calls it, and we have spent hours at a time out of doors practicing at archery, horse riding, and playing lawn tennis, the paraphernalia of which we brought from Kent with us as we have become almost addicted to the game.

Indoors, he has had laid down sheets of maritime canvas matting (purchased locally, where they abound) in an unused room in the older section of the place and has enjoined several of the younger male servants to join him there in Graeco-Roman wrestling of a lighter sort. His diet has become all important, as it has to all of us, and we were excited to recognize how up to date the Ravenglass dinner and luncheon menus had been under my mother's influence. We especially enjoyed the rice pudding cook made us for dessert, a far healthier alternative to other sweets, and have asked for it regularly. The Bordeaux wines she had stocked are healthier than heavy ports and rich sherries.

We are, therefore, quite content, and we plan to invite my new Kentish in-laws for a week or two, especially as the weather while expectedly grey and damp, is not blustery or stormy yet. I'm certain Carrie-Ann's family—now, of course, my family and partly also Lord

Oliver's, as the younger members cleverly enough adore him—will enjoy their stay here. Given how huge and empty the place is, they certainly can't complain of it being "pokey," can they?

We three have begun a furniture-buying expedition about the countryside, as we shall need to furnish those rooms which have been bare since, I believe, your own mama—whom I never knew—passed away. We'll need bedsteads, washstands, all sorts of things.

At any rate, all is well here, you may rest assured. And as you will see for yourself upon your own return, I feel compelled to tell you that Carrie-Ann and I are getting along very well in bed at night, meaning when I choose to sleep in her chamber and not Lord Oliver's. You had made so very of much how unpleasant such nights would be, that I was quite nervous.

Although my wife had no experience, she had fortunately much verbal instruction in such matters from older female relations, and so we have "taken it slowly, for both our sakes," as she put it. I find the act itself to be far less repugnant than you led me and Lord Oliver to believe. My wife and I sometimes pass entire grey mornings abed larking and I am glad of it.

Even Lord Oliver seems interested to try it out, although I have made it abundantly clear that, close friends as we are, he will have to find a girl of his own for that purpose.

That is a joke; and I hope not too forward a joke to your taste, sir.

　　　Yrs.
　　　Roddy

To: The Very Reverend Jasper Horace Quill
The British Church at Campofieri
Town of Fiesoli
Province of Toscana

14 October 188—

Sir,

I am in the very greatest quandary, and I beg you help me what to do. You and I had planned that from Ancona and Bolzano, the lady's way would wend most directly west and south, toward your friend and to safety. The appearance of our nemesis's man so close to hand urges this course of action. But the lady herself will not hear of it. She says to me, "We are but forty miles from Venice. Since I was a young woman, I wanted to see Venice. How can we not turn to Venice now? Write your master and tell him that we shall detour to Venice. What possible harm is there in doing so? What matter if we are a week later in arriving?" Then she adds with no little sarcasm, "We have no welcoming *fête* planned there, I believe."

Before I could respond to this last statement, she lifts volume one of Mrs. Humphrey Ward's most recent novel, and in so doing, blocks off her face and her attention, telling me my own presence is no longer required, and I am stopped cold. This is the third conversation we have had on the subject in as many days, and we have not altered our positions as much as a single inch.

Naturally my fears lie beyond that of the lady's safety, albeit you must admit that with the earl's man skulking about, it is more than justified. The archaic, worldly, and may I write it, *depraved* city of Venice is, as my last letter mentioned, the very scene where one of my own worst temptations lies in wait for me. And already the chambermaid hands us schedules of the train into that horrible place. We would be there already if it were not for certain illegalities required for us to enter, which must be put together so no one knows who we actually are. The city is part of the new republic of Italy, still it retains certain of its own prerogatives, including "marine and inland immigration and customs." I am assured those counterfeit visas arranged for us three shall arrive within a few days.

What shall we do, sir? I await your word. Telegraph it immediately upon receipt of this missive to the address you see at the head of the stationery. I shall hew to your counsel no matter how difficult it may be for myself.

Your friend and most humble servant
Stephen Undershot

To: The Honourable Lady Caroline-Ann Augusta
The Glebe, Ravenglass
Broughton, England

15 October 188—

My Dear Lady Caroline-Ann,
    I am taking advantage of required patience; an unplanned deviation from my planned path necessitates some tiresome papers not in our possession. So I am able to write you again so rapidly, having more leisure than even Mrs. Humphrey Ward's *Miss Bretherton* can beguile from me.
    Unless you are the very great ninny I know you *not* to be, you know more or less where I am. You might, of course, always ask your father-in-law, since he has me followed for reasons of his own to no avail, for I shall never return to him, nor to England. He must make do with that.
    If you wish to write to me, do so via the International *Post Restante* in Venice, Italy, and the letter will in time, albeit circuitously, be delivered to me.
    To return to my narrative: After the death of my mother-in-law, all settled down for several years of comfort and ease for me. This, of course, was the self-deceptive phase of my life of which Lady Bella had warned me. Uselessly, it turned out. I must live through it myself to know it for what it was.
    I had three advantages over my unfortunate predecessor. First, my father and Mrs. Cupp lived near enough at hand that I might take a brougham and visit them often. This I did once Roddy was big enough to be dandled by a nurse. I enlivened my days with watching those two dear old people get along together, not so much the cooing lovebirds of our sillier periodical literature, but rather as two elderly people who have lived long and experienced a great deal amiss in their lives and loves do who at last find themselves in a kind of soft, safe, final harbour. May all of us come to such a place by and by.
    I have already told you of my father's life and his more or less unrequited lifelong love for Livia Jespers, my headstrong mother. A few words about my half-mother ought to suffice to quench your curiosity.

Dora Cupp was born on a rather extensive dairy not far from where she and my father would live out their final years. Her family was not from this vicinity, but from beyond Sheffield, and had been yeoman farmers ousted by forced sale for not paying duties from their lands some time shortly before the Reform Act altered forever that horribly inhumane practice. They moved ever steadily west before settling at last near Ulverston, where a Mr. Frederick Summers had seen the advantages in having various kinds of cows and steers chewing the abundant and nutritious wild grasses that cover the hills above Morecombe Bay. He built a large farm, hired many displaced yeomen from other parts, and provided livings for himself and dozens more.

The second of six children, little Dora proved to be her mother's greatest helpmeet with the other smaller ones. From an early age, she was a housekeeper and child raiser. She married late, at age seven and twenty, after most of the little ones were grown and seen to. Her husband was a lout, a farmer who sometimes worked for Summers and sometimes for her father but wasted his time and his pay drinking and gadding about the area. She bore him no children, and this eventually allowed him to have the marriage voided. Of course, Dora had lost whatever youthful looks she had once possessed in worry over him and in making a household last on the few pence he allowed her.

Alone again after his abandonment, Dora lived with her parents as they settled into poor health and eventual decline. After their death, her eldest brother and his family re-settled into that daub and wattle cottage, and Dora found herself moved out. She had long visited friends who lived in the seaside village not far from our manor house, and there, during my mother's illness, she had taken up duties aiding my father at the vicarage, making certain all was in place when he could find no dean's man nor prebendary for the little financial recompense on offer. She brought into her second marriage as a dowry a very few pieces of good linen, equally scarce but good quality napery, and some assorted silver plate, all secretly given her by her mother before her death.

Mrs. Cupp well deserved her rest in older age as well as company for my father. Although, I one time approached more silently than usual their cottage whilst visiting, out whiling an hour hunting for foxglove and dahlias. I came upon them by surprise, peering through the open window, and I observed that she spoke to my father whether he was listening or not, responded or not, or indeed was in the same room or not.

A second advantage I possessed over the Lady Bella was that I was not head over heels with my husband. As you have already read, if there was anyone I yearned for foolishly, it was for Lord Robert. So, unlike her, I was not heartbroken when Roland failed to appear after sending word that he would appear. I wasn't put out when he remained with us only two days instead of the promised fortnight. I wasn't in the least upset when he did come to Ravenglass and spent all of his time with his bosom friend, since he was my friend also. He did all of that often and with increasing frequency as the years mounted.

My third advantage over my mother-in-law was that I had female companionship. First, I had those sisters from the women's college at Leeds. And when they began to marry themselves off or became less frequent visitors, I had Miss Creswell, surely one of the most interesting persons I've ever met.

All three gratifications would stand me in good stead after the first eight years. For that magical period, I had Baby Roddy, Infant Roddy, Toddler Roddy, then Boy Roddy to occupy me. I suppose I shall never really understand women who are not maternal. I doted on your husband so. Watching him for the first time observe, speak, play, walk, run, ride his little hobby horse, learn to recite, learn to read, become first a handwriter, then a simple mathematician, learn to ride a real pony, take up sport, and become, in short, a little person; that was among the great joys of my life. Without Lord Roland, I believed that would never have happened.

But for every great love, there is inevitable loss. That happened when his father sent Roderick off to school. I didn't understand what that meant besides being bereft of his presence, his voice, his small enthusiasms, and his little difficulties. The boy who returned to me at first winter holidays was still my Roddy, albeit subtly changed. The one who returned after first spring hols was yet more altered. Year by year it worsened, until by the time he was sixteen, I hardly knew the young man who stood in the great hall and spoke to me of his plans for university to which I gave assent, no longer caring what he did.

This inevitable change in Roddy at first came as a great blow. But, in truth, it had been ongoing and was somewhat like an illness that takes hold quietly and saps one of all energy and interest, without one ever being aware of it. I think this is partly what had broken Lady Bella, seeing her innocent golden lad Roland transformed from her heart's ease into an uninteresting stranger in less than a decade.

In Roddy's third year away at school, a minor misadventure arose of far greater import to me and my history.

I mentioned that my school friends would come to visit, and that these visits had naturally tapered off once the young women had themselves been married. All the more of a pleasant surprise for me when two of my friends, including one from the women's college at Leeds, decided to make separate plans to see me: Julia Withersmere, and Astabella Vanbrugh.

Julia had done as she planned and married one of the West Indies heirs, and had been even more astonishing to us by moving herself into the houses those brothers shared in common both in Suffolk-shire and in London town. When she arrived alone at Ravenglass, I didn't dare ask Julia for the particulars of her *ménage*, for I well remembered her saying time and time again how she could not decide between the two brothers who loved her with equal passion. As we drove about our lands, I showing her whatever there was to be seen, I studiously avoided speaking of her situation as I feared to find out that she had espoused the one brother legally only to in truth have wed the both of them bodily, and that she lived with them either together or alternatively, or in some other, unspecified manner. This, my other friend, Astabella, had earlier assured me by post, was the truth. While I could picture it, I tried not to. Our visits were a bit strained if otherwise pleasant.

Astabella herself had not yet wed and, in fact, seemed to be doing her utmost to confound with unmet and dashed expectations several generations of British nobility whom she trod underfoot with alacrity and laughing bundles of charm. Her own fortune continued to grow steeply, so she became ever more of a "target," as she called it, for the young suitors' "pointed marital arrows of interest." As her fortune accumulated, all the more did they go after her and all the more were they shunted aside or bruited about as lacking quality, or pushed into each other to form a sort of hunting pack, and then quite thoroughly dismissed all at once.

It was Miss Astabella Vanbrugh who backed up Georgiana Milton, who had so presciently warned me of my friend, Lord Robert's, unsanctified passion for some unknown lady. And while my own situation meant that I could harbour naught but the merest curious interest in his personal life, still I was surprised to hear of her being in his company more than once. Indeed I witnessed Astabella in Robert's company myself.

It occurred at a county-wide Grange Fair at Broughton town, not far from the manor. This was an agricultural event of great festivity and significance that traditionally capped the early harvest in our local shires. Lord Roland had written to request if I would be "my usual angelic self" and attend in his place. For more than a century, a Ravenglass family member traditionally lit the bonfire that set its evening tone. He, of course, was "too involved in Parliamentary affairs to be able to dash up" for it.

I gathered several of the younger household members who had expressed interest in attending whenever I had mentioned the trip, and we all drove down to that market town in two carriages, my own vehicle as well as another, larger one, expressly hired for us for the occasion.

The first gardener's boy had already attended several of these fairs and so knew all about them, as well as "what good Lord Roland does hereabouts wen we'd come." So I had my rustic young tutor as *cicerone* for the event and felt less uncomfortable. That it was all rather rustic was an unequivocal fact. Even the finest hotel in the fair town we stayed the night in smelled sweetly of feed and hay, being surrounded by cow pastures and stabling.

The following morning, after breaking fast *en masse* at the local publican's, we strode out and encountered a great crowd of shire men and women and much activity. There were contests of strength and of speed by youths, held upon the town green; also a great many booths from which one might obtain oat, wheat, barley, and even sweet maize-cakes; and to wash those down, of course, we had a choice of various colours and strengths of ale. There was a central area, covered over by a two-story high marquee where we might sit and witness a sort of idyllic fashion-plate show, by which the women of the yeomanry displayed their latest designs of bodice, frock, stocking, and head dress. Alas, I was persuaded into judging and only accomplished that by carefully heeding the unbidden and quite loud comments of the girls I'd brought, all of whom held decided tastes and opinions upon the garb thus shown.

There were more games and a sort of May pole and heaps more of the savoury sausages, chops, and varieties of shepherd's pie to be had as the day waned. Just before the bonfire lighting ceremony, I was lifted in a chair by four stalwart young men and placed upon sort of rough throne, from where I might perform the actual ignition. It was there that I first saw Astabella, who I was to meet there later that night, and her surprising beau. She was immediately recognizable by her unique version of a country wench's dress; he for his eminent handsomeness of face and figure, so prepossessing that he stopped older farmer men and women as they passed him, and they must turn and look upon him, not quite believing he trod the earth alongside them.

I was able to obtain Astabella's attention and called her to share a vast tankard of pale ale served to me which, as representative of the local noble house, I was supposed to empty before I retired, an impossible task for anyone not accustomed to it.

"How does milady this nigh?" Astabella drawled as though she were herself a Morecombe lassie.

"Fairly enough," I answered, "although you and Lord Robert must help me empty this five-gallon goblet of brew."

He arrived, and he did pour off flagons of the stuff for himself and for Astabella, who had barely sipped hers when she was suddenly taken with the country dancing that had begun in the large, hay-strewn space set up before my little throne. Soon, she was speaking with two admiring country swains about the dances and how they were "figured." It was only a matter of minutes before one of the lads got up the nerve to ask. She graciously accepted and joined the growing crowd of rustic terpsichorean. This left me thankfully alone with Lord Robert.

He opened our dialogue by saying, "I thought it highly unwise of Lord Roland to make you come here alone!"

"He hardly made me. He asked, ever so wheedlingly. And I'm hardly alone," I replied, for at times, Robert would be so formal and even a bit stuffy. "I travelled with a suite of twelve. And not one of them until two minutes ago ever stopped pestering me as though I were a colic baby and needed my attention constantly diverted."

He smiled that warm and intelligent smile that I think I alone knew from him: his highest form of approval. "Yes, he would assuredly insist they do exactly that," he was forced to admit.

"How is it that our nation's grandest young heiress ends up upon your arm?" I asked.

"Your school friend?" He looked at where she was trying out what I was later told is called a *dos y dos* step, being tutored by a ginger-haired lad. Lord Robert shrugged. "She spotted me in Broughton some hours ago. She attacked me as though I was an enemy city needing to be taken, and she wouldn't let me alone till we arrived here."

Knowing the two of them, he diffident, she enthusiastic, I didn't for a minute question that was exactly what had happened. "Two hundred young London men would pistol-duel you for her attentions."

"I believe she comes after me only because I am *not* of their number," he replied, laughing. "She arrived with some seemingly fine people that she dropped so she might lay siege to me. I'm certain they are insulted."

"That's their lookout—and you might do worse," I added, feeling I must defend Astabella. "For all her talk, Miss Vanbrugh is an intelligent and good-natured young woman."

"Don't I recognize those truths?" he said. "Nor would I expect an iota less from one of your school mates, miss. Pardon me, your ladyship."

"Posh. You may call me miss or even Lillian, as you always have. Well, from what Astabella has said to me, I think she takes you on simply because she lies in no danger at all of your proposing to her."

He must have taken it differently than I meant it. "Did she say that indeed?" he asked with such a cold tone of voice and with such sudden hardness of his facial features that I felt it necessary to explain.

"But of course, she teases men so, especially the handsomer the man is."

He relaxed. "Ah, you mean in the so-called battle of Venus and Mars."

"Yes, in that so-called battle she feels utterly safe with you. Lord Robert. Is she deluded in saying she is so?"

"As everyone in London knows by now, Lady Vanbrugh's charms are many, and they are only overshadowed by her manifold lands, rents, railway bonds, and other possessions, which seem to be ever-developing."

"That's a very pretty evasion. But I happen to believe she is safe, with you," I said, feeling mischievously perverse to want to put him on the spot. "She said so herself, and furthermore, she said your heart is given to another."

"That is news to me, Lillian. I'm unaware of making any such gift."

"Astabella once opined that such an attachment has long existed, so perhaps you now take the connexion utterly for granted. She also said that it was of an 'unsanctifiable' nature, which I would hardly expect you to admit."

His face hardened again, and he with effort must keep his tone light and his voice warm. "If such were true, how would she know?"

"Another of our schoolmates, Georgiana Milton, speculated that Astabella keeps a network of spies about in constant pay. She knows all about everyone."

Now his face drained so, that I felt I must stop myself. "But I think Georgiana was being provocative to draw me out."

He relaxed only a jot. "Do you keep in close contact with all your schoolmates from Leeds Woman's College, miss?"

I knew Lord Robert well enough to know he had some point to make.

"More or less. With Miss Milton a bit less so of late."

"Ah!" he replied. "And here comes Lady Vanbrugh now, out-danced by her young yeoman, perspiring, and quite thirsty, and I would say by now rather thoroughly rusticated." He laughed to see her.

Lord Robert poured cups for Astabella and for Timothy Flagg, her dancing partner. They drank deeply, Lord Robert wiping perspiration off their foreheads with his own monogrammed handkerchief with much joking.

We all drank a bit more, and I felt mollified. Lord Robert was persuaded by Timothy and Astabella, and with poor enough grace, he joined the dance, and she returned to sit next to me.

"And?" said she, with her usual boldness. "What new information have you from our Adonis?"

"None at all. Lord Robert continues to evade and elude me."

"He eludes all of us. You, however, I think he would have in an instant, could he do so legally or morally."

"If it amuses you to think that, then do so," I said, pleased. "It is not true, since he asked after our other school mates."

"Georgiana, most particularly?" she asked, her mouth full of maize cake.

"Why, yes. Surely he's not interested?"

"Who would *not* be interested, as there is no doubt she has made herself quite the most talked about unattached woman in London this season."

I knew that had been Astabella's position the previous several seasons.

"Even so, Lord Robert is, well...nothing of the sort. Yet I believe you ought to be aware Miss Milton has settled herself very grandly indeed in Grosvenor Square in the centre of the May Fair. She has fixed herself up like the millionairess she is become, surrounded by paintings by Greuze and sculptures by Tintoretto. Or is it the other way around? Well, more to the point, she has begun to rapidly gather a glittering circle of gentlemen about herself."

"Just as she always planned," I replied, not at all nonplussed.

"A political circle of the upcoming 'new men,' she calls them. They are seen by political pundits as the 'new men' too. Or so one or another of Julia's husbands—for I swear I can't tell them apart—assures me, since they both read the 'papers, which I myself don't but merely skim for social whatnots. Your own husband," she said darkly, "figures largely among Georgiana's circle. And you might as well hear it from a friend first. This very weekend, while we three are here galumphing about in the hayricks like great yokels, Lord Roland attends Georgiana Milton's first agglomeration where her chosen politicos will encounter the capital to utilise in future to effect their takeover of the governing party."

"He as much as said so in his letter, asking me to take his place," I told her, hiding the more mortifying fact that Georgiana's name was never mentioned.

"Ah, then you are 'in the know,' as they say in London. And you are as ever, happy. How surprisingly clever you continually manage to be, Lillian."

Astabella kissed me on the cheek, then rushed to join the dance.

Replacing her at my side was Lord Robert. Seeing my face, which doubtless had altered since Astabella's news report, he said as kindly as possible, "I wish I had the courage to tell you myself," thus confirming it all. "They already call Miss Milton 'George the Fifth' for the influence she appears to wield among British legislators. Lord Peel is said to be overshadowed, not to mention widely chaffed."

"Georgiana does appear rather Hanoverian from some angles," I had to say, and we laughed over my witticism. "But it matters not, because if you don't already know it, Robert, although Lord Roland is my husband, he is hardly my lover. We are married nine years and this must by now be apparent to anyone close to the two of us." Before he could answer, I went on. "All this time, my little boy has been far dearer to me than his father. Now he too now is gone to school."

"Even so, Lillian..."

"And no, I don't wish to know if Sir Roland and Georgiana Milton are lovers. I assume they will be soon, if they are not yet. I also assume it will be a glittering 'May Fair-match,' as Astabella calls them."

"He cares not for her, personally. He cannot!" Lord Robert said, hotly.

"He cares not for me," I replied. "Nor I for him. So what matter is it?"

"But surely your reputation is at issue. That was the point I most remonstrated with him about before coming down to country."

"You remonstrated with him before coming here? For my reputation?" I laughed. "Oh, poor Robert, you are the dearest man. For my reputation, I am quite content. Stuck away here, none will know of *his* indiscretions but yourself and maybe a few Holsteins scavenging the lea for clover. None of the otherwise ignorant population will think the worst of me. Nor of Lord Roland."

"You are not wrong to think it so," he admitted sadly. "But then, what shall you do?" he asked, quite seriously.

"Do?"

"With yourself? With your life?"

That was the question, wasn't it? And with the unerring marksmanship he invariably displayed with bow and arrow, Lord Robert had once more hit his target at its very centre. I had only just begun to think it out for myself. I had, in truth, not yet allowed myself to really do so for fear of the inward repercussions that might horribly accrue.

"I believe I shall take up Florentine embroidery, which is become all the rage. I shall *not* take up laudanum, like poor Lady Bella did. Yes, that is exactly it. Florentine embroidery. Oh and, naturally, being a country lady, I shall take up a great many more charitable causes."

"You are witty for my sake, Lillian. But you are a rock," Lord Robert said.

"And you, Robert?" I now dared utter. "Since we are of a sudden—can it be all the ale we have swallowed?—so candid. Can you not possibly bring yourself round to be allowed to be happy?"

"Oh, Lillian," he said, suddenly, and with a catch in his voice I'd never yet heard. "I try. I really do try, believe me. But I fear it is far too late for me."

Such sincerity merited my own. "Are you so enslaved by this person?"

"You can have no idea," he said sadly.

Seconds later, Astabella and Timothy drew Lord Robert into the dance, which he joined with his handsome rueful smile. Soon it grew wild. And I grew tired. I took my leave of them all with a wave of the hand, while the dancing and who knew what other rural orgies to follow, raged on and on, loudly even from where the windows were shut against it in my bedroom at the hotel.

Would that I had listened to my own advice to Lord Robert that night? Or even taken up Lady Bella's ghastly solution? But I was headstrong, and I thought myself still young. Worse yet, I thought I deserved more happiness than good deeds and *bargello*.

Lillian of Ravenglass

To: Mrs. Harriett Smith
Post Restante Internazionale
Venezia, Italia

From: Ravenglass Manor
Broughton, England
15 October 188—

My Dearest Mother-in-Law,

My husband is not the monster in waiting
that you paint him to be either now nor, dare
I predict, in the future. I know this with the
greatest certainty as I have looked into his
soul on more than one occasion. What I have
seen is the lovely boy you recall growing up,
not the automaton you believe his father has
attempted and failed in constructing by tutoring
and controlling him since he left your arms over
a decade ago.

That distinguished person, my father-in-law,
believes this marriage of ours was all his own
clever doing and that it came about for political
and fiduciary reasons so he may make a run at the
P.M's. position. Let him think what he wishes.
And yes, it is true my papa is rich enough to
outright buy one borough seat and influence a few
others, if he so wished.

So, the truth is both greater and less. If
anyone wanted the marriage, it was myself. I met
Roddy and Oliver last year at Little Coddington,
Lord and Lady Arbuthnot's "country cottage" of
sixty rooms plus. Over a two-week period, I
threw myself into their company as much as I
could, certainly in a less seemly fashion than
the Countess of Larchmont, who was watching
rather closely, thought quite proper; as she
had no scruples in letting me know, saying I was
"beyond forward."

No matter, by then I was smitten. Your son's
combination of cool, rational, almost scientific

approach to almost everything that does not matter to him, and his quietly intense and quite passionate approach to what *does* interest him, sealed the poor boy's fate. His humour, which I daresay must come from you, and his sheer goodness did the trick. He doesn't even see the other side of the ethical, never mind ever lean to it. Nor do I have to tell you how good looking he is. I'm certain our children will be charming.

I told him all this on our wedding night, which we enjoyed by prior agreement without any possibility of messy conjugal relations, but lying side by side upon that enormous four poster bed, only slightly the worse for all the champagne and eager to discuss the guests. He made me laugh so hard I had to close the windows. And when I told him he'd been my choice and that I had long set my "guns for him," he just laughed the more. "Don't you know, old girl," he said to me, "that fulfilled desires prove in the long run even more trouble than wishes never fulfilled? Some old saint actually said so. I read it once."

What a lovely and wise young man.

As for Lord Oliver, he as much as "officially surrendered" Roddy to me the other day. "Old girl," he said to me, "you've won that tattered, tiny scrap of Roddy's heart, and you are welcome to it. I knew my reign over him couldn't last much anyway. And I've had a wonderful long run." You see how funny and lovely they both are!

Please send me more of your letters, although each of them saddens me so very much to read. Still I must know you better as we neither of us do at all, really. Above all, we must all three of us know the entire truth. I look forward to more letters with the greatest interest and we all read and discuss them with the greatest feeling, I assure you.

Your Daughter-in-Law,
Carrie-Ann

(p.s. If this letter looks frighteningly
official, it is because I have written upon a
type-writer — a writing machine. You did say I
was a "modern.")

To: The Earl of Ravenglass
11 Hanover Square
London, England

20 October 188—

Dear Father,

We await your arrival at Ravenglass and hope you will feel impelled to come some time not too far off in the future. Even if it happens that it will be of your usual "flying visits" of only a few days.

You will find the house, the grounds, and the entire countryside in good order, as I last reported. In addition, you will find the manor house changed in many regards.

Not your own suite of rooms, naturally, as those remain as they were, only cleaned and dusted and repaired wherever required. And the great hall and dining room too will be as your recalled them. My mother's former chambers and those of her guests were also somewhat modernised over the years, and they are quite as comfortable as need be.

Elsewhere above stairs, you will find much altered.

I mentioned in our last letter that we three had decided upon a furniture-buying expedition out of necessity, and so we sallied forth boldly. There are several manufactories not too far off, arrived at in only an hour or so by phaeton and railroad, and we planned our attack as Napoleon did his battles. In one such factory, we found bedchamber furniture of all sorts and sizes, of varied woods and even painted colours for the little girls. Carrie-Anne bargained furiously, and within a week, a large delivery caravan had brought it all. Between their driver and workman and our under-utilised staff of younger men, the great lot of it was brought up the stairs and properly installed.

Other factories were discovered for armchairs, dining chairs, sofas, ingle-benches, and the lot. We again descended upon several of them, found two to our taste—Carrie-Anne's and my own taste. Lord O. *has* no taste in furniture—and again bought them out. Again, they were delivered and placed all about. The second parlour and most of the sitting rooms are also now all furnished, and when my second family arrives, they will all be excellently accommodated.

Yet another two journeys were required to purchase so many new bed linens, curtains, and accessories. Albeit my mother kept a handsome selection of the latter, they are all rather antique and simply too few. We bought scads of the things, including spring mattresses imported from some place called Michigan in the United States, where they are all the rage, and I must say so very comfortable that we donated our own to any servant who would take one, and replaced them with these imported ones. Sheets, down pillows, blankets of all fabrics and colours followed. And then what seemed to be miles of curtains were delivered, and those women servants who knew how to sew took up their needles and happily re-sized them all to the windows.

All the staff seem happy with our alterations and additions, and appear as enthusiastic as we are about it all. Nor were they put out when Carrie-Anne felt impelled to mention that week-long leaves would need to be suspended, as there would soon be many guests, and all the staff required at hand. They were, as my wife put it, "thrilled" that the house would be full again.

Despite all of this purchasing and outlay of money, still we three wandered throughout the newly furbished Ravenglass and while pleased, still found that it lacked somehow.

Lord O. hit it on the head squarely for us all when he uttered what it was that was missing. "It needs pictures. Gee-gaws. Knick-knacks. Furbelows. Surely, old girl"—for such is how he addresses my wife—"you must know the kind of what-nots I mean."

She did indeed. But she thought those could not be acquired at a single or even quadruple blow as we had done so far. Here Lord O. proved once again Providential, as he had read in the monthly county newspaper that such objects would be up for sale very shortly indeed at the Stanforth Estate not far down the coast past Lancaster.

Sir Henry Stanforth, a fellow our own age, although schooled at that other university, had inherited a huge pile down there, and had married as modern as I have. But his new wife had condemned the entire heap and demanded it be razed and replaced by a modern building. You are probably not aware, but there are several very fashionable architects about the country these days whose specialty it is to erect large, modern "country homes," as they call them. Lord and Lady Stanforth hired such a one, and they are about to tear down the old place and put up a new one. The floor plans and several illustrations projecting what the house will look like have been allowed to be published in the county news weekly, and I must say they are spiffily new and quite handsome indeed.

However, much will have to be sold off, as the new construction is to be only two-thirds of its elder's size. Among that stuff would be many pieces of exactly the kind of old accessory that we three require for the newly furnished rooms of Ravenglass.

So we set off on what we believed would be an afternoon lark of a buying spree. We came away with scads of all sorts of old— and a few newer—pictures, several quite old wall hangings, and all kinds of other *objet d'art* and not-quite-art from the sale and auction. Lord Stanforth had one entire room filled with objects, many of them actually from western and northern Africa, which he claimed his grandfather had either brought home or had journeyed back there to acquire. Evidently that grandsire had been something of an adventurer in his younger days. The portrait of that Henry Stanforth, the first of that name, was particularly striking. He'd been painted by Mr. John Turner, who was not quite established at the time as he later would be, and he had been painted in that same chamber containing so many of those exotic objects.

Our host asked the three of us to stay for dinner and overnight and only return home the next afternoon, and therefore we were present when a most amazing personage put in an appearance the following morning.

We were all seated out of doors. As I have continually mentioned to you, for some reason we are experiencing extremely temperate days, albeit so late in the year. Seeing him drive up to the terrace in an open coach, Lord Oliver instantly said to our host, "A king has come to reclaim his knick-knacks stolen by your ancestor." For a royal person he surely appeared to be.

He was a great, brown-skinned man over six foot five inches tall, weighing a good twenty-eight stone. Although he was clad in what appeared to us to be newly tailored clothing of the British style and of a fine haberdashery, he wore a silken turban upon his head, which he would later show was bereft of hair. He also wore several close-fitting earrings, with large diamonds Carrie-Anne assured me were of "the very first water." He was elderly, eighty-five or more years of age, striking, even quite handsome in his way. He walked using two quite stout bamboo canes with silver handholds.

Even more odd, however, was the young lady who accompanied

him. She was about our own age, no more than thirty years of age and possibly much less, also dressed oddly in English clothing of the best tailoring, albeit again she was ornamented with expensive jewellery. But unlike her companion, she was fair-skinned and red-haired and she looked as British as any of us. Indeed, as Lord Oliver again and with his usual naïve perspicuity said, "Stanforth! She resembles your ancestor's portrait up the stairs."

You may imagine then all of our astonishment, when the stranger introduced himself as the Bey Jorma Gorglek and said that he had only recently sought political and religious asylum in the British Isles, having previously been a high official of the Barbary States but now become a Christian.

Father, I am called away from my desk. More shall follow. But this is, in truth, the very man my mother knew to have vanished from her ferry to Calais, several months ago. How wonderful is it that we would encounter him under such bizarre circumstances?

Your son, Roderick

To: The Honourable Lady Caroline-Ann Augusta
The Glebe, Ravenglass
Broughton, England

21 October 188—

My Dear Lady Caroline-Ann,
　　A most unusual encounter happened yesterday and another today, and although we are not intimate, Lady Caroline, still I know you for a great reader of modern novels, and thus I think the following might interest you.
　　The local authorities here in Venice weekly designate an oversized gondola to take foreign lady tourists about to some of the outer islands surrounding the city for a small charge. These isles, some no more than villages erected upon sand bars, are picturesque in the extreme. Their inhabitants are little altered by being in such proximity to a large and bustling city but generally live their lives as they have done for centuries past. Some of these isles, like Burano and Murano, have particular crafts for which they are by now almost too well-known, and one may peep into the manufacture of lovely, paper-thin glass vases or wonderfully intricate lace, and of course, purchase from their makers many lovely pieces. Each tour boat has, as a rule, but two gentlemen on board: its oarsman, or *gondoliere*, as well as a knowledgeable guide, conversant in several languages, although this latter is a voluntary, or at least not a regularly paid, office.
　　I think you must know where this is leading. Two days past, while we were dining *al fresco*, handbills announcing this special tour were passed about by some urchin, and I immediately decided I would like to take part in the very next one, due to set off from a central *mole* the following afternoon. My little *camerista* was equally excited. Since she has been with me, she has travelled a great deal, but I fear, not really had much entertainment from her travel. So this was as much for her delight as for my own edification.
　　Naturally my sentinel disparaged the idea, calling it "a serious contravention of security." But the day was a brilliant one. The waters of the Grand Canal, nearby where we once more luncheoned out of doors, and the entire *Laguna Veneto*, as far as the eye could make out, was still as glass, so my wishes prevailed over his qualms. Nevertheless, he waited dourly at the boat dock, ready, I suppose,

to fly into action should anything untoward happen, though that would mean casting himself bodily into the lagoon and swimming though its very questionable murk.

The gondola was at least eight yards long and three across—six rows of two seats, three rows of three seats, then two rows more. It was in the penultimate that we two placed ourselves. The oarsman was young, tallish for an Italian, and quite slender albeit not more than ordinarily good looking. Note how aesthetically spoiled have we become here. We marvelled that he alone could handle the very large oar. Still, he did so with great aplomb, and since he was young and comely enough, several of the ladies, especially five young ladies from Bremerhaven with a foolish or inattentive chaperone, flirted with him rather much more than was seemly.

Our tour guide was a man three times the oarsman's age and very noble looking. He stood at the front of the boat but was easily heard by us all despite his location. With him was another, somewhat younger, gentleman some forty years of age, to whom the elder turned upon several occasions to confirm a particular fact or word. I'd not seen this third gentleman board with us.

The afternoon passed quickly. We visited Murano as well as Burano, which faces north-easterly as you sail out to sea. As the day was still lovely, a surprisingly democratic voice vote from each lady was taken and, once the approbation was achieved, we continued onward, headed toward the very long islet called the Lido. This is a lovely strand backed by old palaces and old homes, the sands filled with bathing machines and individual bathers gambolling about in the surf. You must know that the Italians scoff at our British prudence and laugh at us for over-garbing in these matters, and they disport themselves as nature first produced them. We stopped also at Torcello and Saint Erasmo, both islets holding tiny, old, and perfectly adorable villages.

Just after we'd left one of the latter, and began back to Venice, some five minutes of gliding, our gondola came to a quite abrupt stop. The North German young ladies who had been so talkative throughout were tossed about the most of us all, or at least made a show of it, but they also made a great joke of it, especially as not one was more disturbed than having her hat knocked off. Yet, try as he may, the *gondoliere* was unable to move us forward. We seemed firmly fixed to the shallow sea bottom, fathoms away from any welcoming shore.

The guide gave some advice and helped the youth, to no avail. Then the gentleman accompanying him stood up and knelt to look overboard at the source of our trapped situation.

At first, we presumed him Italian too, from his colouring, which was tanned, face and arms, sleeves rolled up at the wrists, with a full brown beard, fine brown hair, and large brown eyes. His midsection, evident once his jacket was off and he only in sleeves and vest, was thickset in the manner of Italian men. He was well-fed, though he seemed more than a *contadino*, possibly a well-heeled merchant or, perhaps even more exactly, one of the minor nobility this region is so sprinkled about with.

More the latter, it would quickly appear, from how he now turned and addressed the *gondoliere*. His manner was not exactly abrupt, but his stance at the front of the long boat, if not quite commanding, showed he was at least accustomed to being heeded.

He was. The rower listened to his instructions and thrust his single oar deeply below the boat precisely where he'd been directed and in doing so, nearly bent it double. After one more great heave, which the other man leaned in to help, we suddenly felt a nudge, then a release. The boat shot forward so suddenly off the sludgy reef that the oarsman nearly toppled over, only caught at the sleeve at the last moment by the strong arm of the other man, who shouted, "That does it!" in English. Quickly followed by, "*Ecco! La!*"

So that I knew at once he was one of us.

The dozen or so ladies of all ages who made up the remainder of the gondola's passengers murmured thanks in various dialects as the man returned to his seat.

My own guardian could have done no better to save us, and so I quickly spoke up in gratitude. "Sir! You make a visitor proud to be British!"

His eyes swivelled about and took us both in with such force that I almost felt myself seeing us as he did—the tallish woman in dark violet velvet with a foreign hat pinned upon her abundant greying hair, the tiny female companion alongside her, happy with relief. "Would that I were British, dear lady," he said, inching toward us, "but I only share your language."

"American, then?"

"Guilty as charged. And not, as you see, a howling, painted redskin."

"I've met more than one American, kind sir, and not one was

painted nor howling, which is more than I can say of some of my own compatriots."

Another murmur now arose among the other female occupants, perhaps explanatory of our conversational style, as the righted watercraft slid now upon the oily-looking waters, heading rapidly away from the jetties of Chioggia toward the city itself. The American now swung about his jacket and put it on without bothering to roll down his shirt sleeves, and he strode as best he could in that rocking boat directly to us.

I quickly made room for him, gesturing for my *camerista* to move aside for him to sit between us. He did, but not before holding out a fine if tanned hand to me. "James. Henry Junior, of Boston, New York City, and, lately, London."

"Mrs. Smith," I countered, "of West Lancashire, Cumberland, and, lately, I suppose, of all Europe!"

Up close his eyes were larger, a warmer hue of brown than Venetians usually have and very kind.

"Mrs. Smith," he mused, then, "But of course, your ladyship, I understand."

"Am I so very transparent, then?" I asked, not a little disrupted.

"Hardly, madam, hardly at all. In fact, quite opaque. But it is my particular, shall we say, *donée* to know a person, if she's at all to be known, as surely you must be."

Now I was horrified. "Surely you don't mean to tell me that you are one of those, what are they called? 'Society reporters'?"

"That is exactly what they are called, and I am distinctly *not* one of that scribbling breed. Not a journalist at all. I pride myself upon being a student, a philosopher, and, above all, an inquirer into the human soul. A novelist, if you will."

I was embarrassed to not know his name or fame, until he was kind enough to mention in further conversation "a little pot boiler I dashed off a few years back, titled *Daisy Miller.*"

"I recall it well," I was able to honestly reply. "The book was hardly to be obtained at any lending library in the shire. When I requested someone fetch me a copy from London-town, he was forced to report that every edition was sold out month after month, until, well, I regret to say the book no longer called itself to my attention, and I admit I totally forgot about it. That was some few years ago? You still write?"

"I do, madam, and a few years after that palpable hit, I was fortunate enough to have yet another such, albeit a longer work titled *A Portrait of a Lady.*"

"You will think me a great ninny when I tell you that I read several excellent, if abbreviated, reviews of that novel in some periodicals I regularly take, and from them I concluded your novel was written to a level beyond my powers of comprehension."

"Then the reviewers failed their primary task, madam. You are the very reader I would want for that particular book. But may I be so forward as to offer you a copy of the little novel you were not able to find? It's much shorter, the perfect length and depth for that matter for a *Viaggio Italiano*, and I happen to know there are copies at the English Book Shop on Calle Torre Turco-Agricola."

"You may do nothing of the sort. You may, of course, autograph my copy when I purchase it there later on today. Where shall I find you, sir, for that task?"

He mentioned an address my *camerista* knew of, then mused and said, "Would it be very, very imposing of me to ask you to tea tomorrow afternoon at the house of a very fine lady? She is American born, but raised European and married to an Italian *Principe*, and, as a result, both marvellous and quite *comme il faut*. I feel certain we two must extend greatly our little conversation, which I note is soon to be abbreviated by our arrival. The lady's salon will be an appropriate place to do so."

I looked up, and there surely enough was my stalwart guardian not twenty yards ahead, leaning away from the dock as though to snatch the gondola by its tail fin, if not by its guide, himself. He was quite definitely looking over poor Mr. James Jr. with the most opprobrious of glances.

"Here's her address," the novelist said, handing me a card notable for its florid gilt script capped by a golden crest. "Four thirty tomorrow, if you can appear, as I hope you shall." He then stood up and began to move forward again speaking in Italian, French, and even a guttural German, causing the five sisters to giggle and poke each other's ribs.

We sauntered past that bookshop later in the day, and I *did* purchase not only that well-known novel of Mr. James's—slim indeed—but also another one of more recent vintage on the shelf encompassing two long stories, titled *The Siege of London* and *Lady Barberina*. It was those somewhat distinctly more mature works that I actually had the foresight to peruse the following morning and after lunch before the scheduled tea, not that I imagined he'd have the poor taste to ever mention his writing again. Which meant that surely I must.

My guardian was naturally astonished I would even consider attending such an event, as though tea with quality was equivalent to a bomb-throwing party. "Who are these people?" he begged to know. "How do we know they aren't second story men of the lowest type?"

"Because," I replied, holding out the card for his re-inspection, "Second story men, of even the highest type, seldom have visiting cards to offer one on women's tours. Never mind visiting cards with signets embossed in fourteen karats!"

"It's my sudden death by apoplectic stroke you seek, madam. I know for certain," he over-dramatized, amusing me. And he didn't seem a jot mollified when he left me at the heavy, well-sculpted double doors of one of the largest and most splendid palaces off the Giudecca. "Here shall I be in case of need," he asserated, standing guard by the door, unperturbed by two loose-limbed Venetian fellows larking nearby who were assuredly making fun of his martial attitude.

These Venetian *palazzi* are generally one huge salon opening out onto another, and this one was no different save perhaps in the fine freshness of its furnishings and the extremely good taste withal. The *principessa* was perhaps forty years of age and strikingly beautiful, with hair of that golden wheat colour so prevalent among our former colonial subjects, with a slightly tanned complexion that would instantly set her apart from the subaqueous pallor of an Englishwoman. Her eyes were rather long, light, blue almost grey, and her features generous rather than prim. She was an American beauty rather than a British primrose. Mr. James Jr. was dressed a bit more formally than when I'd first come upon him, in a dark grey swallow coat known as a cutaway with a shirt front that was almost silver in its rich silkiness, pointed with a matte chocolate cravat matching his hair and eyes. He led me to the lady and introduced us. A rather more colourless woman, if superbly dressed, about my own age, was introduced as a Mrs. Nelson of Fifth Avenue, New York, but she kept her peace almost throughout, pouring tea and attending to our prandial wants.

"Mr. James tells me that you travel incognito," the *principessa* began, "which I both admire and approve of as the only proper course for a lady during these times of publicity hounds. Mr. James, of course, believes you do so from motives beyond the usual and wishes me to discover these for him so that you may become an idea he will slowly develop upon. He is filled with these ideas, centring as they do around characters. I've doubtless been one such character connected to one such idea for some time, although I don't think I'm yet a story. Am I, Henry?"

"Not yet," he admitted without a bit of hesitation. "But I think you will eventually become a novel, rather than a mere story."

"Bravo! I only hope I'm to be a desperate character, and that I change nation's histories," she declared.

"Actually, I think you shall be rather desperate in the end, albeit a revolutionary more than a queen," he pronounced.

"Wonderful! And Mrs. Nelson, is she also to become a novel?" I inquired.

"Dear me," the *principessa* said, "Lucretia's long been one of Henry's stories."

The New Yorker smiled at this as though it were very old news.

"The question now must be which character or idea you shall become," the younger woman continued, "because mark you, my dear, do you mind if I call you that? Everyone is so informal around here. You shall be one. For Mr. James is quite taken with your mystery."

"Ah! My mystery!" I said. "My mystery, I must confess, is unendurably arcane, frightful, and indeed somewhat Gothic too."

The *principessa* released an effervescence of laughter into the Titian blue air. "You see, Henry," she said, tapping his forearm, "I told you no English Lady would settle for it. We're horribly polite to you, we silly Americans. But you can't expect everyone to be so willing." Then to me, "Thank you so very much, Mrs. Smith, for clarifying the issue once and for all. But even so, don't be at all surprised to one day come across yourself in one of Henry's narrations, as ghastly as you've just painted yourself. He's frightfully not to be relied upon for being at all agreeable when once he catches onto one of his ideas."

"She'll never come across any such thing," he said serenely, between sips of his aperitif, "since she cleverly enough doesn't ever read me."

"Cleverly *didn't* ever read you, until now," I corrected, reaching into my reticule for the volume of tales.

"I correct myself," he went on imperturbably. "Mrs. Smith has caught up to me—as far as *Daisy Miller.*"

"A distinctly quite early work," the *principessa* delightedly glossed for me, "and thus to be disparaged. Oh, but what's this?" she asked, seeing my volume. "Why, Lucretia," she said to her relative. "It's your biography, writ a bit large."

It was my turn to be taken. "Which? Surely not *The Siege?*" Then I saw my error in Mrs. Nelson's own face. But before I could colour more deeply, Mr. James Jr. took the book I held out and said to the *principessa*, "You see, I was right. Faced with the earlier volume with its drab colours, and this newer one with its femininely appealing violet-coloured boards, she naturally took the latter."

"Henry," the *principessa* now drawled on, still more amused, "has developed a theory of book board design by colour and tint by which he swears novels are unheedingly bought and sold. He drags unwilling artists up the steps of publishers and forces them to madly aquarelle and then forces poor Mr. Publisher to accept those daubs and print them across the books."

Mr. James Jr. signed the volume I'd held out to him. Then he turned to the back and wrote a superscription there, the latter unwitnessed by the American women, who were pointing out a large, festively draped *gondola alla regatta* overflowing with noisy revellers that had suddenly appeared on the canal just beyond the balcony upon which we sat.

Mrs. Nelson vanished and reappeared with a servant carrying a tray of little Italian sandwiches called *pannini* which we hungrily dove into, delicious gobbets of savoury tastes and textures. The gondola stopped, and we were serenaded, and, of course, we must toss flowers to them, before they sailed on.

"I still find it all perfectly marvellous here," the *principessa* enthused, "but Mr. James," pointing to where he stood, apart, smoking a cigarette, "is already quite *ennuye* by Italy. He says Italians have so very little mystery about them. Unlike we deep and many-sided Americans!" She laughed again, deliciously. "Or you very Gothic British. If he were not at this moment writing a tale with a Venetian setting, he'd be long gone, and we poor women the poorer for it."

Looking over the balcony, I happened to note my guardian, brooding below. Checking an ormulu table clock just indoors, I now saw I'd spent more than an hour. So I made my goodbyes and promised to correspond with one of the three.

When I reached our *pensione*, I perused the volume and read on an extra page in the back, "You may depend upon my silence, my discretion, and my aid, no matter what, no questions asked." Two addresses where he might always be contacted, *Post Restante*, were appended.

And so, despite his lovely friend's theories and delightful explications, it seemed that Mr. James Jr. was neither a mercantile scribbler, nor a fool.

Yours, Lillian

To: The Earl of Ravenglass
11 Hanover Square
London, England

23 October 188—

Dear Father,

We have had a bit of a scare here regarding one of Carrie-Anne's brothers, the younger, Theodore, who, when last I wrote you, found himself laughing so hard during his second full tea out of doors, he began choking upon a rind of over-toasted bread.

Lord Oliver—that marvel, that ninth wonder of the world—stepped out along with myself, once we'd been called, onto the big terrace to see the boy turning blue and then purple, and his parents and sibs either laughing yet from the joke or in brand-new consternation at his appearance.

"What's happened?" cried Lord O.

Six of them told us all at once. Still, he understood from the boy's own gestures. And while I made to send off for a doctor, Lord O simply bent down and grabbed the boy up by his ankle. Holding him in the air almost above his head, he swung him around while we all made a circle of space for them, and the women folk all screamed in differing tones and pitches. Naturally enough, I wondered if my friend had gone mad.

But the astonished whirled boy coughed out the toast point, and then began to whimper and cry. Lord O. swung him up in the air again, caught him by his middle, and settled him closely onto the terrace brickwork.

He was soon surrounded and his face washed and he was lectured at while Lord O. sat down in the boy's place and quite finished the toast and drank down his still warm Bohea.

Lord O. had become a favourite of the children upon the Strand near Rye Super Mare during our honeymoon on those occasions that he had deigned to be such a Neptune as he can be with his boating and swimming skills. Now he was a veritable hero and lifesaver, and they would not let him alone. Little Theodore, the choking victim, will not leave his side until ordered off. Lord O. now calls the boy "Coughing Tibbalds," and the others have taken up the name, calling him "Cougher" or "Tibs." They are inseparable. At dinner, when my Kent shire father-in-law mentioned with pleasure the new connexion, Lord O. all but yawned and at last uttered, "Yes. And young Tibs is almost as pretty as Lord Roddy was at that age."

I had quite forgotten I had a story to finish relating to you regarding the ancient Black Jupiter and his pretty white Hebe who made such a surprise showing at Henry Stanforth's house. Well, then I'll continue. We really didn't discover a great deal about the two strangers until Stanforth and his wife, and their offspring *and* their guests arrived here at Ravenglass to visit two days after.

The three of us are most gratified now that we recently spent so much time, discretion, planning, and decision making, not to mention good British sterling, refurnishing the old wing of the house. As I sit here writing this letter, every guest suite but one and every chamber but one is now filled up with its own guest. "'Tis an hotel!" Lord O. said just after our last large luncheon—out of doors once again, for the weather holds remarkably warm. As the kitchen staff served so very many of us, I believe Jannequin counted us all to total up at nineteen, which includes ourselves, Carrie-Anne's parents, their four other children, two young cousins, and an older female one who doubles as nanny, as well as the Stanforths and their three children and the two strangers. We are delighted to be so filled up, as the house seems to merrily ring with all the young people coming and going. Even our very aged head butler Trithers said never in his own lifetime had he actually seen so many residing guests at Ravenglass. "It makes the place seem brand new," he said, and he was both amazed and embarrassed to be using such a term, glossed as I believe it to be off placard adverts in town.

Well, we had invited the Stanforths and were glad they showed up. But it was something that our very own Carrie-Anne had said just before we pulled away from their Redbud Park that encouraged them to visit. To wit, she had recalled letters of my mother referring to Henry Stanforth, the explorer-gentleman so exotically pictured up the stairs at their old house, and how—in her words—"Lady Lillian's own mother was supposed to have married the man, and had instead refused him twice. In fact," she had added just as we'd gotten into our phaeton to take off for home, "I have locked away in an old reticule at home the entire history of that Henry Stanforth when he was believed lost at sea in a hurricane. I believe it was almost six years."

Young Henry and his wife did not at all know of these letters and *must* read or at least hear for themselves, and so their visit. But why then would the two exotics accompany them? Here is where my tale jumps ahead of itself, and so I will straightforwardly relate what happened last night.

Once all the younger guests had been put to bed and their elders had gathered in the newly furbished second parlour, and once a good fire was built and sweet cakes and *aperitifs* were distributed, and the servants all gone and downstairs once more, my wife took out her long letter. She read to us that section of my mother's correspondence which she titled for us *The Love of Lydia Jespers*. I believe you have a copy of it, along with her letters copied to you, and so it shall not be new to yourself.

But you may imagine our astonishment, when the elderly Black man stood up shakily upon his legs and staffs upon hearing it read aloud, and went over to the parlour foyer where his outerwear had been placed. When he returned to us, he handed to Henry a very small packet of silk. He was weeping, which saddened us greatly, but he would not sit. He took himself off to a far, darkened corner of the big parlour away from us all, and there leaned hard against a sideboard and there hung his head.

Henry Stanforth, who was by now the absolute centre of our attention, unrolled the silk cloth and pulled out of it a rough sheepskin manuscript, old and worn. It read in large letters, "For African George, My Great Friend. From Henry Stanforth."

Once unfurled to its other side, it turned out to be a short letter confirming their friendship. It ended, "I know that you will rise high, my friend George. So one day, find yourself an Englishman to read this to you."

We had to all surround the new-found Stanforth family friend and bring him into our midst, with pleas that he remain so, an honoured father to them and also to us, for were we not distantly and by circumstance almost related?

On his visit here, he had just discovered the Stanforths' location when the British Foreign Office demanded his deportation from the country. Although he had been placed on board a ferry bound to France, he had hired a boat to come steal him away in mid-passage. Heading that rescue party was the lass Nyecti, disguised as a French *marin*. So he had vanished from the ferry and made his way in secret, back to England, and by careful stages—for now he and the young girl were both illegal emigrants—to Lancaster and to the Stanforths. This had come about as a result of George reading the same advertisement of sale and auction that had drawn us three to the Stanforths' house.

It is a full circle, closed after sixty-six years, like the clasp on a bracelet. The two Foreign Nationals have requested British diplomatic asylum, and we are all of us so delighted by their history and relation that we have stood as sponsors to them with Henry Stanforth naturally being the primary sponsor. We believe Nyecti to be a direct relation of his through his grandfather. They remain here in the north, and we are hopeful your office will aid us and them in securing their permanent residence papers.

Your son, Roddy

To: The Honourable Lady Caroline-Ann Augusta
The Glebe, Ravenglass
Broughton, England

26 October 188—

My Dear Lady Caroline-Ann,

I am come now, in these letters, to the most difficult ones to write to you, to see in ink for myself.

Lady Bella had spoken to me of disillusionments and of disappointments that she had suffered and that she expected me to suffer equally as a Ravenglass wife. Perhaps because of our very different regards for our two husbands, she never warned me of the potential joy, nor of the great treachery that I alone faced. It was my most thrilling challenge and my saddest trial. Out of it, fortunately, derives that unexpectedly deepening friendship with Miss Cresswell I have mentioned before as well as my eventual enlightenment, leading in time to this long-planned flight.

By this time, Lord Roland pretended to visit Ravenglass only when those in his pay at the house had assured him I would be somewhere else, usually at Ulverston with my father and Mrs. Cupp. The letters between us which had begun as daily whenever Roland stayed in London, had become bi-weekly, then weekly, and then infrequent, short notes requiring me to perform some "lordly duty" he was unable to. Just as well, because with the son gone to university, I needed the father not at all.

My school-women friends visited less frequently, but they visited Lancaster where I would travel to meet them, feeling freer away from the prying eyes and reporting pens in my husband's employ.

Far more sadly yet, Lord Robert also visited far more seldom. At long last, he had decided to marry someone. Although my husband chose her, it was with the greatest foresight. She was the first daughter of a minor baronet located near Nottingham. Not far off in distance, but distant enough. She was reportedly a handsome enough woman, half his age, with the expected ridiculous accomplishments of a girl of her upbringing. Her purpose, like my own had been, was merely to produce a male heir of sufficient physical and mental health to be the new lord once Robert had passed on.

I was invited to their wedding, and I attended it along with my old school mate, Astabella Vanbrugh who, although scarcely younger than I, was still unattached—by now to great scandal. We shared a small parlour between our bedroom chambers at Blackburn House. We contrived to arrive a day before anyone else and to leave later, and so we had nearly a week's time to compare notes and to reacquaint ourselves.

She was by this time the greatest heiress in the British Isles, and also one of the greatest of British society's problems, a fact which fazed her not a whit.

"Do you know that the Empress of India addressed me directly at court?" Astabella told me, referring to the new nomenclature used for our Queen Victoria Regina in the newspapers of late. "That dowdy old frump called me to her side during one of those endlessly long knighthood ceremonies. She wore so much lilac-scented powder that half of her ladies in waiting were sneezing and the rest barely able to hold their sneezing in. Earlier in the day, she had been coerced by her ministers to award me some fantastical gee-gaw, according me to now be a Great Dame of the Empire or some such fol-de-rol title. Doubtless because so much international wealth has been gathered under my name and because of all the import duties that have accrued to her inland revenue as a result."

Astabella went on, mimicking the old Queen. "'There are a great many accomplished, unmarried gentlemen in the British Isles, Miss Vanbrugh,' she said to me sternly. 'It's a great wonder to me personally that you have been unable to accept any of their suits.' To which I replied, 'To the contrary, Your Majesty. I am assured by my financial advisors that at this very moment, I have at least two dozen accomplished British gentlemen quite up to their ears in one lawsuit or another within your kingdom. It's said that in London alone, my lawsuits comprise half the docket of one courtroom and sustain an entire tenant row of Chancery.' When she was at last able to close her tiny, wrinkled little mouth from her great astonishment, she frowned darkly and waved me away, muttering loudly enough for me to hear: 'Evidently money no longer cares *who* possesses it.' As though it ever did, I thought, and further thought that to be a great witticism. I laughed out loud, earning even more of a royal scowl."

At any rate, Lord Robert's wedding was done up in as great a style as might have been expected, and to our collective astonishment, my husband made an appearance, standing as best man. He arrived, I believe, a good ten minutes before the actual ceremony began and left at least ten minutes after he had given a celebratory toast, precisely one hour later. All that time, he was naturally surrounded by his entourage of stalwart young rogues, doubtless protecting him from the perils of satin hoops and dangerously pointed petticoats.

Lady Elspeth Haworth, a very elderly woman, nudged me with her fan and asked who he might be, seeing me stare at him. "Someone very grand," I replied. "A royal?" she asked. "More important by far, ma'am, a political!" Alas, George the Fifth did not also make an appearance. She sent a gift instead—not of ceramic nor even china. I'd not seen my husband for several years, and I thought Lord Roland looked peaky and balding, as the very fair often do rather too early in life. His nose was grown quite as long and sharp as his mother's had become at the end, and his cheeks could have used some of that greasepaint his father counted upon, but I more sagely concluded that despite losing all boyish charm and prettiness, he had at least come to resemble the photogravure of one who ought to be leading his party, which, for one so ambitious, is not a bad thing.

By contrast, Lord Robert looked handsome as ever. He was slender, even boyish, though greying at the temples and, at times, even a bit stoop-shouldered. Thus, thought I, is fair England at age thirty-eight or nine. Imagine all our appearances a decade later? Still, the Family Blackburn put on a satisfactory matrimonial show, missing not a single tradition or ornamentation, and the ceremony and after-rituals went off well. I would return only once to that red brick caricature, Blackburn Castle, with its storybook crenelated towers and frilled-arch carriageways. Now I feel certain I shall never see it again.

I returned to Ravenglass and to that mere sketch of a life I had left behind. But lest you pity me, the servants and neighbours had come to comprise the chief interests of my days, and there I think I did especially well in my charities. Some few years ago, I chanced upon a report composed by a young scholar detailing the "general health and welfare of the rural population," of Ravenglass County as though there was any other population. This stringent Oxonian follower of Mr. Engels judged us to be "of a higher grade than the generally deplorable standards all around that we oft decry;

doubtless due to the less benighted interest and active intercession of one of the less rapacious overlords." Meaning, I assume, myself.

But it was not this social health and welfare that drew to the area the next important player in this lengthy tragicomic charade that I have been writing to you, my dear, but instead its animated life. More specifically, the ornithological or sea-fowl of the northwestern coast of our fair isle, which, as you might guess, abounded not only in its own health and welfare, but in its variety, and thus in its interest for any staunch follower of Mr. Charles Darwin.

Such was the young Alfred Benoit Davison. As he carried upon his person at all times at the very least a "four penny jacket-pocket" edition of the *Origin of Species*, it must be as a committed and utter Darwinist that the charming young man enters my story not a year later.

I first heard of Davison's existence from Miss Cresswell, ever the news-reporter of our little arena. "A young scientist was noted by several in the village yesterday taking chambers," said she during a session of embroidery and gossip, for she is teaching three of our uneducated servant girls to embroider as a prospective fallback for them to earn extra money once they are, in her own words, "pregnant and married to some fool drunken boy hereabouts." Miss Cresswell added in her news report that the scientist had taken chambers "for a surprisingly long period of three months and had hired on a daily lad—one Winston Yawley, a child of ten years, to help carry his specimen trays and sacks."

The scientist's open devotion to the Great Charles was of course a subject repeated to me by Ravenglass's only divine, the less than divine Rev. Rose, later that week. He was first alluded to in an unusually meretricious sermon, to the utter mystification of most of the village, but not myself. At our weekly tea, with his bovine wife, Elinor-Mae Rose, née Cresswell, Rev. Rose came right out and said that he had himself met the young man but had failed to be able to lure him into either Sunday church or—can you imagine?—"a discussion of science and God, along with port and sweet biscuits" in Rose's private chambers. Knowing how drearily all-knowing Rose to be upon any subject under the sun, I could only admire the young scientist's perspicacity.

This then "sets the scene," as the ladies' magazines put it, for Alfred's and my first meeting. To be more precise, the scene itself was a long neglected strand off Morecombe Bay, somewhat south and very much out of the way of any sailors or other local males. The reason for that being I had allowed the younger members of the staff and Miss Cresswell to talk me into taking them out on a seashore outing. The weather had grown warmer inland, and all of us could use a holiday. The younger women wished to be able to enter the tide with their skirts up to their knees, where they would evade the larger waves, gossip, and, of course, titter, screech, and generally have an excellent time of it.

To this end, I had Trithers arrange for my phaeton and an open top cart for the more daring of the ten, mostly younger women who wanted to join Miss Cresswell and myself. Jannequin had made up three pick-nick baskets for us, and we also brought light blankets, and long-worn sheets to keep some of the sand off our faces, food and clothing. The wind was too strong for little single pole "tents" as they are called or even for umbrellas. But we had substantial veiling for our straw and wicker-work schooners of hats to protect us from an excess of sun. The boys driving and our butler carried all this paraphernalia down to a spot of my selection, amid some low-growing, wind-tossed vegetation adjacent to the strand. They set up a little encampment for us among the lower grassy hummocks, and then retired to drive off and return for us three hours hence, by which time we expected to be sated with our experience.

We had only just settled ourselves and had begun to discuss whether devilled eggs and ham salad sandwiches "kept" in the maritime cool air or would be "spoiled" by the strong sunlight and should be gobbled all at once, when we espied and heard a sun-struck figure rushing down the strand toward us, waving its arms about.

As it neared, it consolidated into the guise of a barefoot man with a small boater hat and open jacket nearly torn off him by the wind. Closer, it was a tall young man, and even closer, Miss Creswell identified him. "Upon my word, it's the scientist. Whatever ails the youth?"

He rushed into our little encampment and stopped short, clearly out of breath. When he spoke it was like a purposely loud whisper.

"You must leave at once!" were his first words.

"Have you no concept at all of the thoughtless destruction you're wreaking?" was his second sentence.

"Can you be so inconsiderate? So utterly mindless in your pleasures?" were his third and fourth utterances.

The younger girls withdrew in a huddled group wrapping blankets and sheets about their lower bodies. I could hear them muttering he was "Gone blown daft" and that he must "Hie off! Hie off now!"

Miss Creswell interposed herself between me and the madly flushed whisperer.

"This is the Marchioness of Ravenglass, Lady Lillian. Show respect."

He hushed her all the time. "I do beg your pardon, Lady Lillian," he whispered on. "I'm certain you could not know. But you have settled precisely within a *hatchery* of black-headed gulls. Look about yourself, and you will see nests of eggs upon almost every hummock with cross leafed tops. Unless you leave this area at once, those adult black-headed gulls, hovering there"—he pointed to a spot above the bluffs where Trithers and the lads had left us—"shall *never* return to this hatchery. All of the eggs will remain *unhatched*, and an entire generation of black-headed gulls will never see the light of day."

As he whispered furiously and pointed, I suddenly was able to see the remarkable indicative crossed grasses he was pointing at, and even—since one was not a yard from us—several eggs.

Miss Creswell had drawn herself up to her full five feet five inches as a prelude to making verbal war for my sake. I stopped her with a hand on her arm.

"We did not see," I said to the scientist. "We do now. Help us move. To where shall we move?"

"You oughtn't be on this sector of strand at all. Those bluffs in one week will house the nesting grounds of a local frigate bird not found elsewhere, while striped and white-headed gulls shall nest throughout this middle ground."

"We cannot leave today until others return for us. Point, or better yet, bring us to the spot you think the least harmful to your precious birds, and there shall we remain. It is the only sensible course of action."

"Of course it is. Of course it is," he said, and Miss Creswell slung into his arms first one then another large pick-nick wicker hamper, while I made three of the girls who dared approach take up the third. We distributed the extra cloths among ourselves and took off very carefully lest we do harm, until we were upon the sand, at which point we made greater progress.

He had us slog our way some two hundred yards farther up the beach, pointing out that a certain species of sea turtle sometimes used the path to reach the sea. He was about to leave us when I asked him to sit and join us for refreshments.

As he dithered, I heard Miss Creswell, no shrinking violet, utter, "Why ever should he?" and others reiterate that he was "full-blown-daft," until he coloured rather completely and removed his straw hat. He bowed to me, kissed my hand, and said, "I'm ever so apologetic, lady. You must all believe me to have utterly left my reason, my impertinence was so extreme."

"*Au contraire*," I said. "You were correct. I see the adult black-headed gulls now warily approaching the area we have vacated. We were, in truth, heedless."

"Heedless or not, your manners need correction," Miss Cresswell fumed.

"I believe," I laughed, "Mr. Benoit, or is it Professor Benoit, was completely taken by the emergency of the moment."

"Indeed, I was, Lady Lillian."

"They are your study, then? These black-headed gulls?"

"All the gulls and other sea bird of the area, yes."

"And we were trespassing upon your field of study?"

"It's *your* county, milady!" one of my by no means mollified young women uttered. "How could you be trespassing 'pon what you yourself possess?"

"Indeed! I forgot myself," Benoit allowed. "How may I justify my actions?"

"By sitting down, if you are certain it is quite safe for whatever creature may inhabit the place," I said, a bit archly, I now admit. "And if it is safe, by indulging in the horrors of lemonade and the concupiscence of hard eggs, like any more or less civilized young man."

"You are very kind," he said and did so. Miss Cresswell sniffed, but served him nonetheless out of our wicker basket. The others had imperceptibly moved away and would continue to do so upon one pretext or another. I gathered Miss Creswell remained for my protection and honour.

She needn't have bothered. No male had spoken to me like

him since my brother Rudolph, and he was far away. No young male ever had expressed his sentiments quite so boldly and baldly in my presence. I was instantly taken with Alfred's freshness and his lack of those manners he been found so lacking in.

"I have it upon reliable word," I said, waiting until his mouth was filled with yellow yolk, "that you are to be with us for at least eight and a half more weeks. Perhaps you have already sent in a card announcing your intentions to Ravenglass and it was mislaid?"

I watched him handsomely choke on that a bit before he cleared his lips with a napkin. "My tutor at college assured me that I must contact Lord Roland, and so I did. I assumed..."

"Foolish!" Miss Creswell said. "Lord Roland is too busy for undergraduates."

"I am a graduate. With honours."

"No matter," I said. "This little encounter *sur le plage* shall be as though it never occurred, a mirage of the sun and sea. Instead, you shall send your card to the manor house, and you will be apprised when you may call upon me to take a cup of tea. If I am in a forgiving mood that moment, I shall *not* also invite the Reverend Rose." I could see his eyes startle. "I generally do not like to see him at my tea table more than is required. Miss Adelaide Cresswell," I said, placing my fan upon her bare forearm, "shall, however, be present."

"Charmed!" he said unconvincingly.

To which she immediately replied, "In a pig's eye!"

"We shall both of us expect some accounting of your planned scientific study here on our strands," I continued. "As well as a detailed schedule of when and where my young ladies may feel free to show their knees whenever they wish."

"Is that why you're here! So far away?" I thought his eyes quite as blue as the sky in that moment.

"Of course."

"But why?" he stood up. "Knees are only...knees!" He stood and pulled up his own trousers until they had surpassed his own rather rosy, slightly squared joints. His calves, I noted, were lightly furred. "Everyone has knees," he went on. "Young men. Young women. They only differ in their shape, size, and cleanliness. To show them is no disgrace but proof, in fact, that one has undistorted limbs. And thus a clear sign of health and readiness for childbearing."

At which last, the younger girls who had been looking on in

growing uneasy amazement, screamed as one, rose, and fled away, while Miss Cresswell leapt up, saying "Well, I never, "over and over again. She stormed off some yards away where she gestured at me to follow. I'm afraid I did nothing but laugh until we were alone again, at which point I begged him to unroll his trousers and reseat himself.

"You are nothing unfazed," he said as I poured him more lemonade.

"I am a woman wed nearly twenty years, with a child almost your age. Male knees…?" I shrugged.

"Surely not. You barely look to have three decades."

"Is that the scientist speaking, Mr. Davison, or is it the flirt? For I have no doubt a young man of your prepossessing face, auburn locks, and fine figure must be extremely competent in the flirting arts."

"So long as you are a dead gull pinned 'pon a specimen tray," he said, looking away. "Otherwise, I have no personal arts at all, I fear, spending all my time in the past five years among dull old dons and unsanitary laboratory assistants."

"Then we shall prepare for you a post-graduate course in the more glancing amatory arts," I said, "Which, along with Miss Creswell's course of study in manners, ought to keep you busy, if mortified, all the summer long." It was my turn to laugh at his embarrassment, as he made some excuse, promised to drop his card at my foyer, and made a hasty retreat. When Miss Creswell returned, he was walking rapidly into the distance, keeping to the water's edge, far away as he could from the hatchery.

"Surely you don't mean to receive that man?" she said.

"I was thinking that after some rather required preparations, he might make a suitable mate for yourself."

She looked at me as though I'd grown a third eye.

"Sit down, dear Adelaide. I was joking."

"Don't dare fix me up with such a pretty-looking young man. Promise me, Lady Lillian. Promise."

"Is he very pretty?" I asked. "I hadn't noticed."

"Why would you? With your Lord Robert calling and wed to Lord Roland? Aye, but this one has red cheek and blue eye and broad white brow, and a straight big nose, like one that smells money, the old wives say, and skin like old satin, and hair that curls fine like a babe's and such defined lips that... *You* may be safe, Lady Lillian. But all us single lasses are mere fodder to such as he."

"Mere fodder to such as he," she repeated, I thought rather wistfully.

Lillian

To: The Very Reverend Jasper Horace Quill
The British Church at Campofieri
Town of Fiesoli
Province of Toscana

26 October 188—

Dear Sir,
I require and I rely upon your best advice this day. As I have written before, myself and the young woman are quite prepared to leave this stinking, waterlogged collection of ancient marble and granite and rotting wood that is called Venice. But we are unable to sway milady, who insists upon remaining and would, I believe, remain forever.

In vain are my arguments for our haste and her safety and the little one's daily chattering to her in French that even I can comprehend as good sense. And if we are found out?

To this, the lady replies that we are already followed day and night. That she is not so much of a fool as to believe her husband has not somehow traced her very steps to where she resides. In truth, says she with as much *sang froid* as the crocodile in the river Nile, she would think the less of him and his men did he not know!

Then I suggest travelling on. Why, asks she, when under the circumstances one place is as good as the other, so long as it is far away from England? And why move now when this place is so congenial?

To her, perhaps.

To myself it approaches living within a nightmare.

If you have not already intuited the truth, I have located that place of shame and greatest temptation. When the lady dined out with those American ladies she first visited t'other day, I hailed a passing launch headed toward *Il Ghetto*, and it sped me there easily enough.

No, of course I did not enter. But the reek of the stuff pervaded the exterior brickwork, or at least to my mind it did so. I witnessed two fellows enter, vapid, limp things, not even men, and watched as another was all but carried out by his servants, and so was I strengthened in my resolve to avoid that hellhole.

But other matters of a different if equally unsavoury nature have come up, assuring me that should I remain much longer in this place, its rot and degradation will pull me deep into its yellow fogs and fearful miasmas that seem to hover only inches off the darkly questionable waters.

I provide but one example of many. No sooner had I returned to my on-guard duties that night in front of the doorway of that Ca' Simonato or whatever it is named wherein again dined milady, when a fellow came up to me and asked for a light for his cigarette. As I did so, he cupped my hands with his own and said in a low voice, "Such strong hands!" I replied not, not knowing what to say and expecting him to move off. But he lingered and asked me desultory questions. Was I visiting? Was it my first visit? Did I like Venice? Was I English? Was I American? Did I speak Italian? French? I answered one question after t'other as politely as possible until he finally astounded me by asking how much I charged for an hour of my time.

I thought naturally, that he meant as a protector, and said that I was already employed, by a lady, who was at the moment up the stairs at dinner with her friends.

He then laughed and said, "Why not earn a bit extra on the side?" and splayed out a handful of Italian lira at me. When I looked surprised, he pointed to some bushes near a ruin of a wall and said, "You need do nothing but stand still. And your lady need not know a thing."

At which I still must have looked oddly at him, since I understood not how I could protect him and her at the same time.

Just then two older women passed, and I distinctly heard one of them utter, "*Non te paura, Cara! Suoni* ma *due homosessuale!*"

Even I understand by now enough Italian to know she said her friend ought not be afraid, that we were only two——! You see, I cannot write the word in English.

The other fellow only laughed, but I turned to him and quite angrily said, "Go away! Now! Go!" And lest he not do so, I stumbled down through the two steps into the large wooden door of the *palazzo*. There I awakened an ancient fellow and his smoke-grey cat, which he resembles closely. He bade me sit upon some large old chair to await my mistress.

I think even in that musky, dim foyer, and even though he

fell to sleep again on the instant, the redness of my face and the depth of my dishonour might be easily ascertained. I sat there in a great stew for some time, I can assure you.

Can you not write to her and hurry her forward? Write in care of myself if needed, at the Post Restante, Venice. Or have her friends write to her, especially that one friend who must await her arrival so greatly that he has helped us all in so many ways?

This I beg of you. For her, for my, for all of our sakes.

Stephen Undershot

To: The Honourable Lady Caroline-Ann Augusta
The Glebe, Ravenglass
Broughton, England

27 October 188—

My Dear Lady Caroline-Ann,
    This Venetian respite does me good. But soon we'll move onward.
    Onward too, my history. The very next day, Alfred Benoit Davison left his card inside the foyer at Ravenglass Manor, and two days later he was invited for tea the following afternoon.
    As our summer weather continued warm, we decided to serve tea out of doors. By this time, I had been left to my own devices for a long time, with more than sufficient capital for most sorts of folly. Enlisting Farnsworthy and his lads' aid, I had at last completed the Italian garden behind the house on a rather grand scale, à la Vitruvius. Having seen reproductions of some of Mr. Alma-Tadema's paintings of antiquity and especially of Italy, I had commissioned there a central *terrazzo* in a white marble shot through with verdigris, and with picturesque awnings held up by slender metal rods against the sun, easily allowing in those sea breezes that make our peninsula so accommodating.
    There did Mr. Davison enjoy his first tea at the manor. Present besides myself was Miss Cresswell and an old school friend, Mr. Homer Eagles, visiting from Lancaster-town, where he had become a mercer of note and even some fortune. He kept me up to date with many of the townspeople and farther-flung locals, as Miss Cresswell did with those nearer.
    Unlike his dishevelled self upon the strand, Mr. Davison was dressed as appropriately as possible in white flannels and bi-chromatic lightweight shoes, carrying a sky-blue boater, and matching gloves of extremely loose meshwork, a gift he believed tailored in Italy. His shirt was ecru linen with the palest stripes of blue, and his cravat was a mere cross of silver satin held with a brass pin matching those linking his shirt cuffs. I could easily see that Mr. Eagles, who'd also arrived "well turned out," as the saying has it, was impressed. At one point, the men stood aside and I could hear him asking after the source of several items of clothing, which apparently

hailed from places as far flung as Florence and Philadelphia, and might even have come from the Antipodes.

Miss Cresswell turned her nose up at Mr. Davison on the instant, showing me her own intense interest, for he appeared this day all that she had formerly said he would be at that unimpressive first meeting, a young buck in the rotogravure come to life.

As for myself, by now you must know me well enough, Lady Caroline, to recognize that I am never put off by any Adonis, but merely await his imperfections to show themselves. Mr. Davison showed none that afternoon.

Unless one counted his referring back so often to his own scientific interests, he was a perfect guest. He treated Mr. Eagles as his equal, although clearly he was only a tradesman, he was solicitous to Miss Cresswell, who eventually melted her iceberg under such attentions, and he paid myself the immense compliment of assuming I was as intrigued with the bird life of Morecombe Bay as he was himself.

"Tell us, Mr. Davison," Miss Cresswell said, upon filling our cups with a pungent Assam once again and passing lemon-cakes of her own devising, "how can a person of such evident intelligence be enraptured by our feathered friends?"

"Do you yourself never watch the local bird life?" he asked back.

"Naturally."

"Then you are aware of their intelligence!"

"Intelligence? In birds. Should I not be insulted then to be called bird-brained?" she said, making that face which showed me she was being witty.

"Perhaps only if the speaker is as ignorant as yourself of the *nature* of birds' intelligence," he said, "Which is admittedly limited, but concrete!"

I knew she hated being thought ignorant in any subject, so here I interrupted. "What exactly is it that you study in our local birds?"

"Everything," he replied with great earnestness. "First, how many there are and of what types."

"Black-headed gulls and herring gulls," I began.

"There's those Kittiwake Isle gulls too," Mr. Eagles continued.

"Terns and frigate birds," Miss Cresswell added.

"And so many more," Mr. Davison said. "Like these ringed ouzels, as well as shelducks and teals, and the occasional stork and, of course, curlews. These are their spring and summer grounds as they migrate south in winter. Some of these very birds have been seen as far south as Gibraltar and Morocco. By far, the gulls are the most interesting ones, as they are the most social."

"Wanting their tea at four of the clock?" Miss Cresswell asked.

"Wanting their own mate, which they then recognize, for they mate annually and are loyal to a fault. Wanting their own nest and stoutly defending their territory. Wanting their own family, for both male and female ensure its growth and nurture. This is already known to ornithologists. My study is more specific. I study the entire annual cycle from when they arrive to how and when they choose a mate and a nesting ground, and how they roost, until their chicks are fledged and they fly off south again."

"Ensuring that you will remain hereabouts beyond the summer?" Miss Cresswell stated, with, I thought, some trepidation.

"Ensuring that I shall return upon occasion after the summer when my studies are more specific, and ensuring that I shall then impose upon Lady Lillian's generosity at tea time."

"But...why?" Mr. Eagles blurted out.

"You mean why do I study these birds?"

Embarrassed by his outburst, the mercer merely nodded, and filled his mouth with cake to block any further indiscretion.

"Why, to increase the store of human knowledge! That is the true and only function of science, after all," Mr. Davison said, and in that moment, the afternoon sunlight shafted beneath our canopy in such a way as to illuminate his face with a peculiar stamp of almost classical nobility. I could see Miss Cresswell turn her face away, Mr. Eagles stare, and I, hoping to be a good hostess, said, "You must then promise to tell us all that you learn, Mr. Davison, at the end of the summer."

"I was hoping, Lady Lillian," he replied with a laugh, "that I might report to yourselves on a more frequent schedule."

"If only to enjoy such a tea and cake," Miss Cresswell put in impishly. "Since we all know that the vittles where you are lodging cannot be but barren stuff."

"I readily admit the oat cakes require actual dipping into the tea dish before they are edible," he said. "While the bread baked is of so hard a crust that it requires dipping in harder liquor before it is palatable."

"You shall then come to tea again," I declared. "As well as to dinner and any luncheon wherein a young man may be required as escort or to even out the number. And you know, dear old friend," I said, turning to Mr. Eagles, "you are ever welcome."

When the two men had left, Mr. Eagles by pony cart and Mr. Davison by bicycle, with his trouser cuffs rakishly rolled up to his ankles, I turned to Miss Cresswell, who like myself was waving them away.

"You see, he is not such a savage after all. He never once dipped his shirt front in the gooseberry custard."

She merely bit her lip, as though unwilling to speak her mind. That was such a rarity in this lady that I must laugh and wonder.

I little thought on this visit from Mr. Davison until somewhat later, although Miss Cresswell did refer to it in future, saying, "He had already begun to work in his hooks and claws, like some exotically plumed bird of prey."

The reason being that it was not the young scientist but instead my former schoolmate who carried important information. He had arrived earlier and assured me of news upon two matters: first, my brother Rudolph and second, and more surprising still, that he had report of Mute Matthew, who had vanished from Ravenglass some nineteen years earlier on the night of the old earl's death.

You have read, Lady Caroline-Ann, of the breach with my brother at the time of my marriage. He was dead set against it, and for the first few years, I did all in my power to repair that breach. But as the years wore on and Rudolph's prediction became truer, I began to hold back. By this year, it was evident he had known the character of my husband at a very young age far better than I ever could. What was it he had said then? That I would be thrown aside when I was no longer needed by Lord Roland? Surely that is what had happened.

My pride and my unwillingness to let my brother see his omen made fact kept me from him, albeit it was rare enough that he returned to England and then for only short periods of time.

So long as my father lived on, ever more quiet, outside Ulverston with his new little wife, Rudolph repaired to them when upon shore leave. Never to me. From them, therefore, I learned he had risen at first very quickly due to the favour of one officer in particular, and then more gradually in our Queen's Navy, attaining the rank of commodore, albeit never actually captain of his own ship. He retired after less than two decades, and he did not return to

England to wed and settle down as did most men of his age, station, and pension. But instead, he took on commercial duties as first mate and later as captain out of the West Indies, where he had long served, and then once our father passed away, in the East Indies, from which one day he would not return.

Rudolph never had any companion to our knowledge, but one reason why Navy men did not return home was that they did have foreign born, brown, yellow, and black-skinned wives and preferred them to the home-grown variety. Whenever my stepmother joked with him, Rudolph would always say he had "learned his lesson in love early and hard, and would never tread those paths again," which I never understood until much later on.

He was berthed and changing ships in Singapore colony when the former Mrs. Cupp and I buried my father. She remained in their little cottage, as my husband had other matters than that to attend to now and let her be. Had he not, I would have found her other lodgings. Via his own and George the Fifth's efforts and manoeuvrings, my husband had by then ascended to the starry position of Lord of the British Exchequer. It was my stepmother, then, who reported his increasingly infrequent visits. When she suddenly died, I assumed he no longer stopped at our neighbourhood at all.

So it was that I listened hard to Mr. Eagles when he said to me very quietly, where no one else could hear us, "I fear, Lady Lillian, to bring you disturbing news." When I had asked him to continue, he said, "A regular customer who spends some months in the Far East returned with a tale of your brother at trial of law for his life in Rangoon City."

My heart leapt in my chest like some frightened animal. I barely could utter, "At trial for his life? Upon what charge?"

"The charge of conspiring to murder. The victim was said to be his rival in the affections of a young native person. Or so was it bruited about."

You may imagine my next question. "With what result?"

"He was acquitted." We both sighed in relief. "But my interlocutor believed from other tales and rumours that he gathered in that city that your brother was very likely guilty of the act, for he has altered much of late."

I could feel tears begin to creep down my cheeks at this awful news.

"Did he say my brother then is so lost a cause?"

"I'm afraid so, Lady Lillian. I would hesitate to welcome him into my establishment in Lancaster."

"But...if he was acquitted?"

"Lady Lillian, I have many young women coming into my shop and working for me whose parents most particularly look to me for their morals and behaviour."

Before I could respond more, he went on. "This news shall go no farther, Lady Lillian. I assure you. Only you must know of it all. In the event—"

"In the event that my brother returns?"

"In that extremely very unlikely event, yes, lady."

Regarding Matthew, however, Mr. Eagles's report was almost nearly equally opposite. It mostly derived from our other school friend, Mr. Eldon Creff, who had apprenticed to a mason and then left our shire to find work farther and farther south until he had all but circled London-town. This is what Eldon told Homer, who then related it to me.

Matthew's voice restored, his manner and person ennobled by prolonged contact with the old earl as well as via his now rich clothing, Matthew had used the money I'd given him and travelled to London. Once there, he'd settled in the city home of one of those odd couples the old earl knew well, and who had often asked Matthew to visit.

There, by small degrees, he had ingratiated himself to the family, which, surprisingly, seemed to lack any poor relations. When that host baronet, only a bit younger than Matthew's old master, developed a catarrh of especial severity, the loving young man had cared for him as though he were his own father. This earned him an inheritance, as well as bonding him to that eccentric new baronetcy which also lacked a younger brother to its newly minted lord. Papers of adoption were drawn up after the fact and somehow or other made legal, so that should the new baronet and his single male heir somehow die out, the estates would not go to strangers living far off in Northumberland but instead to someone they knew. In this manner, Matthew gained several learned tutors and a noble-born brother, and had been taken along with him a grand tour of Europe. He also gained a calling in the Church of England as well as a new name, and eventually a young wife and a small clerisy in Suffolk.

After all that tragic and happy catching-up, you will well understand, Lady Caroline-Ann, what fresh air Mr. Davison, with his eternal birds, proved to be when he arrived a bit later that afternoon looking so...

I am interrupted by news.

Lillian

27 Octobr

We are here still in The Venis

I have late to-nite espy the Lord's Man. That pretty, bad one.

He pretend to fondle a boy and not see Her Ladyshippe as we pass on Fondaco as they call here.

The boy too I have espy here be-for. Out the side. Upon the street. Many places.

Why wait you?

Must I wait too? Or go?

Tell me PLees.

Henriette

To: The Honourable Lady Caroline-Ann Augusta
The Glebe, Ravenglass
Broughton, England

30 October 188—

My Dear Lady Caroline-Ann,
We have left Venice by short stages quite suddenly and are proceeding via a tiny railroad of only four cars drawn by a minuscule steam engine onward. It goes slowly at times, although the land is mostly flat. It also stops often enough, seemingly without reason, unless to look at cows is a proper reason, and stays still for long enough periods like this one, to allow me to write.

I have come to think that that my young companion, whom I had taken for a Frenchwoman, and to whom I spoke naught but French, is instead a native of this land, perhaps of this very country-side, as she stares out at it for hours at a time, silent and wistful. When I asked her once, she looked at me in pretended horror and insisted she was *une fille de la cite*.

The decision to leave Venice was mine, furthered by my companions' daily misgivings and more particularly by friends awaiting us farther along our road.

I might have remained in that blessed city of canals far longer, but my watcher-over was indeed correct in believing us to be more at risk there than elsewhere, given the narrowness of the *calles*, the preponderance and thickness of the fogs during the night hours, and the general dilapidation of the local populace, whose fortunes have steadily plummeted since Napoleon conquered the city three-quarters of a century ago and then let it fall into non-French hands. My dinner hostess, the charming American *principessa*, assured me that she only travelled *en retinue*, since crime is rampant and often senseless and foreigners are often the choicest victims.

I return now to the events at Ravenglass: I shall never return there alive.

The young scientist continued to visit at afternoon teas whenever they were of a non-private nature. He was, I'm afraid, subjected to the meretricious company of Rev. Rose and his wife a few times, the latter continually irritating us all by asking Alfred if he was related to the Cheshire Davisons or the Yorkshire Davisons or the Cantabrigian Davisons until the scientist declared his family was all and ever from Kent since the invasion by sea of the Celts in the year six hundred and two.

Also, and more to his liking, we had the company of Mr. Homer Eagles, who was at the time more often about the neighbourhood of the manor. The mercer had taken a local house in the town and was planning to buy up land and erect himself an estate worthy of his bank accounts. Naturally, Alfred Benoit Davison would leave upon his bicycle from those teas with extra cake and sometimes other food from our large and under-utilised pantry where, even with our largish staff, waste still occurred.

Only one dinner did he attend, and that at Mr. Eagles's leased house, where I attempted to introduce him to some of the very few acceptable younger ladies of the town, all the while being certain to compare them unfavourably with Miss Cresswell.

I was pleased to notice then how, since that first tea, she had softened considerably in her tone of voice and attitude toward not only Alfred but toward all of us. Surely that reduction of sharpness of sight and of her need to voice her insights must, I believed, be a sign of her being, if not in love, then at least most interested in Mr. Davison. This misconception, for it soon proved to be one, had one crucial drawback for myself. I rather relaxed when I ought to have been alert, and where I believed myself to be acting as a sort of benevolent substitute mother toward him, he took it wholly otherwise.

Thinking back as I have often done in the years since, I've concluded that one visit in particular was the turning point which at the time I completely missed.

It occurred almost a month after that first encounter, when during tea at the manor—albeit not outside in the garden, as the summer had returned to its usual state of being cool and damp—Mr. Davison proposed another visit to the little peninsula inlet of Morecombe Bay, this one to be tour-guided by himself.

Earlier, I'd had Samson and his fellows go out to the strands with Mr. Davison and quite publicly post it against trespassing along a five-mile stretch.

Rumours in the town rose on the instant, such as a shipwreck had occurred carrying a plague; one of the feared black-wrack tides of medieval times had returned, and the beach was littered with dead fish and sea mammals. We chose to correct nothing anyone said.

So there, one afternoon in mid-July were myself, Miss Cresswell, and Mr. Eagles being led about carefully and in a low voice by Alfred, who showed us the varied colonies and hatching areas.

Rather foolishly, I was immensely pleased by this outing, for wasn't I, after all, owner or at least co-owner of it all, anyway?

No matter. I felt I was seeing it all for the first time through Alfred's eyes. Facing south and east, we could make out over the seashore not only the top towers of Lancaster Cathedral, but also through some optical effect of the flat and nearly unmoving tides between, peaks of the Pennines and the Lake Country.

"A magnificently pretty picture-book," Mr. Eagles said for us all. But following that, he and Miss Cresswell did linger behind. All of my constant calling to them to hurry and catch up the rest of that afternoon did no good. That, too, I ought to have noticed sooner.

Instead, I let myself be led away by Alfred.

"They nest so closely together," I said.

"For greater protection. And because arrayed in such number, each has a lesser chance of being attacked by a predator. Do men act any differently?"

"Yet they defend their tiny little territories so valiantly."

"Professor Jansen of the Norwegian Institute believes that is a type of socializing for the males. The females only join in when the fight worsens."

"Where have we seen that?" I asked with a laugh.

"In your people's cottages, doubtless."

"Doubtless, but also in the so-called best of homes."

"But here, in truth, it's all gull cries and preening and facing off upon each other. More posturing than pecking. Little real violence is ever done."

"Unlike our manor lads brawling at a publican's. Not but one of them under the age of twenty but has visited our sponsored new medical office in town because of some brawl or other."

"Some of the black-headed gulls arrive here at their nest already mated. They often do so while flying from their winter sojourn," he explained, "while others will wait and find mates here at the nesting grounds. As you may imagine, there is much gull-calling and posturing. Much chasing after females by males, and posturing and then hesitation, pretending indifference and then flying off, returning yet showing uneasiness and sometimes even displaying fear. And then it all begins again until the female shows a distinct preference for one male over another."

I laughed. "It sounds like a provincial ball." I had officiated at one or another over the years. "How do they know how to choose a nesting spot?"

"I've seen them hovering, circling, hours at a time, the male and the female. First he, then she drops down for a visit, then off again. This sometimes happens a half dozen times."

"As Mr. Eagle hovers and circles, searching for his own nesting ground," I said still full of mirth. "I fear Lord Roland will have to part with some recently acquired land, or my old friend will not rest."

"Mr. Eagles appears to be hunting for both a nesting ground and a mate simultaneously," Alfred said, looking behind us to where the two were very slow in catching up.

This surprised me, and I was a bit shrill in urging the two to join us.

"Surely you are wrong, Mr. Davison. Miss Cresswell was especially eager to join *your tour* today."

"What could I possibly offer a lady like Miss Cresswell?"

"Surely you are modest, because you are fishing for a compliment," I replied.

"Black-headed gulls fish, Lady Lillian. Not I. Her condition in life would be no better than it is now if she were married to me."

"But her station would!"

"If one is to believe the current literature, it is American girls who seek to better their station and British girls who prefer to better their fortunes."

"I am offended for my friend," I said.

"You need not be. I applaud her good sense."

The object of our discussion and her companion had just then arrived at where we had stopped. Miss Cresswell thrust a parasol into the sand and said, "I declare this spot to be for England, and I require instant settling lest I fall over. Do you not agree, Mr. Eagles? These two are clearly in training for some arctic expedition where they shall trudge over frozen wastes weeks on end."

Her wit and good cheer saved the situation and did anodize my annoyance. We all sat then and there and partook of our refreshment.

Later on, I heard the mercer asking Alfred what we had been speaking of.

"Mating!" he said, and our two companions flushed rather suddenly.

"Among black-headed gulls," I added.

Could it be, I wondered, they had reached an agreement while lagging?

A second such inspection tour took place two and a half weeks later. We entered from a different place, as the several colonies were in different stages of breeding, hatching, and fledging their young than before.

Again, Miss Cresswell joined us, only this time Mr. Eagles did not.

He had arrived the previous day to confirm that a neglected property north of Ravenglass some twenty miles was his choice. He asked me to look over the letter his clerk-attorney had drafted to purchase it from my husband. I did not comment upon their decision to several times mention our mutual past as children, but I did comment that the price paid would be significant to my husband, who seemed always short of pelf. I said Mr. Eagle ought to, in addition to that, remark his unquestioning support at the hustings once elections were held. This because Lord Roland's inherited holdings had, through some machinations that I did not understand, become a double political constituency for both the Houses of Lords and Commons. This newly sold land was part of a good-sized Rotten-Borough where the election of a Ravenglass lord was *not* already ensured, as was his other one. I knew from Lord Robert and Astabella Vanbrugh that the House of Commons was where my husband now sought power over the bureaucracies and eventually influence over the throne. I said so to Homer Eagles.

"I can see now, lady, why your husband values you," my old friend commented, little knowing Roland and I seldom if ever even corresponded on this or any other matter, and that I was looking out for Mr. Eagles.

Miss Cresswell had been present then, and pleased as punch at how matters were evolving. It was she the next day who proudly told Mr. Davison of this little exchange, to which the scientist replied, "The damned fool!"

"Mr. Eagles?" she asked, mortified.

"No, his lordship," and then stalked off a bit on his own, not returning until he was himself again.

And that, Miss Cresswell later described as "the moment her

ladyship was first so lightly knotted in a tether that none of us noticed it."

The train has started up again. This note is left at the next station.

Lillian

To: The Very Reverend Jasper Horace Quill
The British Church at Campofieri
Town of Fiesoli
Province of Toscana

29 November 188—

Dear Sir,
A most astonishing and awful occurrence! I almost do not know how to write it.

We had returned from the main *piazza*, where my lady repairs daily here in Venice, and where I fear by the minute to have her discovered. She has encountered a little group of seemingly well-bred Americans who either live here part of the year or visit for lengthy periods. The scribbler I mentioned before is the main male member of this seemingly innocuous entourage. A woman his own age, who my lady tells me is also a well-known writer, is his female counterpart. She is in some way related to a novelist of some repute whose books my friends and I hid to read under covers in our school dormitories, all about American Indians, and the British and French who lived among them—a Mr. James Fenimore Cooper.

Henriette, the little French (?) wench, also enjoyed going to St. Mark's *piazza*, as she may flirt to her heart's content with whatever manner of person may come her way while the lady is distracted by her literary company. Since the incident with the note I intercepted, I now have to keep my eyes more closely on her as well with the proviso that she not see me watching her.

All of which is guaranteed to irritate my already worsening dyspepsia, which has struck repeatedly. I can barely tolerate most of the food served and am reduced to eating their ubiquitous *macaroni* with a little butter and salt or their rice dishes, surprisingly varied and also bland enough.

The several *ristorantes* here fortunately keep a loo open behind their kitchen, and I had been forced to use this commode yet again when I heard a dialogue beyond the flimsy door, recognizing the voice of my lady's companion.

"Where are you?" she chastised someone. "I have been five days waiting you."

"'Ow in blazes am I to know you 'ave come 'ere? You said you wuz all off to Bolzano."

Here I peeped out the crack of the door, where I saw the French tart and an Englishman of the lowest ilk, given his speech, but dressed well and with a little European beard called a goatee. He carried a walking stick with a fine carved head of silver.

"Did I not, as told, leave a note at ticket booth two of the terminus?" she now asked.

"I found no note at any place agreed upon," he replied. "Why do yer t'ink I dare accost yer 'ere out in the open?"

"And the other one?"

"'E's here too. But e 'aves not the latest word from 'im! That I 'ave."

"Will you then meet up and tell me how it is to be done?" she asked in a low voice.

"We shall plan a time on 'er usual route from the 'ouse to Sain' Mark's. You shall distract the big lout. If 'e gives yer trouble, shout out and one of us'll dispatch him to his maker. Then you'll push 'er grace in our direction. We'll take care a the rest."

"Yes. That plan is best," she said.

Then they were gone. I waited not very long to exit and followed them some yards behind but always in sight. As they entered the *ristorante*, he went left and she right. I followed him with my eyes for a while as he sat and ordered himself a lemon fizz. She returned to my lady, who had not seemed to have missed her.

That night, as I walked my lady home from that American writer's home not far from where she had gone to dinner, I disclosed Henrietta's second passport.

"Why would she need two passports?" her ladyship asked.

"If she is known to have committed a crime and wishes her presence not known."

"Ah! I was afraid of something of this sort."

"How did you come by this maid?" I asked.

"Fortuitously," the lady admitted. "At the time, much that was fortuitous was occurring, our own connexion, for example. I assumed she was another boon."

"I fear she may have been *placed* in such a way as to *seem* a boon." I then told her of the note I had read and what I had then overheard, all of it to Henriette's discredit, if that is even her name. "Three confederates against two is not a number I am at all pleased with, lady."

"Nor I. I will talk to her tonight."

Two hours later, the lady flew into my room. "Quickly. She is fleeing. Quickly."

Still in my shirt sleeves, I rushed out and down the stairs to the lower floor and courtyard. I could hear Henriette shouting and someone answering.

By the time I got there, the Italian concierge had relented, and I could see him escorting the traitress to the front door. It is kept locked and bolted after the sun has set, as is usual in this place.

"She denied nothing," I heard the lady on the stairs behind me saying. "When I faced her with it, she denied nothing. She simply ran out."

I shouted to the concierge not to let her go, but I was too late. I reached the doorway and shoved him roughly aside to see Henriette rush out on the street such as there is and spin around as if expecting to see someone there. Spotting a gondola and oarsmen coming, she shouted to him in Italian.

I reached her before the boat could slip into place, and she pulled herself from out of my grasp with unexpected strength, turning to make a great leap for the approaching gondola, all the while shouting and waving at the *gondoliere*, yelling for him to not dock but instead go.

She miscalculated, fell short of it, and instead struck her head on the boat's high side at its rear. I heard the dull report of her head striking the wood and, in horror, I witnessed her turn about, her eyes to Heaven, before she sank beneath the craft. Behind me, the lady and concierge both cried out.

The *gondoliere* dove into the canal where he thought she must be, and he was under for some minutes. I reached for the unmanned boat, shoved it into a berth, and fastened it, so he would not strike it himself coming back up.

We saw his head up away from the dock and his hand pointing down, then he dove again. When he came up this time, Henriette was in his arms. Myself and the concierge aided him in getting her small body onto the dock, and then helped him also. He went into the house for a blanket and brandy against the water's coldness.

"I told her she was forgiven," the lady said over and over, as we attempted to pump the water out of the small, chilled breast. Too late, however, since clearly the blow to her head, a deep gash already bloodied, was what had undone her.

"She was undressing my hair," my lady continued, her voice hollow with dread. "She stood dumbstruck by what I told her I knew. Seeing that, I said to her, 'Stay with us. You are safe with us!' But she said to me, 'What will he do? What he will do now?' Then she ran from the room madly and I called to you. Why would she do such a thing, Mr. Undershot? Why? When I offered her haven!"

"Not to disparage the dead, my lady, but she was a bad one. She and those she dealt with. I believe she wisely enough knew what to expect, and that she feared for her life if she could not be relied upon to deliver you."

"Everything he touches," my lady said then. "Everything! He turns into something evil or dead!" She looked at me. "So far, thank God, you have held steadfast."

And I thought, for how long, Undershot? For how long?

Well, sir, I can tell you we had several hours of it with the local *polizia*, who luckily enough were headed by a worldly, easy-going old fellow.

"We see this often, *Dama*," he said to my lady, attempting to comfort her, though she barely listened, she was still so much in her own dark thoughts. "They meet a young man. They think they are in love as never before. Then they are betrayed!" He threw a hand into the air in a theatrically, fatally useless gesture.

I still have her note. And now we are very much warned. I doubly so.

Stephen Undershot

To: The Honourable Lady Caroline-Ann Augusta
The Glebe, Ravenglass
Broughton, England

1 November 188—

My Dear Lady Caroline-Ann,
   Our little train rattled onward from Mestre to Padua and Padua to Rovigo and Rovigo to Ferrara across the ancient, gigantic plains of the Po River, as vast I think as anything in nature but the Austrian Alps that I have ever seen, and as imposing, in its contrasting manner.
   From Ferrara, we rattled on to Bologna, where at last the flat lands conclude in the loveliest and most harmonious of fertile, agricultural beauty spots. We spent one night in Bologna, a lovely city, medieval in parts and older than any I think I have seen in our homeland. We then were moved onto a different, so called narrow gauge rail and another sort of train. So we began rising into the foothills of those very mountains which, when we had awakened, took up our entire view from the bedroom windows of our Bolognese hotel, stretching from one side to another.
   Up here, our speed is reduced as we have risen by corkscrew and double ess turns higher and higher until below and behind we can make out our recent train tracks as nothing but a double metal glitter in the now deep green hills and bare brown escarpments. Our train takes us by the least altitudinous of treks, or so am I informed. Seldom do we rise above one thousand five hundred feet above the sea level, yet it seems a strange new land we inhabit. Because of the slowness of ascent, we have already stopped two nights in tiny, cold towns which I believe barely existed before the iron monster of modern travel arrived to give them life and their goat-herding inhabitants newer employment as station masters, linemen, ticket sellers, innkeepers, and tea shop owners.
   On the morrow, I am assured, we begin our descent into the flowered valley of the Arno, and then to our next, most welcome, resting place.
   If naught else, these past sixty-odd days have given birth to the most wonderful external alternations of my life. Lucky is the British young man of means who is so often allowed such a journey early in life, and unfortunate are we poor British young women who

are most often not. But while I have caught in turn the brass, the silver, and even the golden rings on this carousel, soon too, one ring beyond value is due to me.

If I go on and on like a travelogue scribbler, it is because I am putting off a sadness also to report—the loss of my young female companion, who was discovered by my sentinel to be in my husband's pay and confederate with yet another stalker. I attempted to regain her confidence, but she would not listen and ran herself out of my room, out of the building in some harum-scarum attempt to escape punishment, I must suppose. It ended fatally for her. Now just my man and I travel on.

❖

I had, I believe, arrived at that moment in my life where despite having lived nearly four decades, I was still a girl in my mind and my knowledge of the world. And this despite what I had witnessed of what had happened to those about me: the old earl, Lady Bella, Mute Matthew, my mother and father and Henry Stanforth, Mrs. Cupp, Astabella and Lady Julia, Lord Robert, and my brother Rudolph. All of their histories ought to have been significant lessons, but evidently they were not sufficient for my hard-headedness. I was as deeply asleep as the little princess in the fairy story, and then all of a sudden, I woke up.

Three events occurred, one rather momentous, the other two very small indeed, but I get ahead of myself.

We continued all that summer and early autumn to observe the various seabird colonies, Alfred Davison, Mr. Eagles, Miss Cresswell, and myself. At times, although rarely, other company joined us at these forays to the seashore. Mind you, we stood many dozens of feet apart from the birds, peering at them through field glasses and, at times, settling behind makeshift blinds composed of white-painted fisherman's nets to resemble natural rocks, as well as other more ingenious objects of Alfred 's construction, which the birds soon became accustomed to seeing, and thus disregarded.

Oddly enough, it was at this time that my school friend Georgiana Milton decided to pay a long-overdue visit to Ravenglass.

I first supposed, and Miss Cresswell tartly offered her agreement, that Georgiana did so to gauge the effect of all the talk about herself and Lord Roland upon the manor and its denizens—meaning myself.

Like Astabella Vanbrugh, she had remained unwed and had grown immensely wealthy. Unlike our friend upon her own arrival two years previous, Georgiana arrived in state, I must admit, with what she however alluded to as a "much reduced travel retinue of only four servants," and she almost immediately told me she was planning to marry. She admitted the nuptials were of greater political than personal importance, as she did have nieces and nephews aplenty to leave her fortune to. But she was hesitant to have it divided in a single generation.

The gentleman to be so munificently affianced by her already possessed several children of his own by a long-dead wife, and also what Georgiana referred to as "a small fortune, a larger intelligence, even greater experience of life, and an enormous heart." He also stood for a large manufacturing borough in the House of Commons, which contained most of those factories from which she derived her vast income. A borough, I must add, not yet gathered into my husband's party, which this alliance would thus help to enfold.

She produced a sizable diamond beautifully set and attached to a string of pearls—representing the proof of engagement—and at the end of a week's visit, she produced the gentleman himself, Mr. Gilbert Brewster, whom I liked on the instant.

"One supposes," Miss Cresswell saucily opined, well out of our guest's hearing that first surprising night of her visit, "that the gentleman accommodates himself to infidelity, since the going rate is forty thousand pounds per annum. I know I could bring myself to do so."

Somehow or other—had she spies like Astabella?—that quip arrived at Georgiana's ears, and she accosted the two of us at breakfast in my rooms the following morning to demand that we repeat whatever libel we had heard lest it damage her repute with her fiancé.

She found us open-mouthed at this astonishing request, and it was Miss Cresswell, blushing redder than the damask curtains, who then quietly uttered, "It is known, miss, that your friendship with Lord Roland has for years been beyond that required for political expediency."

"What? Nonsense!" Georgiana laughed. "Rubbish! Poppycock!" she said rapidly and with, I thought, some real relief in her voice. "It's all utter trash. Lies! Smoke and persiflage!"

"Truly?" I had to ask.

"I said it was, didn't I? Lord Roland has never so much as kissed my lips."

"Then what woman is he unloyal to Lady Lillian with?" Miss Cresswell asked for the two of us.

"Absolutely none that I am aware of, and I am about Hanover Square all of the time, privy to the comings and goings there."

Later on in the day once we were alone, Georgiana did admit to me that we had her anxious for a short while since she had an extremely covert *affair de coeur*. She admitted it had been with a very discreet, rising young party member of no especial significance yet, but to be watched. I believed her.

"Anyway," she said, "I am certain to others it looked as utterly innocent as your taking such an interest in that young scientist, Mr. Davison."

"My interest *is* utterly innocent," I said.

"Not if *he* could help it."

"What do you mean?"

"Don't be naïve, Lillian. You've toyed with men long enough to know when they are wrapped about your little finger."

This struck me as greatly unfair until she said, "Have you not for decades danced a gigue about Robert of Blackburn?" At which point, I was forced to be silent. But she continued.

"It *is* achievable, you understand, Lillian, what I've done. So long as everyone is kept looking at the *surface* of the relationship and believing like yourself that I am interested in another man! It's achievable so long as you can maintain that surface *quite eventful* enough. All will feel in the know and none will bother to look beyond and see the true connexion occurring *beneath* the surface. That is how I and my Sidney were able to effect it for nearly a decade. In public, we would quarrel mightily over political trifles. He would appear to drop me or I him, for tumultuous weeks at a time. There would be equally public reconciliations with never more than a handshake to seal it. It was quite the most amusing political spectacle in Britain, and the popular press ate it up like spicy sausages. They never knew we were virtually husband and wife! I have since heard rumoured other such goings-on, of even greater endurance than ours."

"I am ever the student and yourself the teacher."

"*Your* interest might be innocent, your Alfred's is not."

"Join us at the strand and see for yourself," I said. And so she did, she and her husband to be. As my girl was brushing my hair before bed that night, Georgiana knocked and entered and replaced her behind me.

"You are both innocent of any indiscretion," she said. "He, however, is smitten with you. And I swear I have seen him before."

"At his university?"

"I have no recollection where."

"He is not uncommon looking?"

"Bosh! He is uncommonly *good to look at*, and I am certain I have seen him before. I simply don't recall where. I have seen *so very* many young men, among them *more than a few* uncommonly good to look at, that I'm of no use to you."

Unknowingly, she had been of great use to me.

No sooner was Georgiana gone from Ravenglass and I walking upon the inlet shore with Alfred again than I repeated her words in order to gauge his reaction, including her assessment that he was uncommonly good to look at.

"I had hoped..." He seemed unable to complete his sentence and tried another tack altogether. "Women of the world like Miss Milton are forever the greatest mystery to me. I don't know how to respond to anything they say."

"Very prettily avoided," I responded. "No bullfighter was ever quite so adroit with his cape."

"What would you have me say? That Miss Milton is not wrong? I will, if I for a moment thought you would allow me to do so."

"By now you must realize how generous and liberal a lady I am, despite my advanced age and hoary title. You may say whatever you wish."

"So you may laugh at me?" he asked, and I thought his voice strained.

"I didn't plan to do so unless you planned on being particularly amusing."

"I'm sure it will seem infantile and infinitely amusing to you." He was very red faced as he turned on me and almost angrily said, "Well, if you insist upon stepping all over me, then..." He dropped his collection kits upon the sands, got himself upon one knee, and reached a hand out to me.

"Surely, Alfred, you know I would never dream of stepping all over you. Whatever are you thinking?"

"I am thinking," he said, "That, like all women, you wish to make a fool out of a man. I accede to being made so."

"I thought you had a higher regard for me. For all women."

"Then my suit has merit in your eyes?"

Just then Miss Creswell and Mr. Eagles approached, and it was the latter who, seeing Alfred on his knees, asked, "What did you lose? Shall I help you search?"

Thus, I found out that Georgiana had seen what I had not—or at least what I'd kept myself from seeing. Alfred did indeed care for me.

The next five days proved stormy ones outdoors, and they allowed me to keep Alfred at a distance and at the same time to meditate upon my situation. After only two days, I found I missed him. Upon the third day, Miss Cresswell—who visited daily when she did not sleep at Ravenglass—asked if I was not going to have our regular tea with visitors, which would include Alfred and her Mr. Eagles. I invited him but not Alfred. At that occasion, I heard them wonder where Alfred had gone off to. From Jannequin, I later heard that tea cakes and other sundries from the kitchen had been packed for Alfred, and as he wasn't at our tea, one of the garden lads assigned to carry them to him in the village. For that I was grateful.

Alfred sensed that a crisis had been attained, and he did not attempt to communicate with me. This continued until Sunday sermon, when lo and behold, there he was, in a rearmost guest pew of our little church when Miss Cresswell, Mr. Eagles, and I walked out under the tepid sponsorship of her buxom sister, the vicar's wife.

Alfred said hello sheepishly and thanked me for sending on the extra tea-things.

"Mr. Davison seemed pale and somewhat crestfallen," Mr. Eagles opined during our ride home to Ravenglass for Sunday dinner. "Do you think he has come down with a fever?"

"It's more likely one of his herring colonies has come down with a fever," Miss Cresswell suggested, "since that is all he thinks of, day and night." I had to kiss her cheek for her wit and quick thinking.

"If he *were* ill, he could benefit from a hearty broth and a roasted joint," Mr. Eagles went on. I knew he and Alfred got on well. He already missed his conversation and would do so again at dinner in one hour's time at Ravenglass.

"Then the garden lad will bring him portions of both broth and mutton," I said with finality.

"You are too good, Homer!" Miss Cresswell said with real pleasure. "Thinking of your less fortunate friends." The manner in which she took his arm and held it somehow told me that, indeed, they had arrived at an understanding.

After our dinner and our indoors walk throughout the lower floor hall and chambers because of the rain, I approached my subject by saying, "I had hoped you would miss Mr. Davison's company more than you seem to have. Instead, it's my old friend, Mr. Eagles, who misses him the more."

"He's an excellent fellow," Miss Cresswell allowed.

"Mr. Davison?"

"Him, too. I meant Mr. Eagles."

"Then Mr. Davison has no chance at all with you, Miss Cresswell."

"None at all. Despite what you had hoped for, Lady Lillian, I think you will be happy for me."

"I will be happy for you. Is it all then settled with Mr. Eagles?"

"Not quite. For one, we wish your blessing."

"Which you have."

"For another, our continued close friendship."

"Again, it's yours."

"If I may be so forward, Lady Lillian, what are your own plans?"

"Plans?"

"Regarding Mr. Davison?"

"I hope we can remain friends even when our little beach-quartette is ended, as it must be, whether by season or circumstance."

"Yes, of course. Naturally."

What mattered now, I concluded, was how to keep our friendship alive, since I realized I'd come to depend on Alfred for more than I could express in words.

This could not be effected at a distance and I must see him at tea.

He was beaming, gleaming, I almost said. The laughter and the good spirits among him and my other guests were never at a higher pitch.

A letter from Astabella had arrived that morning. In it, she reported what Georgiana had written her about my situation, which she described harshly if truthfully. I was abandoned, solitary, and unwanted lawfully by Roland, and at the same time I was adored unlawfully by one beloved by all around me. My course, the two of them had agreed, was all too evident.

So, I knowingly and recklessly entered on a course of action that should lead me into breaking my marriage vows. I took up with Alfred Benoit Davison once again, saw him far more often, saw him without the chaperone of Miss Cresswell, who was now spending far more time at Mr. Eagles's—soon to be her own— estate. Only girls from the house accompanied us on our seashore adventures. Emboldened, he made love to me, at least verbally. As the August torpor dropped over us all, I began to persuade myself I was otherwise mistreated and deserved whatever happiness I might snatch at. This undoubtedly dangerous course included several kisses upon the terrazzo at night, and I was looking forward to how we might achieve an assignation away from prying eyes.

We had decided on a dower house built on the estate centuries earlier and, I suppose, at some point actually used to house a widow who had outlived her lord. It had been leased out over the years to old family retainers, now deceased. It lay vacant and thus came to my attention. I was drawn there by our estate foreman Rocksmith, the old acquaintance who had brought my husband and me together so long ago. He suggested his aged yet still lovely wife and I take a look and see what the house was in need of most, so it might be leased again and turn a profit.

It could use a general overhaul of fabrics, mattresses, smaller furniture, and other furnishings, which she noted down in a notebook and said she would see to.

But what struck me most was its extremely quiet prospect, too far from the manor or its grounds for prying, and far from the village, with, however, a lovely view from one second-floor bow window of the strand of an inlet of the Morecombe Bay surprisingly nearby.

Alfred visited the dower house and assured me it was private and inaccessible except by a meandering path from the road, while it lay in a direct line from the sand.

That was where we would begin our tryst. The time was set for the day to come, late afternoon. I'd taken to afternoon rides in the phaeton from which I would step down, sending the lad back, while I ambled home. I knew Miss Cresswell and Mr. Eagles were at Lancaster that day, and I expected no one to call and miss me if I arrived home later than usual.

But it's always some funny little detail that changes our lives, for better or worse, and so it was that August day.

Our afternoon mail had not yet arrived when my ride and its momentous aftermath began. On our path, my driver and I encountered a postal delivery man who asked might he shorten his rounds by leaving the manor's post with us. I fanned it out on the seat next to me and saw a note in Georgiana Milton's thick stationery and masculine handwriting. I was so quietly excited yet anxious about what I was about to go and do that I tore it badly opening it, and so stuffed it into my frock's single large pocket without reading it. The next moment I entreated Thaddeus to stop so I might get out and walk home.

I don't think I intended to read her note until much later, so distracted was I by impending events. I ambled on, looking about cautiously. Seeing no one, I approached the dower house, which seemed deathly still. Once inside the downstairs back foyer, I could see Alfred's collection kits, overshoes, and sunhat dropped on the bench and floor. I stole up the stairs to the hallway and still heard no sound.

When I reached the room we had agreed to meet in, I tapped once and, receiving no reply, edged the door ajar.

Alfred lay naked on the bed upon his back with one arm thrown over his flowing hair. He was asleep, almost silently so, his white breast rising and falling, and I remember thinking he was the first man I had ever taken the time to look at in such a natural state. Lord Roland had only appeared in the dark, as though by stealth, too quickly for me to know much except pain and, eventually, regret. The whiteness of Alfred's body contrasted to the deep suntan of his legs up to his knees, his arms up to the elbows, his neck and his face. It was as though he were some fabled beast of antique mythology, half man and half...what? Faun? Satyr? Some type of outdoor creature.

He seemed so content that, for a moment, I thought to leave and not bother him. Then I thought, as he exposes himself for me, so should I expose myself for him so we are equal. I knew from what my girl servants all said without any prompting that my own form remained youthful, despite the two births. My mother had remained slender to her end. I must share this with her, never mind I walked and rode more than ever she had. I began to undress.

Although I'd worn only the lightest of clothing without a bustle or other excrescence in fashion, this still meant a great deal of unlacing and unbuttoning and unbuckling. During it, Georgiana's letter fell out of the pocket and spread upon the floor. In picking it up, I was drawn to read it.

As I expected, her news was of her upcoming nuptials. I was about to stuff the note back in my outer pocket, now off and lying upon the floorboards, when I arrived at the *post scriptum.* "I have not utterly lost my memory, as we both feared that last visit. I now recall when and where it was that I encountered your young Darwinist. Right there, in Lord Roland's town house, and the young man was exiting the office and being congratulated by your husband, I suppose over some achievement or other. I recall it well, since we were introduced, and Lord Roland specifically said to me, 'I have the greatest hopes for this young fellow to produce results where no one else has yet had even a ghost of success.' This occurrence was in February this year, I think perhaps even St. Valentine's Day. Your scientist will confirm it, I'm certain."

I remember the light entering the room at that moment, so golden through the white muslin curtains, so golden and so ethereal, touching everything there—his skin, the chestnut wood headboard, his hair, my fallen clothing, the stationery itself, tinting it all ever so delicately with gold, as though signalling the treachery of what men do not treasure enough in life.

Then he awoke. From a dream, I suppose. He looked up and furrowed his brows, perhaps trying to remember it or brush it away, since the hand closest to where I sat on the floor rose and seemed to push something away. Then he turned to me and smiled, and it was such an ecstatic smile that for a moment I almost tossed her note away and rose to him.

"I waited…" he said.

"I arrived."

"And…"

"And this arrived with me," I said, and I rose up onto my knees so I might look him over, all the better, as I handed him her note.

Alfred looked confused and then read the post scriptum and he looked up at me sharply, his face not a mass of questions but instead one question only.

That was all I need to know. I slumped back down onto the floor and reached forward, gathering my clothing. Trying too late to cover myself.

"I don't deny it," he said, sitting up. "The meeting. The mission."

"The mission being to succeed where no one else has yet had even a ghost of success?" I asked.

"The mission being to compromise you because you were otherwise untouched and untouchable."

I held up my hands, "Well, and you have succeeded. What more is needed? Witnesses? A photograph as proof? Here I am for all to see."

"I forswore it," he said. "I wrote him a week ago and forswore it all."

"All? The money and what else? The promised university position?"

"No. Yes. I don't recall what else."

"But having foresworn it all, can't he now do you great harm?"

"Possibly. Probably. I wrote and told him he was daft and evil to wish you harm, since you are the best person who ever—"

I put a hand up to his mouth.

"Now he undoubtedly *will* do you great harm. He will *not* be crossed."

"I'll put myself where he can't reach at me," Alfred said. "The Continent. Perhaps America. Science is, after all, universal."

We sat looking at each other, and I swear in those moments more truth and goodness and understanding passed between our two faces than ever I had been blessed to exchange with any other person in my life but one!

He broke the silence. "No one knows. No one will come."

"You mean no one will catch us?"

"No one knows but you and I."

"I still must leave, you understand."

"I understand," he said sadly. "When I forswore it all," he added darkly, "I did it for the right reasons. So, I understand."

I rose and began slowly dressing myself.

To my surprise, he rose and helped me dress, very gently, very delicately, and very discreetly. I felt like one of those Titian Venuses, accompanied at their toilette by nude *putti*.

He angled me toward a looking glass and we affixed the details of my dress. He hovered behind, a large, naked, two-tone, fallen Lucifer.

"There," he said, replacing my collar. "Now no one shall ever know."

"I shall know. And you."

"Yes, but that can't be helped!" he said, and I thought he caught a sob in his throat before he spun out of the room and thundered down the stairs out the back doorway.

From the bow window, I could see him running across the flat turf through the empty sands and into the surf, running and then diving, surfacing after so long a time that I lost my breath waiting. He swam so far out, he was soon gone from view, and I thought he surely would drown himself.

I waited until he was safely back on the sands, albeit exhausted. Then I left the dower house and walked home. I was accosted by a rent-farmer in a dogcart. He stopped and helped me up and to the front door of the manor. There, all were dozing. No one had missed me at all.

The day after our disappointed assignation at tea, Miss Cresswell reported that Mr. Davison had removed himself from the neighbourhood with no intention to return. Did I know of it? I said I did not and had heard naught.

Some weeks later I asked if Mr. Eagles knew how to communicate with his friend, as I believed I had something to return to him. Rather solemnly, he said he did. But I returned nothing, and we never spoke of him again.

Instead, I fell into as deep a despair as ever Lady Bella had. For I had understood at last that no matter where or to whom I turned, my life was forever hemmed in, controlled, and manipulated by a man hundreds of miles distant who had not the least care for me, except to do me as much harm as possible whenever he might, and for no reason I could descry.

Fortunately, Mr. Eagles and Miss Cresswell's nuptials took on a great present dimension at that time, and so none but she ever knew had close I had come to utter despondency.

It was many weeks before I could bring myself to tell her what had occurred, and I only did so in the most glancing and innocuous of terms. Clever Mrs. Eagles understood and said, "Your wish, my lady, is my command. Even if that wish means my most valuable friendship in life comes to an end."

And she said what was now apparent to us both—that I must prepare to leave Ravenglass and England forever.

Yours, Lillian

To: The Earl of Ravenglass
11 Hanover Square
London, England

2 November 188—

Sir,

We are all well here at the manor and do well. There are no problems to report. But my wife shakes her head and says to me, "Now! Tell him now." And so I will.

If any problem exists at all, it is that my mother's letters continue to arrive, and they cause Carrie-Ann doubts and require explications that I have to admit I cannot begin to provide. For days on end she wouldn't show them to me, saying I was quote a "hard-hearted male person" and "couldn't possibly understand the female heart."

Once I persuaded her that wasn't true—I don't believe it is— she thrust the letters at me and hovered while I read them through. They are lengthy and this lasted a good while.

When I had done so, she cried in triumph, "You see! You are not in tears as any sane person would be."

I drew her to me, and I told her that rather than be in tears, I was deeply saddened by what I had read. Saddened, and I have to admit, to her—and to you too, sir—very angry.

As always, they are copied and forwarded to your office. But I must write it now—Carrie Ann and I await some explanation of these horrendous, these inhuman charges my mother has made against you.

Roderick

To: The Honourable Lady Caroline-Ann Augusta
The Glebe, Ravenglass
Broughton, England

4 November 188—

My Dear Lady Caroline-Ann,
"When you are in your deepest despair, go to my sewing box," Lady Bella had said to me, her last words I remembered hearing. Eventually, I did, going to what had been her chamber, abandoned for years, closed up, collecting dust and spiders, but none of those so wonderful as Precita. I found the old rectangular carved wood box among her few remaining articles, and I remember cradling it for her memory and her agony, which only now I shared and only now fully appreciated.

There I made my second small, yet oh so significant discovery, for when I had almost dropped the sewing box, a slender drawer, until then altogether hidden from sight without any handle or method of ingress, slid ajar, and in so doing revealed a glimmer of pale grey silk.

I slid the drawer fully and opened the silk, and what did I see but a treasure trove! What had she told me so many years before? That every time the old earl had returned to Ravenglass, he had done so with some rich tribute or bribe for her. She had tossed me that jewelled ring I still wore on the hand that no longer bore the mendacious wedding bands. Now, within this royal wrapping of silk, I found more: emeralds set into a ring and matching golden necklace; clear-as-ice diamonds in a silver bracelet and matching pendants for the ears; black pearls set in a double choker matched with a brooch; ruby earrings cradled in red gold; and topazes and amethysts in white gold. She had kept these near herself as she wheeled about madly in her creaking contraption of wood. Now they were mine—her gift.

I saw their utility. Converted into pounds sterling, they would help me vanish. But how could this be done?

I took Mrs. Eagles née Cresswell into my confidence and she her husband. A few weeks passed before Mr. Eagles called on me, and as we strode along that terrazzo, now fallen into desuetude as I'd become newly reclusive, he told me he had heard of a trustworthy man in Lancaster who I might approach.

"He's a recent emigrant to our shores. He has many connexions abroad, where large gems may be easily traded without many questions asked or given. He'll expect a percentage of the value. But my fellows have dealt with him, and none feel him to be miserly nor a usurer."

This was recommendation enough, and I requested he set up an interview. I had long put off a needed shopping trip to the city, and now I took it, with two servants from the house, one of whom was sure to be in my husband's pay. Even so, once in Lancaster, I gave them time and money to entertain themselves and to purchase sweets for their companions, while I remained at Mr. and Mrs. Eagles's town residence.

Homer and I then stole out the back door and then to where Mr. Eduard Golding kept an establishment. Looking into its single display window, one might take it for a draper's shop, and inside I found some lovely drapery, apt for bedrooms at Ravenglass Manor.

Mr. Golding was not in when we arrived, despite our appointment. His young wife and her baby were, however, and she assured us he would soon return.

She spoke little English, but some French and Dutch. We conversed the while we waited over the baby, a girl five months old, very pretty and very blond, as I recalled my own firstborn to have been. The crib and swaddling and all her clothing were of the finest quality of lacework, cotton lisle, and silk, as though she were a princess. Mrs. Golding allowed me to hold little Ruth and dandle her, which brought tears to my eyes, recalling my loss of Hannah so long ago and for no good reason that I ever knew. We spoke like old friends.

Mr. Eagles had left to hurry Mr. Golding on, and they returned together. Like his daughter but unlike his dark little wife, Mr. Eduard Golding was fair, his hair and sideburns and moustache that orange shade called strawberry blond, his eyes pale green. At sight of him, I paled because he somewhat reminded me of Mute Matthew.

Husband and wife spoke a few moments, and then Mr. Eduard Golding took me aside from Mr. Eagles and said, "I had expected a great lady of the realm, due homage and obeisance. I was fearful of this meeting, I must tell you, afraid of this great lady's stern manner and her great worth so far above my own. This was why I held back.

But I have come home to find a woman—please forgive my poor English—a woman like my own wife, who loves little children."

"Your wife is a fine woman. Your child is lovely. I am the beggar here, Mr. Golding. Whatever my title and estate, I need your help now. How would I dare appear other than as a supplicant?"

"You are no supplicant, but I hope will prove a friend," he said.

That said, I opened the sewing box and silk and showed him what I had brought. He inspected them with his jeweller's *loupe*, and he smiled.

"These are excellently cut, rare, heavy in carats, and valuable. We may realize a great deal from these, my lady. But in Amsterdam, not here in England. I suggest a course of action that will take a little time and will require your utmost trust in me. If they are sold at once, the market will drop, and their value be less. If you can give me three months, I may sell them in several voyages and realize a higher profit."

He asked if I had more to sell, but I had received little from Lord Roland and, anyway, I would have left whatever he had given me, so I could not possibly be accused of theft.

And so my current course was set in motion.

For its greater implementation, I would need other help, and this arrived in two forms upon my second visit to Lancaster-town, to actually hand over half of Lady Bella's jewels. As I was taking coffee with Mr. and Mrs. Eagles a late morning in his town house, she brought me a newsletter of the town, exclaiming, "Don't you know these people, Lady Lillian?"

Indeed I did. The page she had handed me was marked in black flower type, as though in a funeral crepe. Enclosed was a paid obituary for a Mrs. Matthew Partlett, dead at age thirty-seven.

"Isn't this the wife of your old friend?" Mrs. Eagles asked.

We read on, and it appeared to be a local death of Kentish born Iphigenia Partlett, née Vernon, bereaved by Mr. Matthew Partlett, husband, of Phillipson Hall in Surrey. The funeral was to be held that afternoon in Lancaster, and there was a showing until one o'clock.

"This is Mute Matthew's wife," I said. "Poor Matthew. We have nothing else important to do then. We should go to him."

We quickly dressed funereally for outdoors and were conveyed to a handsome town house, where two footmen in crepe led us in to a large parlour. A coffin was placed for viewing and within it lay a youngish, not unattractive woman. Several female and one elderly male mourner sat nearby, and when we asked for the deceased's husband, we were led to an upper chamber.

It had been so many years since I had last seen Matthew that I was about to call the gentleman who met us a complete imposter. He possessed the same lineaments, the same slender grace and fine bones of my old friend. But *he* had been a boy, and whom I *met* was a man, and a gentleman at that. He was dressed like fine gentry, and his bearing was that of a man of estate. He recognized me and bowed. "My Lady Lillian, you do us the greatest honour," he said. He did not know my companion, but was gracious to her.

He was engaged in some critical business pertaining to his wife's family estate and begged our pardon for ten minutes, but asked us to remain above stairs and had refreshment brought, while he re-entered the chamber he'd been in before.

"I am astonished," Mrs. Eagles said, "to find your poor waif of a lad, of whom I had heard so many tales, turn out to be a handsome, mature man of such great parts."

"No more than I am, Mrs. Eagles," I replied, for I was equally astonished.

"Of course, you had been told of his recent fortunes."

"I had. Even so, it is difficult to understand the two persons as one."

"You naturally fear for his affections."

"I have no fears. Nor expectations."

"There, my Lady Lillian, you would do well to hold fire," she said.

When his business was completed, the two men exited and Matthew, or Mr. Partlett, as he was now known, joined us.

He brushed aside our condolences at his wife's death. "Hard it may sound, ladies, but Mrs. Partlett was a trial for many years to us all, myself less than her family and friends, luckily. But that is the truth. For years she was weak of mind and needed a friend and caretaker more than a husband. Such I was to her. She could no more be a true wife or mother than any inmate of an asylum, and it was only with the tenderest of care that she escaped that particular fate. It was you, Lady Lillian, who taught me so. Your care for myself when all else shunned me or mocked me, and then later on, your care for poor Lady Bella…"

"Then," Mrs. Eagles asked what I feared asking, "This was a marriage in name only? Without issue or affection?"

"Yes. A little affection," he admitted. "Which of God's creatures cannot be loved for some virtue or other? But no issue, as there could be no real marriage."

We spoke some minutes and others visited and had to be spoken to.

When we were alone, I said to Matthew, "You are always so good. I could never understand why you alone of all my friends never came to my wedding?"

"I would not sanction it with my poor presence," he said, sheepishly.

"I thought perhaps there was some other reason."

"You deserved better than he. But I see I was wrong, and you are happy."

"Whether I deserved better or not, you alone were right to think as you did. I am not happy. I am as unhappy as ever a creature could be. And, aside from Mr. and Mrs. Eagles, I am friendless."

"After the funeral, you will come to me and tell me all. All. Don't hold back a single word or incident."

I was surprised at his anger.

"This will be useless, Matthew. Only one course lies open for me now. If you wish to help me, then you must forswear all thoughts of vengeance against Lord Roland and concentrate upon securing my freedom."

"I agree in all, Lillian. You have been my lodestar all these years that we have been apart. In all that I have done and said, I always first considered how it would appear in your eyes. If you can bear to be with me, I'll concentrate upon your freedom and your happiness."

"Bear to be with you?" To my surprise, I said, "It is my wish."

So easily as that, then, did I find my greatest friend and support in an old friend whom we both discovered I had never stopped caring for, nor he for me. Without him, I could not have made this great change so late in my life.

But one more incident needs to be told, and that is the death of my great friend Robert Graham, Eighth Baron of Blackburn.

But it must wait. Some emergent news has come and I must go.

Lillian

To the Earl of Ravenglass,
11 Hanover Square
London, England

12 November, 188—

Sir, we are, Carrie-Ann, Lord Oliver, and myself, extremely perplexed. How is it that you do not respond?

The most recent of my mother's letters tell us in some detail how it was that she effected her escape from Ravenglass Manor. As Carrie-Ann said to me, "This was a bold and remarkable action of your mama's. I could think of no one even of my own age and my greater knowledge of the world who could have done it unless she was in the most desperate straits. That a sheltered older person like Lillian has done so speaks of how desperate she was. And her letters give us the reasons so plainly. It is worse than ever I could have expected when I began reading these so light-heartedly weeks ago."

Lord Oliver and I agree. Unless there is some explication forthcoming for this decades-long cavalcade of deception and abuse—although what explication would even be possible, I cannot think.

I—we—await it impatiently.
Roderick

To: The Very Reverend Jasper Horace Quill
The British Church at Campofieri
Town of Fiesoli
Province of Toscana

13 November 188—

Dear Sir,

I bring you sad news, although not about her ladyship, who is well and who is at long last safe from harm at the hands of those dastardly men who had sought her life. Yes, your friend was right in believing that the earl's men would stop at nothing.

The one you have been apprised of for some time as following us, is indeed the earl's man. A very dangerous fellow indeed, by his own admission. But through I cannot say what stroke of fortune I surely never deserved, he turned out to be someone dear to me. Indeed, my own baby brother, not seen for two decades. I enclose a copy of his very last letter, intended for the exchequer himself. In it, you will be brought up to date.

❖

And now that you have read Addison's letter, know this. By the following morning, I had told her ladyship some of what had occurred the previous night, amending for the sake of brevity the scene in which it occurred—the opium den here in Florence—which surely would have revealed the depth of my degradation. And of course, not revealing how my brother was almost the instrument of my demise, as he and his confederate had been sent to murder me while I was in the grip of an opium dream. Recognizing me by the scar on my throat, which he as an infant watched done, instead he roused me and drew me away into safety. Whatever the lady thought or intuited, for she is a strongly intuitive woman, she was overjoyed for me and my discovery of my long-lost brother. She agreed to have Addison join our little company.

We spent hours catching up, and this morning I walked across the street from the *palazzo* where we are guests to meet with Addison in the *pensione* he had taken, and he had his travel packet stuffed and ready to come with me. He had sought in vain the young man he had hired. His hope was to ask the lad to accompany us, and if he would not, then to return him to Venice with sufficient money. To this, I agreed. But what of the third confederate, I asked? The murderous one from the night before.

Macllhenny had vanished at nightfall. Addison said he believed Macllhenny was infuriated with him after the abortion of their plan to murder me in the opium den. He did not know to where he'd gone. But Addison said it was of no importance, nor was he of any importance to us.

We embraced again. I picked up one of his bags and he the other, and we went down those narrow stairs into the street. There the two fellows I have just written of stood waiting, the Venetian lad and the British confederate, whom Henriette called Macllhenny.

Addison went to the younger and made him understand by his command of Italian and by gestures that he was welcome to come with us. That lad agreed happily and went inside to retrieve his own smaller travel packet.

"And what of his lordship's mission?" Macllhenny asked, petulant, while we waited.

"I have written to his lordship," Addison said.

"Saying what? That this one lives and that you are turned traitor?"

"What business is it of yours, Lobs? 'Tis mine alone."

"So say you."

"What do you mean?" my brother asked.

"'is lordship knew to have this job well done, he needed me-self," Macllhenny said, "Why is why he sent me after ye. If ye cannot do the job, then I am to do it. To do him," he said, pointing to me, "and then her! That is my mission."

As we stood there in front of her ladyship's guest rooms in the *palazzo*, he unsheathed one of those Italian stilettos and rushed at me. I was able to step aside and received only a slash of my jacket sleeve and not even a cut to the arm.

But Addison was incensed. He withdrew his own knife, and before I could stop him, the two went at each other.

A small crowd quickly gathered, for these Italians like nothing better than to see blood flow in the street. I rushed into the *pensione* to call for help. Addison's lad leapt down with me, and we got to the street in time to see Addison stumble backward and fall, at which MacIlhenny was upon him in a flash and stabbed him but missed his heart, hitting him lower in his abdomen. The lad had scooped up Addison's dagger, and he stabbed MacIlhenny in the back. As he drew back, the Venetian grabbed him by the throat and slit it. He fell, spouting goblets of blood.

The lad and I both shoved him over to get to my brother. "Get my man away!" my brother croaked at me. "I'll live."

My lady had seen the affray from her windows, she later told us, and she rushed down to the street. She was held indoors by the owner. But the lady broke his hold and rushed out. Seeing her, I shouted, "I must off with this lad for his safety," and pushed through the crowd of onlookers, rushing past that intersection into a labyrinth of alleyways, from whence he led me to a doorway, saying "*La cugina mia.*" His cousin. She let him in, and I ran back to the *palazzo*.

The irritated crowd was dispersing at the command and rough handling of the *carabineri*, the local police, but there MacIlhenny lay, blood pooling on the stones of the street. I hid my face as much as possible and rushed into the *palazzo* we'd been leaving, to find the lady guarding my brother, who lay upon some kind of trestle on the ground floor of the place. With her was a young medico, who commanded several Italian women carrying pots of water and various other objects. Addison had lost consciousness.

"It is serious. But he will live," the lady said to me. "This doctor assures us." I noticed then that the lower part of her dress was askew. "Leave it be," she said, wearily. "My petticoat served as your brother's bandages. So much was needed to bind him closely to stanch the wound, only that would serve. He will live," she repeated. She conversed more with the doctor. "He's sleeping now. It will be a day or two until he is able to…" She then seemed almost to faint, so I moved her to a wooden chair nearby and helped her into it. "The boy? He's safely away?" she asked. Imagine, sir, her concern for all but herself.

I confirmed that. "The *carabinieri* arrived. Too late, as usual."

"Would you please call in the driver who was to take us to our haven?" When I had done so, and the baffled man was standing in the hallways, she stepped out and handed him a note, telling him to take it to her friend and say we are delayed by a mischance.

The driver listened still not too clearly, then the young doctor stood forward and, taking the note and the driver, walked him outside again repeating, I suppose, what she had told him.

"Had Addison *not* defended me," I said, "both you and I, Lady, would have perished surely enough. The blackguard's *poignard* had both our names written upon it. So seemed to be your husband's, and this confederate, MacIlhenny's, darkest intention. Also their intention to have it happen here and to be bruited about at home as though it were a foreign misadventure, so none would think to see his hand in it so deeply."

"His black hand reaches this far, it is true," she said. She took to her chair again and covered her eyes.

The young doctor, the lady, and I held vigil there all evening and during the night. Food and drink was brought to us. A cot was brought in for the doctor to rest upon. The lady and I remained in the large wooden chairs, but cushions and eventually blankets against the night chill were brought to us for some comfort. The owner of the *palazzo* and his grown son came by to see to our further comfort, ignoring the questions of the police, who demanded entrance, as the owner had locked the gate and door to the street as they do at night time.

The following morning, the doctor and the lady were already awake when I woke. My brother had come to, well enough to complain of the pain in his abdomen. The doctor administered a small tincture of laudanum, enjoining him to sleep. We were just beginning to drink some *caffè* and eat some bread when her ladyship's friend arrived. Another Englishman, to my surprise. He paid everyone and sent the doctor away, although the latter would return again during the day and just before we slept.

Her ladyship's friend knew what he was about. He has resided in this land some years along with his now late wife, who apparently had been very troubled in her wits and so only comfortable here, far away from England. He told us that the *carabinieri* would deal with the matter of a foreign man dead in the street as they ordinarily do—efficiently and ruthlessly. Anything we might do or say, her friend assured us, would only be considered interference or admission of guilt and would cause great trouble for all of us. We must say nothing at all. And as soon as possible, we must leave.

This they accomplished the following day, her ladyship and her friend, Mr. Matthew Partlett, who made all of the arrangements and the needed payments and bribes. My brother was moved up one floor—very carefully, by the doctor, myself, and another, and he continues to be on the mend enough that he was able to sip some broth and complain and hold my hand and kiss it time and again, saying, "I found you and then I almost lost..." I enjoined him to not think of what might have been. In a few weeks' time, the doctor assured us, we will be able to travel by slow carriage to join her ladyship and her friend.

The Venetian lad returned too, and has joined us. Although I cannot truly understand my brother and this lad's affection for each other, it seems strong and possibly enduring. The lad sends me to sleep, sends me out of doors, and he remains with Addison. My brother told me he will remain with him from now on, saying, "He is more than a servant to me. You must understand that, Stephen."

Her ladyship also wrote, asking us all to stay on awhile in her service and to live with her and Mr. Partlett at his estate, as much for our own comfort as for *all* of our safety. She feels responsible for us, and as the young Venetian has already learned some rudimentary English, perhaps he might be of use to the couple. For who knows, she wrote, if there is not a third assassin sent out by Lord Roland, in case these first two failed? And will we two not be needed then to assist her and Mr. Partlett? None of us would be at all surprised if there was a third. Or a fourth.

After receiving some mail, Mr. Partlett a few days after, said that much is afoot in England, as a result of her ladyship's many letters to her son and his wife. This should ensure our safety, but for a time it would be best if we three joined them. It is a large, secure manor estate and we are most welcome for as long as we wish. I do not know how Lord Roland shall pay for these crimes, but in only a few months, I myself am of sufficient age to be able to return to England to claim my adopted father's estate in Suffolk. We shall see then what I and my father's friends may be able to achieve.

We wrote back agreeing. Our next destination is that Italian country home which Mr. Partlett he says is a long day's distance from here, near the town of Fiesole, where you reside, sir. And so it is with expectation that I look forward to meeting you, sir, my unknown correspondent during this adventure, and introducing my brother, Addison, to you. Mr. Partlett asks me to inform you that he will thank you in person, tomorrow, before sunset, for all of your aid to us and to myself in particular, when we join you and when he returns with Lady Lillian safely home to the Villa Roccambi ed Piave.

Your friend, Stephen Undershot

To: The Honourable Lady Caroline-Ann Augusta
and to her Husband, my son, Roderick
at Blackburn House,
Cumberland, England

15 November 188—

My Dear Roderick and Caroline-Ann,

I have received copies of the various letters written since I last sent you a letter, and I know the situation is, as you, dear Roddy, write, "well in hand" for the time being regarding "that person."

By now you have also received notice of my application for divorce, which given the circumstances, will be allowed. I filed those papers while still in the British Isles. You should know that upon the dissolution of our nuptials, banns will be read in what they call the English church here, to be followed by a private marriage to Mr. Matthew Partlett of Fiesole, Italy, and Suffolkshire, England, the nuptials to be held here in Italy. You are, of course, invited to attend, but I must warn you, it will not be a jot as grand as your own ceremony and festivities.

You are at Blackburn House because Lady Blackburn has wished it so. She requested your presence several months ago when she was first widowed, but it is only now, after all this correspondence from myself, that you can begin to understand *why* she requested it, and why I too requested it.

I referred in my last letter to one large and two smaller incidents that altered my life and now, I'm afraid, yours too. Which are the smaller and which the larger of them will, I believe take many years for us to all sort out. All three were ultimately of importance.

The two you already know of: The first my arranged meeting with Mr. Eduard Golding, the jewellery-factor, and through him, the making of my financial independence from your father which allowed me to leave Ravenglass. The second was my re-encountering, shortly after that, Mute Matthew, now newly widowed Mr. Mathew Partlett, who offered me his protection, his love, and his hand—all of which I accepted. Which I *ought* to have accepted many years before, except that in that case you would not exist, Roderick, and I would never wish that.

But one more incident needs to be told, and that is the death of my great friend Robert Graham, Eighth Baron of Blackburn, and it may not be put off any longer.

He had acquired a disease of the blood, what used to be called a "flux," which began to sap his strength and health not long after he wed. I had, in fact, noticed this quickly enough at his wedding, and within a year Robert was bed-ridden. My own life was complicated and agonizing enough at this time. Still, when he called for me, I went immediately to Blackburn House.

I found him abed in that silly round tower which he had made his "Corsairs Cavern" as a lad, and he was poorly indeed. He had lost much weight, and earlier his young wife had said that no matter how much he was fed, none of it remained with him. His own surgeon, Dr. Sharpless, who had attended both my childbirths, said it was a wonder Robert had lasted so long. He ascribed the illness to an as yet undiscoverable cancer.

Whatever the cause, you may naturally understand how distressed I was for poor Robert.

But not he. He had come to terms with his mortality. He claimed he would have died all the sooner, if it weren't that there was one matter he must tell me.

Here I must ask you to look back on those letters I sent your wife in early September, all about the early days of my marriage and of Lord Roland's—I suppose I must call it mating—with me.

What I did not know was that my husband was unable to *be* a husband with me. Nor with any other women. Males only, and usually younger males, aroused Roland to that state in which he would be able to mate at all. It was these younger males, always in his company, always about him, even at Ravenglass, whom he must utilize to arouse him in his own chamber at the manor for a longish period, so that he might then rush in to me as he had first done, near naked and breathless, hot from their arms, to be a husband to me to make an heir.

From Lord Robert I learned that evidently my brother Rudolph had been Roland's plaything in that when young. As we now understand, poor Rudolph had been corrupted by Roland, and he had then gone on his life to corrupt young girls and and—who knows—young sailors, too. Lord Robert himself had briefly been Roland's amour in their college days, only to be thrown over for someone younger and of a lower class, since this became Roland's preference thereafter.

Perhaps you two "moderns," Roddy and Carrie-Ann, have already reached this conclusion about Lord Roland. You both know a great deal more of these private matters than I ever did at your age, I was so utterly sheltered in these matters of the world.

According to Lord Robert, that was a Ravenglass family trait Roland inherited and carried. The old earl, we now know, required man and woman together for many years for his own pleasure-seeking, and then later only a lad alone, playing love-games with him. Nor, apparently, was he the first of his line to harbour this propensity. He had warned young Roland what to expect later in life, as he had been told by his father, and he by his father back, for how many previous generations? All, evidently, were unable to love women. This also, Robert said, was the reason why no Ravenglass girl child could ever be allowed to survive. The family fear was that the girl too would become "turned," as Lord Roland was, toward *only* her own kind. While this tendency was apparently controllable, and not too difficult to cover up in a man, it would—or so they all awfully believed—never be so easily controlled or covered up in a woman. And so, all living Ravenglass children *must* be males.

This was awful enough to hear from a dying man who I had thought was my great friend but who ended up being so complicit in this extraordinary deceit for so very long.

What Robert next told me, however, put all he'd previously exposed to me quite in the shade.

By the second year of our marriage, after I had given birth and "lost" my little girl, Hannah, Lord Roland found he could no longer mate with a woman even under those strict circumstances that had earlier aided him. He attempted to do so with someone else and could not. But by this time, an heir was absolutely required. And so, during those few last, brief, reckless, and yes even I had noticed, more passionate matings, his friend, Lord Robert, had secretly taken his place in my darkened chamber.

There, I have written it. I almost believed I could never write it.

Robert had to overcome all of his natural scruples to do it, he said, but it was after all, he admitted, also his greatest desire to take his friend's place. Lord Roland had known and played upon this weakness. And although Robert wished it had been done by light with my knowledge, he admitted to me, "It was better than nothing at all, which was the alternative."

Of course, those relations too ceased as soon as I was *enceinte*.

So, it is with great relief and even pride that I can inform you, Roderick, that you are the natural son of Robert Graham of Blackburn. You therefore end once and for all the generations-long bane of Ravenglass husbands and also their war against a line of Ravenglass wives.

I hope this will not be too great a shock to you.

You will discover after you have read this letter that Robert's will has left you as Blackburn heir. Certain smaller properties and other benefices go to his young wife, of course. It is not as great a fiefdom as Ravenglass would have been, but it is honestly your own, since the will names you Robert's son and heir.

What will happen to the manor where you and I lived for so many years, I cannot say.

Carrie-Ann has sent me copies of your last two letters to Roland, and so I know now that you have taken up cudgels against him for legal redress.

Roland will, doubtlessly, fight like a tiger for his life, his freedom, and for his estate. For myself, I want none of it. Although by terms of our marriage agreement, in the event of a failure to conceive by either party, a certain large section of the estate should devolve upon the wounded party, which in this case is my own self.

I shall someday return to England, if only to see you two happy together.

Come here first and see me at last happy.

Your loving mother, Lillian

To: The Earl of Ravenglass
11 Hanover Square
London, England

15 November 188—

Sir,

The bearers of this letter will arrange for you to gather whatever belongings you require for a preliminary sojourn in Her Majesty's Prison for Felons at B——, there to await trial for the murder of my sister, Hannah, as well as implication in the death of one Henrietta Acropila of Milan, Italy, by the hand of your factor, one Allister MacIlhenny, a.k.a. Lobster Tail, now deceased. Also by that deceased one's words, witnessed by myself and my brother, for conspiracy to murder one Stephen Undershot, as well as conspiracy to murder your wife and my mother, Lady Lillian of Ravenglass, all by various hands under your control and in your pay.

You alone well know the motives behind all these charges.

You may not know how it has all come to light, but so it has. My mother's many letters, received by my wife and myself, as well as those missives of Mr. Undershot and others to which we became privy, will be the very first proofs entered in court against you. Mr. Undershot, a citizen of Leicester and London, is eager to return to his home and will bear witness under sworn oath in court to all that is charged to you.

Other living witnesses to your earlier atrocity upon my elder sibling have been located, and are already deposed by the law to support that allegation.

No matter the outcome—and I don't doubt you already have many on the highest benches suborned to you—at the very least, the scandal of arrest will put a stop to your career in Parliament as well as in the Lord Exchequer's Office. Also, now utterly dashed are your hopes to become Prime Minister of England.

I despise you, sir, and I hope never to lay eyes upon you again unless it is as witness to your execution via the hangman's noose.

Roderick Fitz-Graham. 9th Baron Blackburn

FINIS

About the Author

Felice Picano (http://www.felicepicano.net) is the author of thirty-six books of poetry, fiction, memoirs, and nonfiction. His work is translated into seventeen languages; several titles were national and international bestsellers, including *The Lure*, *Like People in History*, and *The Book of Lies*.

Four of Picano's plays have been produced. He's considered a founder of modern gay literature along with other members of the Violet Quill. He's won or been nominated for numerous awards including being a finalist for five Lammies, and he received the Lambda Literary Foundation's Pioneer Award. He is a teacher and international lecturer on Gay Literature, Gays in Hollywood in the Golden Age, and Screenplay Writing. Picano's most recent books are *Justify My Sins: A Hollywood Novel in Three Acts* (2019), *Songs & Poems* (2020), *City on a Star: One—Dryland's End* (2021), *City on a Star: Two—The Betrothal at Usk* (2021), *Pursuit: A Victorian Entertainment* (2021), and *City on a Star: Three—A Bard on Hercular* (2022).

Books Available From Bold Strokes Books

Pursued: Lillian's Story by Felice Picano. Fleeing a disastrous marriage to the Lord Exchequer of England, Lillian of Ravenglass reveals an incident-filled, often bizarre, tale of great wealth and power, perfidy, and betrayal. (978-1-63679-197-5)

Murder on Monte Vista by David S. Pederson. Private Detective Mason Adler's angst at turning fifty is forgotten when his "birthday present," the handsome, young Henry Bowtrickle, turns up dead, and it's up to Mason to figure out who did it, and why. (978-1-63679-124-1)

Three Left Turns to Nowhere by Jeffrey Ricker, J. Marshall Freeman & 'Nathan Burgoine. Three strangers heading to a convention in Toronto are stranded in rural Ontario, where a small town with a subtle kind of magic leads each to discover what he's been searching for. (978-1-63679-050-3)

One Verse Multi by Sander Santiago. Life was good: promotion, friends, falling in love, discovering that the multi-verse is on a fast track to collision—wait, what? Good thing Martin King works for a company that can fix the problem, right…um…right? (978-1-63679-069-5)

Fresh Grave in Grand Canyon by Lee Patton. The age-old Grand Canyon becomes more and more ominous as group of volunteers fight to survive alone in nature and uncover a murderer among them. (978-1-63679-047-3)

Loyalty, Love & Vermouth by Eric Peterson. A comic valentine to a gay man's family of choice, including the ones with cold noses and four paws. (978-1-63555-997-2)

Bury Me in Shadows by Greg Herren. College student Jake Chapman is forced to spend the summer at his dying grandmother's home and soon finds danger from long-buried family secrets. (978-1-63555-993-4)

A Different Man by Andrew L. Huerta. This diverse collection of stories chronicling the challenges of gay life at various ages shines a light on the progress made and the progress still to come. (978-1-63555-977-4)

Busy Ain't the Half of It by Frederick Smith and Chaz Lamar Cruz. Elijah and Justin seek happily-ever-afters in LA, but are they too busy to notice happiness when it's there? (978-1-63555-944-6)

Pursuit: A Victorian Entertainment by Felice Picano. An intelligent, handsome, ruthlessly ambitious young man who rose from the slums to become the right-hand man of the Lord Exchequer of England will stop at nothing as he pursues his Lord's vanished wife across Continental Europe. (978-1-63555-870-8)

Best of the Wrong Reasons by Sander Santiago. For Fin Ness and Orion Starr, it takes a funeral to remind them that love is worth living for. (978-1-63555-867-8)

Coming to Life on South High by Lee Patton. Twenty-one-year-old gay virgin Gabe Rafferty's first adult decade unfolds as an unpredictable journey into sex, love, and livelihood. (978-1-63555-906-4)

Death's Prelude by David S. Pederson. In this prequel to the Detective Heath Barrington Mystery series, Heath discovers that first love changes you forever and drives you to become the person you're destined to be. (978-1-63555-786-2)

His Brother's Viscount by Stephanie Lake. Hector Somerville wants to rekindle his illicit love affair with Viscount Wentworth, but he must overcome one problem: Wentworth still loves Hector's brother. (978-1-63555-805-0)

The Dubious Gift of Dragon Blood by J. Marshall Freeman. One day Crispin is a lonely high school student—the next he is fighting a war in a land ruled by dragons, his otherworldly boyfriend at his side. (978-1-63555-725-1)

Quake City by St John Karp. Can Andre find his best friend Amy before the night devolves into a nightmare of broken hearts, malevolent drag queens, and spontaneous human combustion? Or has it always happened this way, every night, at Aunty Bob's Quake City Club? (978-1-63555-723-7)

Every Summer Day by Lee Patton. Meant to celebrate every summer day, Luke's journal instead chronicles a love affair as fast-moving and possibly as fatal as his brother's brain tumor. (978-1-63555-706-0)